THE CORSAIR

Abdulaziz Al-Mahmoud

Translated by Amira Nowaira

English edition first published in 2012 by

Bloomsbury Qatar Foundation Publishing
Qatar Foundation
Villa 3, Education City
PO Box 5825
Doha, Qatar
www.bqfp.com.qa

Copyright © Abdulaziz Al-Mahmoud, 2012
Translation copyright © Amira Nowaira, 2012

First published in Arabic, 2011
as *Al Qursan*, by Bloomsbury Qatar Foundation Publishing, Doha

The moral right of the author has been asserted.

ISBN 9789992194720

10 9 8 7 6 5 4 3 2

Map by ML Design, London

Typeset by Hewer Text UK Ltd, Edinburgh

Printed and bound in Great Britain by CPI Group (UK) Ltd, Croydon CR0 4YY

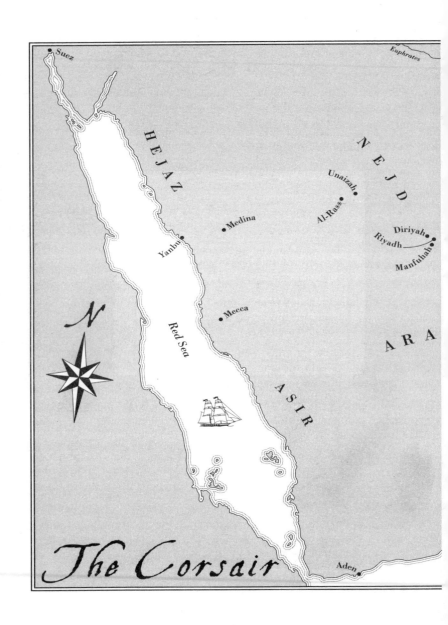

Suez

HEJAZ

NEJD

Unaizah

Al-Rass

Medina

Diriyah

Riyadh

Manfuhah

Yanbu

Mecca

Red Sea

ARA

ASIR

Euphrates

Aden

The Corsair

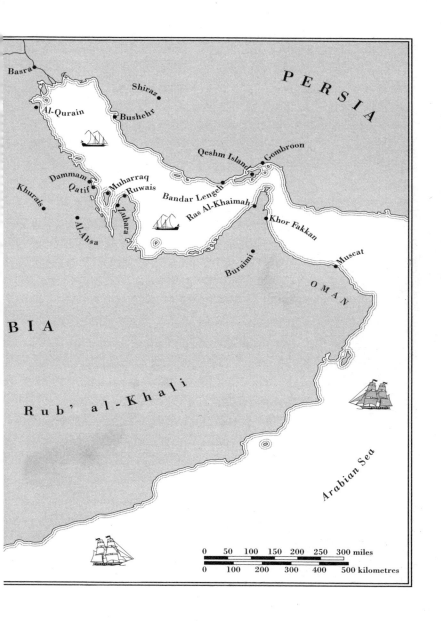

Basra

Shiraz

PERSIA

Al-Qurain

Bushehr

Qeshm Island

Gombroon

Dammam

Muharraq

Qatif

Ruwais

Bandar Lengeh

Khurais

Zubara

Ras Al-Khaimah

Khor Fakkan

Al-Ahsa

Buraimi

Muscat

OMAN

BIA

Rub' al-Khali

Arabian Sea

| 0 | 50 | 100 | 150 | 200 | 250 | 300 miles |
| 0 | 100 | 200 | 300 | 400 | 500 kilometres |

Chapter 1

Plymouth

PLYMOUTH'S OLD HARBOUR AREA was still called the Barbican even though the fortified gate and battlements that had encircled the port in medieval times had given way to a large fish market and a motley array of squat fishermen's cottages, merchants' homes, inns and public houses – all vying for space in a maze of alleyways. The residents were similarly diverse: one could tell their place in society with a glance at their clothes, from the rags of the fishermen and cabin boys, to the loose-fitting slops and rugged wide-legged trousers favoured by sailors, to the unimaginative but practical attire of the merchant class. Only the luxurious garments of the well-heeled and the landed gentry were distinctly absent from the Barbican's cobbled alleyways.

The well-to-do could be glimpsed only fleetingly as their carriages tore down the lanes on their way to or from the docks. Indeed, the coachmen driving the carriages instinctively picked up speed when they entered the Barbican as though fearing the pervasive smell of rancid fish and open sewage would offend the delicate sensibilities of their passengers. Even on the hottest days of summer, unsavoury pools collected everywhere. The coachmen would whip their horses almost to a frenzy and gallop wildly through the tortuous alleyways, with little more than a hurried shout to warn pedestrians to seek cover from the resulting spray.

On this particularly hot summer's day an ornate carriage entered the Barbican. Alerted by the sound of thundering hooves and shouts, several pedestrians moved swiftly to the sides of the lane by the fish market and watched the carriage fly by in a golden blur. The full beauty of the vehicle could only be appreciated later when, after its dash through the labyrinthine town and its harbour area, it came to rest by the docked HMS *Eden*. The coat of arms of the aristocratic Loch family was visible on both sides of the carriage. As the door facing the ship swung open, the family shield glinted in the sun and reflected a deep yellow glow.

Plymouth had played a pivotal role in Britain's conquest of the world ever since Sir Francis Drake had sailed out of the Barbican with his fleet to confront the Spanish Armada in the sixteenth century. In the intervening two and a half centuries, the kingdom had gone from strength to strength and its maritime power was firmly rooted in its ports, in the merchantmen that imported and exported goods from the outer reaches of the colonies and in the men-of-war that protected trade and sought out new markets, by force when necessary.

Captain Francis James Erskine Loch stepped out of the carriage and put his cocked hat firmly on his head. He filled his lungs with the pungent air of the docks, gazed briefly at his beautiful ship in her berth and then turned to offer his hand to his wife, Lady Jesse, to help her out of the carriage. She opened a parasol to protect herself from the sun and walked daintily, her hand on her husband's arm, as they made their way on board the ship.

Loch was just a little past his thirtieth year, a man not much given to compliments. He was born into a wealthy family and both his father and uncle had served in the Royal Navy. The family owned a great deal of land in the north of England and Scotland and had high-level connections both in His Majesty's Government and in the colonies across the world.

As soon as they stepped on board the *Eden*, a shrill whistle sounded and an officer bellowed, 'Captain on board!' As one, the entire crew of sailors and marines in their military uniforms stood to attention on deck. The officers saluted their new captain, who promptly reciprocated, while the captain's ensign was hoisted to rest just below that of the Royal Navy.

All eyes were on Loch. HMS *Eden* was to be dispatched to fight in distant lands, and her 120-strong crew took in the features of the man who would be in charge of their lives for the next months, perhaps even years. The marines waited to be inspected by their new captain in the time-honoured tradition, and were visibly disappointed when Loch nodded perfunctorily towards them and instead headed straight for his quarters.

He entered his cabin on the quarterdeck followed by two officers who took off their caps and waited for him to notice them. When his eyes finally fell on them, he smiled as he registered the features of Lieutenant John Mansen.

'My dear John,' Loch said warmly. 'Good to see you, old chap.'

They shook hands and Mansen turned to kiss Lady Jesse's hand. 'How do you do, ma'am?'

The captain patted him on the back and teased, 'How have you managed to stay so young after all these years?'

'Thank you, and a pleasure to see you, sir,' said Mansen with a grin. 'The messages you sent to the Admiralty bore fruit and they agreed to transfer me from the second fleet to the *Eden*.'

The captain flicked his right hand as though chasing away a fly. 'The Admiralty, indeed,' he said with a nod. 'Took me a full fortnight to convince them to assign you to me.' Loch chuckled and spoke to his wife. 'Our friend Mansen is deemed the brightest officer in the entire navy.' He turned to the lieutenant. 'The second fleet was certainly most unwilling at first to see you leave them to come with me.'

'I have always wished to serve under your command again, sir,' replied Mansen formally and, with a sweep of his arm, introduced the second officer in the cabin. 'This is your number two, Lieutenant Duncan Williams, who has just arrived from London.'

Loch peered at the lieutenant and offered him a thin smile. 'Williams, yes – good to have you on board. The Admiralty talked a lot about you as well,' he said, adding cryptically, 'I hope we will be in agreement during the journey or else I might have to feed you to the whales as I usually do with those I dislike.'

Williams was unsure whether to take this as a joke or a veiled threat. He opted for a wan smile and said, 'You'll never doubt my loyalty, sir.' He, too, bowed as he reached down to kiss Lady Jesse's hand, while looking furtively at Mansen. His first meeting with the captain seemed to have got off to an inauspicious start and he searched the other officer's face for any cues.

The captain moved to a sideboard where he found a bottle of brandy. He poured himself a glass and gestured vaguely with his finger for the officers to help themselves. Mansen complied straight away, but Williams hesitated: the captain had not explicitly offered them a drink, thereby ignoring the unwritten code of conduct.

Mansen had become acquainted with the captain during a long voyage on HMS *Mistral* and the two had managed to overcome their differences. Owing to his aristocratic breeding, Loch regarded those around him as little more than servants; in truth, had it not been for his family's position, he never would have acquired his commission in the navy. From Loch's perspective, sailors were just sailors because their minds had been created that way, and all social distinctions were divinely ordained.

Mansen had learned to accept that the captain rarely paid much attention to the crew, even though good relations on board were essential for morale on long journeys at sea. He knew the captain would often remain in his cabin for days on end, writing his log and talking to no one, acknowledging the crew's salutes with little more than a nod whenever he emerged on deck. Mansen had come to forgive this brusqueness because Loch was not devoid of positive traits. The captain was brave in combat and a skilful strategist. He would treat his men kindly after having tested them for a long, seemingly endless period.

Mansen poured a glass for himself and one for Williams, urging him with his eyes to accept. Mansen downed his drink in one gulp, the veins in his neck and face bulging and then relaxing. Taking his cap in his hand, he tapped Williams' arm to signal the meeting was over. 'With your permission, sir, we'll be on our way,' Mansen said.

The captain glanced at his wife, who was busy unpacking. 'Yes. Let's call it a day. We have a long journey ahead of us.'

The men saluted and turned smartly on their heels. As Williams was leaving, his eyes fell on Lady Jesse, and he thought of the scent of the perfume on her hand when he had kissed her.

Once outside and out of earshot, Williams asked, 'Do you really like the captain?'

'Yes, I do. Why do you ask?'

Williams shrugged. 'Wouldn't you say he was, um –' he struggled to find the appropriate word, 'unusual?'

Mansen was amused. 'The man has several personalities. The worst is the one you just saw, but you'll see other personalities that may be better. My advice to you is to pray that he will come to like you. Once he does, this journey will be like child's play.'

'And if he doesn't?' Williams asked.

'Then you should pray we don't encounter any starving whales.'

They emerged on deck and Mansen reminded him that, as the deputy, it was the lieutenant's duty now to give the order to weigh anchor.

There was a flurry of activity as soon as the order was given; scurrying like ants, everyone knew where to go and what to do. The crew pulled on ropes to unfurl the sails and the ship slowly slipped out of her berth at Plymouth, opening her sails to the wind like a seagull that had come to perch on top of the crow's-nest.

As darkness fell, Loch opened the captain's log, dipped his pen in the ink bottle and stared at the blank page. This was the first of what would be many logs and he paused to reflect and imagine the reams that he would no doubt write over the course of this difficult mission.

He began with his name, the date and a brief inventory of the ship:

I am Francis James Erskine Loch, Captain of His Majesty's Ship, Eden, weighing four hundred and fifteen tons, with one hundred and twenty souls on board and twenty-four cannon. We set sail from Plymouth at one o'clock in the afternoon on this ninth day of June, one thousand eight hundred and eighteen. The winds were favourable.

Loch was not sure he liked Williams – time would tell if he would ever warm to him – but at least he had succeeded in securing Mansen, who had proved his reliability and friendship on board the *Mistral*. He would need all the loyalty of his crew on this voyage.

Loch closed the logbook, lit his pipe and blew out the candle on the desk. Enveloped in darkness, he heard his wife's voice from the adjoining cabin.

'Don't you want to get some sleep, Francis?' she called out.

He drew on his pipe and gazed into the night. The *Eden* was setting sail for one of the most remote and hazardous locations in the world. Soon enough, she would be plying the waters of the Persian Gulf, looking for pirates who had taken to blocking sea routes and plundering British ships that travelled to and from Asia.

When Lady Jesse repeated her question, he replied, 'Yes, in a while. I'm thinking of the pirates we're going to meet, my dear.'

'Which pirates do you mean?' she asked.

In the darkness his wife was little more than a black silhouette. He placed his pipe in his mouth once again and said, 'The pirates of Arabia, those who block sea routes and plunder ships travelling to and from Asia. They are the reason for our journey.'

Even his officers did not yet know the nature of the mission. He did not know how they would react, though many would be grateful they were not heading for South America, with its mosquitoes and endemic diseases.

'Arabia?' said Lady Jesse with distaste. 'You know how I hate going to these places. I'm told they're suffocating and hot, and their people are backward and barbaric. You simply had to accept this damned mission.'

'Good night, dear,' he said curtly as he emptied his pipe into an ashtray. They had discussed this subject on several occasions and he did not feel inclined to talk about it now. He looked forward to dropping his wife off in Muscat before any actual fighting took place.

But Lady Jesse was not so easily dismissed. 'Always thinking of invading and killing so that you can be called a hero and attain higher military honours. I would remind you that we're the ones going to them while they haven't thought of coming to us.' She paused. 'Hardly a chivalrous endeavour.'

Loch opened a porthole and stuck his head out for a breath of fresh air. He loathed the stagnant smell of ship cabins.

These were difficult years for him, but they were necessary if he was to advance within the Royal Navy. This was an assignment of singular importance, and he had seized on it to strengthen his military career. A success in Arabia could translate into a position of vice-admiral. But first, he had to ensure the safety of British trade by removing the threat from the Arabian buccaneers.

The *Eden* sailed in a southwesterly current towards the West African coast, and Loch was still brooding when he caught sight of dolphin fins shining in the moonlight in the ship's wake.

He smiled at this good omen.

Chapter 2

Bushehr, Persia

T HE PORT OF BUSHEHR was the only harbour in the eastern
side of the Gulf with facilities to receive merchantmen. It
handled merchandise that originated from as far afield as India,
the Bay of Bengal and China, as well as from the nearer cities of
Shiraz and Basra; from Bushehr, the goods were shipped to the
rest of the world.

In any given year, the port accommodated some fifty ships,
in addition to small fishing vessels and boats used for transport
between the ports of the Gulf. Its five thousand inhabitants
were a mixture of Arabs and Persians who lived in abject poverty
and competed endlessly for trade. The calls to prayer rang out
five times a day from three mosques – two for the Shias and a
third for the Sunnis – and small communities of Christians and
Jews also vied for space in the town. The traders were in constant
contact with their counterparts in such cities as Cochin,
Bombay and Basra.

Although Bushehr was ethnically and culturally diverse, it
enjoyed stability and was free from tensions – mainly because
everyone was busy making a living. The inhabitants spoke
Arabic or Persian and, most often, a pidgin mixture of both,
which the merchants and sailors had been compelled to learn in
order to communicate successfully. Illiteracy was widespread

except among those lucky enough to have been taught the rudiments of reading and arithmetic at the religious schools. Most of the inhabitants were sailors who had learned their trade through a timeless oral tradition: they knew the prevailing weather conditions from the colour of the sky, the direction of the wind and the shape of the waves, and they navigated by the stars.

The British governor's official residence, Government House, stood conspicuously on the coast. Its façade of white plaster set it apart from the other houses, built either of clay or palm leaves. The scorching sun had faded the colours of the Union Jack that fluttered in front of the building. Outside, a Persian soldier stood guard to prevent curious passers-by from entering.

Government House was rendered all the more striking by a collection of lemon and palm trees at the entrance and a lane paved with white stones that led from the street to the building.

Many British governors had been posted to Bushehr, and while some had concentrated their attention on the building itself, adding new wings or repainting, others had focused on the garden and on planting a variety of trees and shrubs. Consequently, Government House reflected a jumble of tastes that only emphasised its oddity as a landmark on the coast. Locals had taken to calling it 'the strange building with the tattered flag'.

Not far from the governor's residence and overlooking the harbour was a popular coffee house where traders met in the evening to talk, smoke and make deals. This was also the hub for illicit trade – where money was exchanged for goods stolen by pirates.

David Matthews knew about the illegal traffic, just as he knew he was the butt of many jokes. As the administrative official and second in command at Government House, he began his days at the docks, picking his way through the stacks of merchandise and crates of livestock that had been earmarked for import or export. Matthews had spent an entire year in the town, monitoring the movement of cargo and calculating the taxes due to the East India Company.

He was not happy to be assigned to Bushehr and complained incessantly about the dirt, the flies and the heat. He was considered effeminate by the traders and sailors he came into contact with; they mocked him on account of his formal Western attire, his conspicuous hat and, especially, the scented handkerchief he covered his mouth and nose with, to guard against the pervasive odours of the harbour. Matthews kept the handkerchief on his face even when he spoke to the sailors, which only added to their derision. While he knew they were having a good laugh at his expense, he did not take much notice as long as they paid the taxes owed to the Company.

In shielding his face he unwittingly resembled the women of Bushehr, who concealed their faces for altogether different reasons. The women wore garments studded with metallic ornaments that sparkled in the sunlight, and which covered their faces except for a small slit for the eyes. The veils were similar to those worn by Bedouin women in the Arabian Peninsula, but were slightly shorter, revealing the lower lip. Almost all the women in Bushehr wore the face veils, with the exception of the few who came from the interior of Persia.

As an unmarried man, Matthews considered his life in Bushehr to be a living hell: dust and grime were everywhere and he never felt clean despite scouring his room and washing himself and his clothes every day. He hated the food, which invariably had the taste, texture and even grit of sand. He often spat it out at mealtimes, cursing the day he had arrived in this land.

He spent most of his time at the harbour talking to traders in broken Persian or even more hopeless Arabic. They never fully understood him, and he would enter into lengthy negotiations with them until he lost his nerve and resorted to warnings and threats to put an end to the conversation.

Matthews had no friends in the town and only one regular companion, a Persian called Abbas, who spoke English interspersed with Farsi words. Abbas was a guard at the governor's office and, over time, they had established an understanding whereby Matthews took Abbas with him to act as interpreter and even to resolve disputes and arguments. It also suited Matthews to have a native of sorts with him who was quick to show others the correct way to address an Englishman.

Matthews had just emerged from a long argument with a trader and was wiping the sweat off his face when he noticed three ships in the distance coming in to harbour. He stared at them blankly through a telescope and thought wistfully of his home in England. He frowned as he realised they were not the regular dhows or junks used by traders.

'Good Lord!' he exclaimed and, without another word, handed Abbas the telescope and hurried away from the docks.

The Persian guard looked at him in bewilderment and turned to squint at the ships, wondering what demon of the sea had suddenly appeared to the Englishman.

Matthews sprinted the short distance to Government House, causing many traders and labourers to grin and point at the flustered foreigner.

With barely a knock at the door, Matthews rushed in to see the governor, Colin Bruce.

'What the devil?' Bruce held a fan made of palm leaves and was beating the air furiously in front of his red face. He pointed the fan at Matthews as he added, 'You'd better have a jolly good reason for barging in like this.' He reached for a cup of tea on the desk to which he had added a generous dash of rum. 'Well?' he said impatiently, bringing the cup to his lips.

Matthews was out of breath and spoke haltingly. 'Pirate,' he said. 'Erhama – b-bin Jaber's ships, sir. I think he's here.'

The governor nearly choked on his drink. He hastily deposited the cup on the desk, splashing some tea. Matthews made a mental note that the office smelled faintly of rum.

'Are you sure?' asked Bruce anxiously. 'Are you absolutely certain of this? It's too early, much earlier than we expected!'

'I've seen his colours on the masts, sir,' replied Matthews. 'Three ships coming into Bushehr. One must presume he's on board one of them.'

The governor jumped to his feet and strode to the door, pausing only to pick up his hat. 'Come then,' he announced. 'Let's not waste any time in meeting him.'

By the time the two men reached the docks to stand by Abbas, the ships had drawn closer to the harbour and it was almost possible to make out the ensigns with the naked eye. But Bruce held out his hand for the telescope and focused on each ship in turn.

'You're right, Matthews,' he said at length. 'Those are his colours. That's Erhama bin Jaber alright.'

Ordinarily, the sight of three pirate warships coming in to harbour would have been terrifying and, as governor of the district, Bruce would have barked orders to arrange some form of defence. Instead, he turned to Abbas and asked him to prepare some tea and sherbet as well as some tobacco for the arrival of his guest.

This was not an ordinary, dull day in Bushehr, and Erhama bin Jaber was not an average, run-of-the-mill corsair. Everyone, including His Majesty's Government, sought his friendship; a directive from the highest levels in London – via Government House in Bombay – had instructed Bruce to make overtures to the pirate. He knew he would have to record every detail of his meeting with the pirate, which he would then pass on to his superior in India, the Governor of Bombay.

Matthews noticed that, as the ships drew nearer, the general din in the harbour died down and silence crept over the port. Traders and sailors were well aware of the ships' identity and many left the docks out of fear of what might happen. Even the livestock – the horses, camels and sheep that usually added their clamour to the general hubbub – were eerily quiet.

The ships dropped anchor and their sails were hastily folded.

Erhama bin Jaber stood on the deck of the first ship – the *Ghatrousha* – and took in the town with a steady gaze.

The pirate's reputation was well-known on the maritime trade routes from India to Basra and from Bushehr to Madagascar, though no one knew for certain where he actually lived. Some believed he lived in a private fort in Dammam near the Arabian coast of the Gulf. Others claimed he had a special hideout on the Qatari coast, while still others said he had a pact with the Qawasimis and had a home and a wife in their region. But all these were no more than unconfirmed stories.

Erhama bin Jaber's life itself was the stuff of legends and lent itself to endless embellishments by sailors as they sat drinking tea at night. His chronicle of deeds was a mixture of fact and fiction, constructed according to the needs and wishes of the narrators. Though the versions of the pirate's life were bizarre and inconsistent, Erhama, who was in his late sixties, never bothered to correct any of the details, preferring to create an aura of mystery around himself which served him well. Whenever he gave an order in his distinctive booming voice, his men carried out his command without question. They were a mixture of Arabs, ethnic Baluchis and slaves, as well as a few Malabar Indians captured during assaults on commercial vessels.

Erhama made ready to disembark. His beard was unkempt and he wore a small white turban. His cotton gown, creased and visibly grimy, came down to mid-calf and was partly covered by a black woollen cloak on his shoulders. But the Englishmen who were waiting for him focused on his belt, which held two pistols and an expensive gold dagger, and on the sword slung over his shoulder that accompanied him wherever he went.

His injuries revealed a lifetime of battles: he had little movement in his left hand because of shrapnel that had lodged in it a long time ago, and his face was disfigured by a scar running from the left side of his forehead down to his cheek across his left eye. That eye, or rather its absence from the ashen socket, was the first thing people looked at.

Erhama peered at his hosts as he advanced towards them. The governor held out his hand and the two men shook hands, each with a guarded smile.

Bruce spoke Arabic fluently and said formally, 'I welcome you to the port of Bushehr. Would you like to come with me to Government House where we can talk?'

Erhama acquiesced and, as he was led away from the docks, the few traders, labourers and sailors who had remained watched him warily, hoping that the newcomer would soon disappear so that trade might resume.

Erhama's son, Bashir, followed the three men. The twenty-year-old was good-looking, unlike his father, and he was keen to learn English fluently. He already had picked up a little Persian, Hindi and English from his father's crew. Bringing up the rear was Erhama's faithful slave, Dirar, who was his master's right hand and confidant.

Once inside the governor's office, Erhama sat in a wooden chair and was offered tea by Abbas. Slightly uncomfortable because of the weapons he carried, Erhama laid the pistols on the table, leaving the gold dagger in his belt. He placed his sword beneath his thighs and mechanically drew the blade out a little way and inserted it again into its scabbard, only to repeat the process. It was a particular habit of his: he liked the rhythmic sound it made, like the ticking of a clock, as hilt met scabbard.

It was a habit Bruce found particularly irritating, but he forced himself to ignore it as he asked genially if he could get Erhama anything else to drink.

Erhama shook his head. 'I'm here only for a couple of days. I know my visit bothers you so I will not stay long.' The governor was about to protest, so Erhama added, 'I have many enemies who might make trouble for you if they knew of my presence here. All I need is to get some supplies for my ships and give my men a little breathing space – then I will leave.'

'We will offer you what we can,' said Bruce, 'on the understanding that your men will not attack any of our – um – interests or the interests of the Shah of Persia. But I am *very* glad that you are here.'

Erhama raised his eyebrows in surprise. 'Oh?'

The governor cleared his throat. 'His Majesty's Government would like to enter into a pact with you, according to which you would agree not to attack commercial ships coming from or going to India.' Bruce paused briefly and then continued. 'I have also been instructed to invite you to be an ally of His Majesty's Government in the region by fighting the Qawasimis and the Wahhabis who are fomenting trouble for us.'

Erhama frowned. 'And what would I gain from such an agreement?'

'The full support – and gratitude – of His Majesty.'

There was a long silence that was interrupted only by the clicking sound of the pirate's sword on the scabbard.

Erhama sipped his tea and spoke again only once he had finished it. 'I stand to lose a great deal,' he said slowly. 'As you know, I'm an ally of the Wahhabis. As for the Qawasimis, I cannot afford to become their enemy as well.' He placed his cup firmly on the table and peered at the governor. 'I know there have been unusual movements in Bushehr for quite some time now and that many Persian soldiers who serve the Prince of Shiraz have pitched tent some distance from here. So why don't you tell me what's really happening?'

Bruce nodded. 'Well then, you will know that the Wahhabis have recently taken over in Bahrain. We intend to remove them from the island with the cooperation of the Sultan of Oman.'

The pirate narrowed his eyes. '*We?*' he said. 'Who is this *we*?'

'His Majesty's Government,' Bruce replied evenly. 'We have been in conflict with the Wahhabis for many years, but their influence has grown lately in a manner that seriously threatens our interests. We've coordinated plans with our friends in Oman and they are willing to provide a military force and ships. The Prince of Shiraz has also agreed to supply us with two thousand soldiers to be part of a campaign to put an end to the Wahhabi presence in Bahrain.' The governor paused. 'We are planning for war,' he stressed, 'and we need to know on which side Erhama bin Jaber and his men will fight.'

The sword momentarily stopped clicking. When Erhama next spoke, it was in an uncharacteristically low voice. 'Are you aware of what you're saying? In doing this you will be turning back the hands of time. As you know, I took part in the battle to kick the Persians out of Bahrain. You'll be handing the island back to them. But neither you nor the Sultan of Oman will be able to do anything about it afterwards.' The sword began to move rhythmically again. 'I fought with the Al-Khalifas to liberate the island from the Persians. I lost my left eye and the movement in my left hand. Others lost far more. It's a high price that cannot be forgotten.'

'We are planning for war,' repeated Bruce, 'and not just in Bahrain. Our victory will be across the Arabian Peninsula. Those who are with us will appreciate how generous His Majesty's Government can be.'

Erhama asked to smoke and Dirar reached for some tobacco on the table and lit a pipe for him. As Erhama inhaled the smoke long and deeply, he fixed his gaze on Bruce with his one good eye. He released the smoke, stared at the ceiling and inhaled again.

'Let me think it over.'

'I really must insist on knowing your decision,' the governor said somewhat brusquely. 'We have no time to waste, Erhama.'

The pirate rose to his feet, gathered his pistols and stuck them back in his belt, then slung his sword over his shoulder. 'You will have my answer in a day or two,' he said and strode out of the office, swiftly followed by Bashir and Dirar.

Erhama was not in the habit of sleeping away from his crew, for life had taught him that sleeping on the *Ghatrousha* was much safer than sleeping in a house. He hurried back to his floating home surrounded by his loyal entourage, which anxiously awaited his decision.

As darkness fell, the heat became less intense and a refreshing sea breeze sprang up.

Outside Government House, Bruce and Matthews could just make out the mixture of sounds and voices coming from the direction of the pirate's ship – even the clicking of Erhama's sword slamming into the scabbard drifted in from the docks. They could also discern a group of shadows around the fire.

'What do you suppose they're talking about?' Bruce asked.

'Don't know, sir, but it's clear the pirate knows what he wants,' replied Matthews. 'He's a cunning old fox, isn't he?'

The governor gazed long at the fire that blazed on the *Ghatrousha*. 'We need him on our side so we can concentrate on the Wahhabis.'

Matthews had little faith in agreements, knowing that not everything written on paper was respected and that interests had the upper hand in the end. 'Even if we do convince him to sign, what makes you so sure that he'll honour the pact? In my work at the harbour I've seen countless deals that were broken even before the ink had dried.'

Bruce lowered his gaze to the waves breaking on the shore. The sound of the surf seemed to echo Erhama's sword. Placing his hand on Matthews's shoulder, he said, 'You're probably right. But those are our orders from London.' The Governor of Bombay had relayed the orders and Bruce still hoped to be able to report back that the Arabian corsair had been neutralised and would not attack merchantmen coming from India. He said out loud, 'Did you know that Erhama has never attacked a ship flying the Union Jack? I suppose, with the coming war, our friends in Bombay are rather worried he may change tack.' He led Matthews back inside Government House. 'Let's call it a day, shall we? I bet the pirate and his men will stay up all night mulling over our offer.'

There was an uneasy calm in Bushehr. The main coffee house was deserted, as were the streets. But residents of the town, who, in search of cool night air, would often sleep on the roofs of their houses, looked out at the harbour and the fire on the pirate's ship that burned until just before dawn.

In the morning, Bruce made his way toward his office feeling heavy. Outside the office sat the guard who most days slept continuously until he was scorched by the blazing sun and stung by flies. Bruce was about to enter his office when he spotted a knife sticking out of the door that held a sheet of paper in place. He read:

I will make no deal with you. We may meet as friends today and as enemies tomorrow. But since I need you as much as you need me now, let us agree that for six months we will not fight each other.

He snatched the paper, cursed and hurried to the docks. Once there he was stunned to find that Erhama's ships had already gone. He grabbed a labourer and asked him about the ships, but the man was too terrified to answer. The governor let go of him and turned to another, who nodded and said, 'They took their supplies and weighed anchor before the dawn prayer.'

'Damn!' Bruce swore. 'What a damnable disaster! Damn!'

He walked back to Government House, talking to himself and kicking the ground. Those who saw him thought he had undoubtedly gone mad.

Chapter 3

Bombay

MAJOR GEORGE FORSTER SADLEIR sat in full military uniform as he waited in the hall to be admitted to see the governor at his headquarters in Bombay.

He took out his gold pocket watch and looked at it. He had been waiting for a long time and hoped that the meeting would begin and end quickly. It was particularly hot and humid in this palatial mansion; putting the watch away, he began to fan himself with his hat. Sadleir had worn his best uniform for his meeting with the governor – a uniform designed for cold European weather rather than the blistering heat of India.

He desperately wanted to be out of this stuffy palace and to take off all his clothes and immerse himself in cold water as he usually did after training or a game of polo.

The place was virtually empty, as if even the employees of Government House had found the heat too unbearable to come in to work.

After what seemed like an eternity, he heard the sound of footsteps in the corridor and saw the man who had admitted him and who now asked him to follow him to the governor's office.

Sadleir walked behind the tall Indian, who wore a turban with a feather at the front, and a gown that came halfway down his calves. They reached a door with the words 'Sir Evan Nepean, Governor of Bombay' written on it. The man stopped and gestured for him to wait.

The Indian knocked several times and, without waiting for permission to enter, opened the door and signalled to the officer to go in.

Sadleir marched into the room towards a man sitting behind an imposing desk. He stopped a few paces away and saluted smartly, the heels of his shoes coming down with a resonant click on the wooden floor.

Sir Evan beckoned to the officer to sit down and peered at him over some loose sheets of paper as though he were evaluating him. 'So you're Major George Forster Sadleir,' he said at length. 'I was going over your file.' He glanced down at the sheets as he continued, 'You joined the 47th Regiment at the age of sixteen and took part in several battles in South America and Afghanistan. Then a few years ago you trained some Persian officers – and made rather a good job of it by all accounts.' The major had shown some proficiency in Persian and Arabic, one of the reasons his file had been singled out. 'I see the Shah even gave you an honorary rank in his army, isn't that so?'

'Yes, sir,' answered Sadleir. 'But that mission was by no means a pleasant experience – I lost two of my friends from the 47th Regiment in Persia.'

'I see,' said the governor pensively. 'And how are you faring here?'

Sadleir was taken aback by the question; his general welfare was not often the subject of discussion, particularly not with one so senior in the government. 'Very well, thank you, sir,' he said with obvious hesitation. 'The regiment is fond of travelling and fighting for king and country. Ever since we moved to

Bombay, we seem to have spent most of our time hunting and playing polo.' He stopped abruptly, worried that he had said too much.

But Sir Evan's face remained impassive. Bushy, overhanging eyebrows practically concealed his eyes and long, white sideburns grew down his cheeks, almost meeting at the chin. He placed the sheets of paper on the desk and, clasping his hands together, asked the officer, 'What would you say then to a highly confidential mission?'

'What would you like me to do, sir?'

'Nothing less than safeguard the future of the Empire, my boy.' He unfurled a nautical map on the desk and asked the officer to join him. 'The future of British trade in this region will depend on your success in carrying out a most dangerous and secret assignment.'

Sadleir came to stand by the governor and realised with a start that his heart was pounding. Sir Evan scratched his sideburns, removed his glasses and returned them to his face once again.

Then, placing one finger on Bombay and another in the Gulf, Sir Evan began, 'With favourable winds, our ships can cover the distance from Bombay to the Gulf in three weeks. They usually carry spices, wood, perfumes, dried fruit, and textiles from China and Asia.' In rapid succession, he tapped on the ports of Muscat, Basra and Bushehr. He explained the strategic value of those ports and how goods were sent through Oman, Iraq and Persia, and then on to the Levant and Europe from where huge amounts of merchandise were shipped on to Africa and America. 'This is a flourishing trade that we can ill afford to lose. Do you understand, Major? Have you any idea what it took Britain to gain those trading rights – the wars over generations with our competitors?' His voice trailed off and he shook his head at the thought. 'I mean we lost some of our finest ships and our best young men at sea.'

The Governor of Bombay proceeded to list the wars that Britain had waged in order to rule the waves: a catalogue of conflicts with the Spaniards, French, Portuguese, Dutch, Arabs and Turks. The battles that changed the course of history had been hard-fought and had cost Britain dearly in terms of human and material losses.

'His Majesty's Government most certainly does not intend to lose these trading rights now.' The governor spread both hands across the area between the Indian subcontinent and the Arabian Peninsula. 'This region is vital for our interests. It is the life artery for which we must fight tooth and nail. Do you understand?'

'Yes, sir.'

'There will be many challenges ahead of us. Your role will be to bring together all the available resources in the region that will enable us to face these challenges and overcome them.'

Sadleir was feeling particularly hot and sticky, but he resisted the temptation to take out a handkerchief; he certainly did not want the governor to think that the prospect of the assignment was making him sweat.

'Do you know where Nejd is, Major?' asked Sir Evan abruptly. 'No? And why should you?' His finger landed in the heart of the Arabian Peninsula. Explaining that the name came from the Arabic word for 'plateau', he traced an invisible line down the peninsula: piracy and tribal conflicts were rampant in the east, while the Muslim holy sites were located in the west. Whoever ruled Nejd, he said, would control these two important regions: the commercial and the religious. 'About a hundred years ago,' he continued, 'a man called Mohammed Abdel Wahhab was born in a miserable little village in Nejd.'

The governor took great pride in his knowledge and he sketched out the growth of Wahhabism from the earliest calls to fight new ideas that had been introduced into Islam, to Abdel Wahhab's pact with an important tribal leader, Sheikh Mohammed bin Saud. By 1775, Nejd had adopted Wahhabism; ten years later, the eastern part of the Arabian Peninsula had done the same. Many people on the coast had also adopted Wahhabism and declared war against infidels.

'That would be us,' said Sir Evan. 'This was when they created a strong naval force and began to attack and destroy our trade.'

Now his fingers moved out towards Persia and the Ottoman Empire as he explained how not all Muslims had been persuaded by the zealots; the Wahhabis were especially unwelcome in the courts of the Shah of Persia and the Ottoman Sultan. Acting on the orders of his suzerain in Istanbul, the Khedive of Egypt had sent his son, Ibrahim Pasha, to the Hejaz in 1811.

He pointed at the western half of the Arabian Peninsula. 'This is where the Egyptian army is currently striving to suppress the movement and stop Wahhabi expansion.' His hand moved swiftly to the southeastern corner of the peninsula. 'Meanwhile, we have a friend in the Sultan of Oman who is also playing a pivotal role in stemming the Wahhabi tide, which has reached his region through his neighbours, the Qawasimis. He is helping us to resist this expansion both at sea and on land.'

The governor paused to see if Sadleir had digested the intricacies of the regional politics. 'We must put an end to Wahhabism and piracy in the Gulf,' he said forcefully. 'We must get rid of anybody who threatens our trade – the vital maritime route must remain safe and secure and, more importantly, it must stay under our complete control. That, my dear chap, is your mission.'

The stifling heat in the office had finally got the better of him; Sadleir reached for a handkerchief to mop the sudden stream of sweat from his brow.

'It is far from an easy assignment,' conceded the governor. 'But you will have a priceless object to help you.' He moved away from the desk. 'Now let me show you what you will use to accomplish your task.'

Sir Evan led the way to the other end of the office, to a large table on which was placed a sleek wooden box that was decorated with striking pictures and an intricate, Arabic script. 'This is the key to your mission, Major,' he said, opening the box. 'You must defend it with your life.'

Chapter 4

The Island of Madeira

THE WEATHER HAD BEEN fine and the winds favourable all the way to Madeira. The island, now administered by the Portuguese, had been under British rule for many years and still retained a strong British presence. As soon as the *Eden* docked at Funchal Bay, the port officials sent a messenger to the British consul on the island, who arrived to receive the captain in person when he disembarked.

Loch invited both his lieutenants, Mansen and Williams, to join him on the island. After eight days of sailing, it was a pleasure to walk on dry land, a pleasure that the captain did not wish to deny his officers or, for that matter, his wife. It was also his way of making amends for his absence from the wardroom since, during that first leg of the voyage, he had not felt inclined to socialise with his officers. In fact, Loch had rarely emerged from his cabin, and then often only to accompany Lady Jesse on deck late at night, after the sailors had retired, in order to allow her to stretch her legs and have a breath of fresh air.

The consul met them with a smile. 'Captain Loch,' he said, holding out his hand. 'A pleasure to meet you, sir.'

'The pleasure is all mine,' replied Loch as he shook the consul's hand. 'You really needn't have taken the trouble to come in person to meet us.'

The consul bowed and took Jesse's hand to kiss it. 'We don't receive visits from many beautiful ladies,' he said. 'It's a pleasure to meet you, Mrs Loch.'

He reached over to shake the lieutenants' hands. They exchanged pleasantries as he led them away from the docks and up a steep and winding road. The houses in Funchal Bay were built on the mountain slope facing the harbour. They were huddled together in a random fashion, leaving narrow paths for the passage of people and goods. A large square stood in the middle, where celebrations and seasonal markets were held. Alongside the well-paved road were bright flowers and green grass, and residents who saw the group raised their hats and caps respectfully.

As they climbed the hill, they could see the city beneath them. On their left was the summit of the mountain, overgrown with fruit and olive trees. They finally reached the consul's residence, a beautiful, whitewashed villa with a breath-taking view from the garden. At the entrance was a finely-sculpted fountain of a winged Eros carrying a bow, with water gushing from his mouth. The sound of cascading water and the smell of the mountain flowers added to the irresistible charm of the place, and Loch asked whether they might stay in the garden rather than going indoors.

The consul welcomed the suggestion and signalled to the servants, who quickly started to clean the chairs, lay the table and bring drinks and fruit.

Loch turned to his host. 'By bringing us here to this fabulous place, you've made me regret my decision to join the Royal Navy. I should most certainly have been happier in the diplomatic corps enjoying such beauty.'

Once they had been served refreshments, the consul asked them where the *Eden* was heading. The ship was one of the navy's finest men-of-war and he was curious to know to which continent the battle would be taken. The consul was well aware of the details of maritime movements and conflicts in Asia and Africa since all ships on their way to or from those continents called in at Madeira. So when Loch informed him that they were sailing to the Arabian Gulf, he nodded and was not at all surprised. He had read some of the dispatches about the simmering conflict between the East India Company and Arabian ships in the region.

'And what do you hope to achieve?' asked the consul.

'Ah well, that is a matter purely for the Admiralty.' Loch's response had been a bit curt, so he added more affably, 'It's a secret mission that I haven't explained yet to my officers.'

'Yes, but does the enemy know about your mission?' asked the consul with a twinkle in his eye. The consul went on to describe how, from a historical perspective, there were no real secrets. The consul, who was widely travelled and a voracious reader well versed in various cultures, had written books on geography and history. 'In any conflict,' he said, 'I find it most instructive to understand the motivations, to put oneself in the enemy's shoes, as it were. For instance, quite aside from the specifics of your secret mission, you are clearly going to wage war against Arabs. Have you asked yourself why they are fighting us in the first place?'

'These are backward tribes, sir – piracy is a way of life for them,' answered Loch coldly. 'There is similarly little to be gained in knowing why a bushman throws his spear at a European.'

'Yes, of course, but it would be interesting to know if, from their perspective at least, we are the pirates and plunderers. Do you not think this is intellectually interesting?'

Loch did not think so and chose to remain silent out of respect for his host.

Lady Jesse spoke now and asked the consul, 'I say, are you one of those who call themselves "enlightened"?'

The consul smiled broadly. 'We live in the Age of Reason, my dear lady. This is a time for civilised men to make the world brighter.'

It was Mansen who spoke next. 'That is all well and good, sir, but there are still entire continents that are dark.' He picked up on the analogy of a primitive African as an indirect way of offering support to his captain. 'You assume that all men are born equal, whereas many will have beastly instincts and throw spears simply because they cannot know otherwise.'

'My dear Lieutenant,' replied the consul, 'I too started my career as a young officer in the Royal Navy and had the opportunity to come into contact with various nations and peoples. I found that people are generally kind and peaceful by nature. All they want is to live without anyone forcing them to change their ways. They want neither an unjust ruler nor an invading army. I do believe there is an inherent humanity that binds us all.'

He was interrupted by the servants bringing trays of food to the table.

'Oh, what a feast,' cooed Lady Jesse and, taking in the vista, she said, 'Tell us a bit about this delightful island.'

The consul related a particular myth about two lovers during the reign of King Edward III who, finding objections to their union from their families, had decided to elope to France on a small ship. During their voyage, a mighty storm had struck their vessel and, after several weeks at sea, they had landed on the island. They had stayed on and had a family and, reputedly, all the inhabitants of the island were the offspring of that love.

Lady Jesse was particularly enthralled by the tale, and Williams could not help wondering how she had ended up with such an unromantic soul as the captain.

'But we are of course very close to the African coast,' added the consul. 'You'll find here communities of Arab as well as of African descent.'

Loch had been listening politely and he now looked up, astonished. 'Do you have Arabs here?'

'Of course, my dear Captain. The people you're going to fight are just a tiny part of a vast population stretching from the African coast to the Gulf. On my journeys, I have met Arabs living in Java, in the coastal regions of India and in Quanjiao in China.' He paused. 'Arabs lived in Europe for more than seven hundred years before they were kicked out. I do believe it's uncharitable to compare them to Bushmen with spears.' He then turned his attention to Lady Jesse and described the beautiful palaces that the Arabs had built in Spain. 'They left books, forts, gardens and irrigation systems. They were creative in the fields of medicine, astronomy, travel and geography. All this was burned down or destroyed in the name of heresy. Some of their best scientists were burned at the stake along with their cousins, the Jews, because they would not convert to Christianity. Some were burned because they refused to eat pork. Can you imagine that some of them were burned alive because they took a bath on Friday?'

The consul looked again at the captain and continued, 'There's talk that Christopher Columbus used a map drawn by an Arab to reach America and that some of his sailors were Moors. I don't want to bore you with this talk, Captain Loch, but you might do well to study the history of the people you wish to fight.'

Loch said nothing and went on eating. The consul continued the speech he had given to more than one visitor. 'I think people, my dear Captain, become creative when they live in an atmosphere of freedom, in a society where tolerance for others flourishes, where the government is an integral part of the society it governs and where justice prevails. Once the balance is lost, people become corrupted and their national traits change. When this happens, it becomes difficult to return things to their original state.'

When they eventually came to take their leave, Loch thanked the consul for his hospitality and said, 'You seem happy, sir. You lead a quiet life here, perhaps a bit too quiet for my tastes after all.'

'Of course, Captain. I wish you, your lovely wife and your officers a safe journey. I also hope to see you on your return from your mission.'

'We'll certainly stop by on our way back to Britain,' Loch replied. 'Perhaps we'll bring you one of those Arabian pirates so you may hammer some reason into him.'

'Please do call on me again,' insisted the consul. 'I've seen many men passing through here on their way to wars. They invariably return as different human beings. I would be keen to know if that will be your experience.'

The *Eden* set sail again after two days in Funchal Bay, which Loch duly recorded in his logbook. He also wrote how the Empire would certainly be doomed if more British began to believe in the universality of men as the Consul of Madeira did.

Chapter 5

Off the Coast of Bahrain

E RHAMA BIN JABER'S SHIPS left the port of Bushehr at night, heading west. Whenever he drew near to Bahraini shores, between the peninsula of Qatar and the Al-Ahsa coast, Erhama would contemplate the palm trees in the distance and his breathing would grow so loud that his crew could hear it. The mere mention of Bahrain would cause his mood to turn morose. The hatred between Erhama and the rulers of the island was mutual.

As they approached Bahrain, Erhama asked Dirar to signal to the commanders of the other two ships to board the *Ghatrousha* for a meeting. They joined him at the stern, where he sat drinking coffee and smoking. He opened a small box that lay near him and took out a rough brown sheet of paper and a piece of coal that had been pared at the tip and served as a pencil. He gave them to his son, Bashir, and began to dictate:

> *Dear Ibrahim bin Ofaisan, may God keep you!*
> *I write to tell you I was in Bushehr a few days ago where I was met by the British governor. He proposed an alliance with them under which I would pledge not to attack commercial ships heading from India to the Gulf or those flying the British flag, though I have not done that for many years now.*

But this is not the most important matter. There were around two thousand Persian soldiers at a camp a few hours from Bushehr. They were certainly not there on a picnic. Their presence, plus the request for an agreement and the governor's confession that his government plans to invade Bahrain in order to return the Al-Khalifas to power, make their intent clear. The British are planning a huge campaign, and do not want any interference from me.

The invasion of Bahrain is inevitable. But there is also another British plan, which the governor kept secret, that aims to build on their anticipated success in Bahrain and that relates to the entire Arabian Peninsula. If they wished to fight the Qawasimis they would have amassed their troops at the port of Gombroon or in Bandar Lengeh or Qeshm Island. Given that they are amassing these forces in Bushehr, it is clear to me that you are the target. Be prepared, brother, to make your escape.

Peace be upon you,
Erhama

Erhama asked Bashir to stamp the letter with the seal kept inside the box. 'Deliver my message to Bin Ofaisan but beware of spending the night with him even if he insists. Do you remember where we last met him three months ago?'

Bashir nodded. 'Off the western coast of Bahrain.'

'That's right,' he said and, turning to his commanders, he gestured to one of the other ships. 'We will remove my flag from the mast of the *Munawara* and place wooden planks and furniture on board to make it look like a commercial ship. Bashir will be accompanied by ten sailors and the rest of the crew will join us here.'

He addressed his son again. 'You'll lead the *Munawara*. Once you arrive in the small bay off the western coast of Bahrain, wait until nightfall, then light a lamp, raise it high and move it from left to right seven times. Stop and wait until you have counted to fifty and then repeat the process three times. When you see a light on the coast returning the signal, put out your lamp and wade in to shore. After you have delivered my message, return to the ship and head for our hideout in Qatar, where we will wait for you.'

The *Munawara* sailed quickly westwards, while the other two ships headed south. Once Bashir reached his destination, he waited for nightfall before lighting a lamp and giving the signal as his father had instructed. The response soon came from the shore, so he left the ship and waded through the shallow waters until he came to the source of the light.

He was greeted by a dark, elderly man who asked him to follow him. Bashir scrutinised the man's face in the dim light: he was around sixty, with a shining white beard and kind eyes that inspired trust. On his head was a piece of cloth that was tightly wound, and he wore a short cotton gown and a leather belt with a cheap knife.

The two men walked a short distance until they reached two tethered donkeys. The old man mounted one of them and invited Bashir to ride the other. There was nothing around except the all-consuming darkness, and Bashir asked the man what he had been doing in such a forbidding place.

'Waiting for you,' he replied simply.

'For me?'

'Erhama sent you, didn't he?' said the old man. 'Our work requires us to remain here. Servants bring us water and food every three days. When we see the light signal, we reply, knowing that it is from Erhama or someone he sends. It's our job to escort you safely to our master Bin Ofaisan and bring you back here when you ask.'

Astonished, Bashir said, 'Who is *we*? I don't see anyone else here other than you.'

'Yes, sir – there are two of us. After we see the signal, my companion heads off at once on his horse to our master, who will meet you in a secret location away from prying eyes.'

'Prying eyes?'

'Bahrain is a tiny island and our master has many enemies,' the old man said.

Bashir knew that could mean the British, the Al-Khalifas or even the Omanis. The port teemed with all sorts of people, including spies.

They travelled in silence for what seemed an eternity. The man was not disposed to talk and it was so pitch dark that Bashir could barely see his own donkey's ears, let alone the path ahead.

Eventually, Bashir spoke merely to break the silence and hear another's voice in this blackest of nights. 'I forgot to ask your name.'

'I'm Yaqout, sir. I'm one of Bin Ofaisan's slaves,' he said. 'We're almost there, sir.'

What at first appeared to be a sinister wall loomed in front of them, seeming to have come from nowhere. It looked like a gateway to hell and it was only as they approached it and Bashir squinted that he realised that it was in fact an unbroken line of palm trees. The dark night had been playing tricks on his eyes.

Once past this barrier, it seemed as if they had entered a black tunnel. Putting his trust in God, Bashir closed his eyes and let his donkey follow the old man's, finding a path through the dense grove.

After a while, a few scattered houses appeared at the edge and he opened his eyes to a clay candlelit house with a wide doorway. He climbed off his donkey and followed Yaqout into the squat dwelling.

In the centre of the single room sat Bin Ofaisan, drinking coffee and reaching for a date from a wicker plate.

Bin Ofaisan did not appear remotely surprised to see him; he grinned and got up so they could shake hands. To Erhama, Bin Ofaisan was a friend and an ally, so out of respect for the older man, Bashir kissed the top of his head.

Bin Ofaisan wore a clean white gown that almost reached to the ground when he was standing, a woollen cloth wound around his head and a leather belt about his waist. He had a long white beard that came down to his chest and he held a small stick which he used to tap the ground from time to time in a way that reminded Bashir of his father's habit with his sword.

Bin Ofaisan had come to Bahrain at the head of a Wahhabi army to help the Al-Khalifas expel the Omanis. After the Wahhabi troops had completed their task, Bin Ofaisan had remained in Bahrain and, backed by his soldiers, had compelled the Al-Khalifas to accept him as the uncrowned prince of the island.

Bashir remembered everything that his father had told him about Bin Ofaisan. The man's prolonged stay in Bahrain had provoked the anger of the Al-Khalifas, the British and the Omanis. It did not surprise him that they were all conspiring to force him out in any way possible.

'Please be seated, my son,' Bin Ofaisan said to his guest. He then asked Yaqout to bring more coffee.

They exchanged pleasantries and, once the coffee was served, Bin Ofaisan offered his guest a date from the wicker plate. 'What can I do for you, son? What brings you to Bahrain?'

Bashir reached for the message in his pocket and handed it over.

Bin Ofaisan took his time to read the letter. His face gradually turned pale, and the hand that held the sheet began to shake almost imperceptibly. He looked up. 'When will you sail again?'

'Tonight, sir,' replied Bashir. 'My father ordered me to leave the island as soon as I had delivered this message.'

Bin Ofaisan nodded and promptly ordered his slave to bring him a pen. On the back of Erhama's letter he wrote:

Dear Erhama,
They have united against us. I sense the many conspiracies around me. A large group of my companions has lately been recalled to Diriyah following the news that Ibrahim Pasha, who wishes to use his army to quash our blessed Wahhabi movement, has arrived in the Hejaz. I now have only a small number of men, who would be useless in full-scale combat.
I will meet you in the north of Qatar in our usual place ten days from today.
May God protect and preserve you,
Ibrahim

With a message to deliver, Bashir asked Yaqout to lead him back through the darkness and took his leave.

Chapter 6

Bombay

T HE GOVERNOR REACHED FOR the sword in the sleek wooden box and held it out to Sadleir.

Though the box was beautiful, it was the scabbard that caused the officer's eyes to widen as he took in the array of encrusted jewels and precious gems. Sadleir drew the sword gently, his fingers tenderly running over the inscriptions engraved on the blade as though fingering the softest silk.

'Good Lord!' he exclaimed with awe. 'I've never seen anything like it.'

'Yes, Major,' said Sir Evan. 'It's worth a small fortune. One of a kind, actually. It was meant as a gift for His Majesty, but, given the situation in the region, we've decided to put it to better use.'

The officer was still busy scrutinising the blade, so the governor patted Sadleir's arm to attract his attention. 'As I said, this sword is the key to your mission, Major. You cannot succeed without it. Let me explain what I mean.'

He took the sword from Sadleir's hand and replaced it in its scabbard and box. Then, once he was satisfied that he had the officer's full attention, he turned to the map on the desk and swept his hand across the region. 'The Shah of Persia is our ally,' he began, his finger tracing the extent of Persian territory. He spoke about the Crown's special relationship with the Shah, particularly the military and commercial ties that allowed Britain to trade freely in Persia and to collect taxes from ships that docked at Bushehr.

'But there's a new power,' said Sir Evan darkly. 'A band of zealots that is beginning to take its toll on our trade and presence.' His hand closed in a fist to hover over the Arabian side of the Gulf.

In recent years, Britain's traditional enemies in the region, the Qawasimis, had become more than mere irritants. They had adopted the Wahhabi strain of Islam, which had filtered in from the hinterland of the Arabian Peninsula, and had taken control of a swathe of territory extending from Al-Ahsa to Ras al-Khaimah.

A finger shot out and landed firmly on the coastal town of Ras al-Khaimah, at the mouth of the Gulf. 'This place has become a den of pirates,' the governor continued, as if squashing an invisible pest that had crawled onto the map. 'This is where the likes of the outlaw Erhama bin Jaber are based.' He paused to see if Sadleir had recognised the name of the infamous brigand whose ships terrorised the Gulf and the Arabian Sea. 'That rogue is backed by the pro-Wahhabi ruler of Bahrain, an unsavoury but shrewd character called Ibrahim bin Ofaisan. So let me tell you our plan, Major. It involves getting the Egyptian army led by Ibrahim Pasha, which is camped two days away from Diriyah, to join forces with our ally, the Sultan of Oman.'

The Crown needed the Sultan because he was fighting the Wahhabi menace on his territory from land and sea; the Sultan needed Britain because of his aspirations for an independent homeland. But he was reluctant to cooperate with the bloodthirsty Ibrahim Pasha, who was notorious in the Arabian

Peninsula for his plundering and looting. The Sultan had made it clear that he would not tolerate the Egyptian army close to his borders.

In the Byzantine politics of the region, Ibrahim Pasha also needed Britain's support in order to strengthen the nascent state that his father, Mohammed Ali Pasha, had carved out in Egypt.

'Your mission, Major, is as crucial as it is confidential,' the governor said, speaking slowly. 'You are to draw Ibrahim Pasha into a pact that includes the British troops in the Gulf area and the Sultan's men. With such a pact, we will easily get rid of all the pirates and our trade will be safe.'

Sadleir nodded slowly as the governor explained the strategy that he should adopt with every leader and the itinerary that had been set out for him. First, he would travel to Oman on HMS *Thetis*, a man-of-war that had been transformed into an innocuous merchantman in order not to raise any suspicions.

In Muscat, a representative of the East India Company would receive him and arrange his meeting with the Sultan. Sadleir was to use all his powers of persuasion and any means at his disposal to convince the Sultan to join this new pact.

Next he was to set sail for Bahrain on a naval ship commanded by Captain Loch, taking advantage of a six-month truce with the pirate Erhama bin Jaber. He was not to set foot on the island, but rather remain on board until Ibrahim bin Ofaisan had been killed or detained, and the Al-Khalifa family had regained control of Bahrain. Then, travelling westward to the coast of Al-Ahsa, he would be met by the sheikh of the Bani Khaled tribe, who would arrange for him to join a caravan heading for the Hejaz. Along the way, Sadleir would leave the caravan in order to meet Ibrahim Pasha, at which point he would offer him the priceless sword and persuade him to join the secret pact.

'You will tell him that the sword is a token of friendship from His Majesty and that he should expect more valuable gifts as soon as he moves his army eastward and once his fleet arrives in the Gulf.' The governor handed Sadleir some correspondence and letters of introduction for his mission and then reached for the sword again. But this time, he did so wearily, as though he had just climbed an impossibly high mountain. 'Do you understand the gravity of your task, Major?'

'Yes, sir,' said Sadleir, saluting smartly. He stood to attention for a while, the box with its precious prize tucked firmly under his left arm.

Sir Evan nodded slowly as he collapsed in his chair and signalled Sadleir to leave. Simply the thought of the intricate and dangerous mission was enough to drain him of all energy.

The port of Bombay was one of the most crowded places in the world, with ships constantly arriving in the harbour from all four corners of the globe. There were ships from Arabia, China and the Gulf of Bengal, as well as from the various islands and parts of East India. Sadleir stood perfectly still as he took in the hive of activity. He could make out many ethnicities and races in this intoxicating mix of ships, currencies, weapons, drugs, precious gems, spices and perfumes.

The docks made his head spin in every respect. It was a dirty world, where the natural stench of the harbour – with its stagnant water and putrid fish – had to compete with the smell of sweat from the fishermen and sailors.

It was with a sense of relief that he found HMS *Thetis* and hesitated only briefly before boarding. He had not expected that a British naval ship could be transformed so convincingly into a nondescript – even ugly – commercial vessel. The captain of the *Thetis* saluted him and, as his aide led the way to his cabin, Sadleir made a note of some of the changes that had taken place. The ship had been repainted and her sails exchanged for the type used on merchantmen, the cannon portholes had been tightly and carefully sealed, and the interior of the ship had been comprehensively altered to reflect its commercial credentials, complete with a cargo of goods and livestock. With the exception of the captain and his aide and one Arab sailor, the crew consisted entirely of Malabar Indians.

As soon as Sadleir was in his quarters, he took the priceless sword from its box, wrapped it in a rag that was tattered enough not to attract anyone's attention, and found a suitable spot under his mattress to hide it. He stashed the box under his bunk and decided to keep the Governor of Bombay's letters in his inside pocket. Sadleir left his cabin after locking it securely, and made his way back on deck from where he watched the ceaseless commotion and smelled the permanent reek of the harbour.

He wished to set sail immediately, not least because, according to the plan, he had barely three weeks to get to Oman.

He gazed out to sea, where he spotted a flotilla of small boats that habitually followed the big ships, like parasitic creatures, with their pedlars on board trying to sell monkeys and exotic animals before they docked and had to pay taxes on their cargo.

His attention was drawn to a knocking sound coming from the side of the ship. Sadleir looked down and saw a young man in a small boat striking the hull with one of his long oars. '*Lorki?*' shouted the youth expectantly when he saw Sadleir.

The captain of the *Thetis* came to stand beside Sadleir. 'He offers sexual services to seafarers,' he said with a chuckle. 'If you wish to contract a disease that will torture you to death, you can try your luck with him.' The captain seemed so amused by his own joke that he was still laughing as he moved away to prepare for their departure.

Sadleir turned to the young man and shouted down, 'Get lost, you bastard, or I'll tear you apart!'

The youth turned his boat around, driven away not so much by unfamiliar words as by the tone and the look of sheer disgust.

Later that day, HMS *Thetis* set sail, driven by favourable winds.

Ten days into the voyage, Sadleir wrote in his logbook:

16 September 1818: We met the Connoy *yesterday – a British merchantman under the command of Captain Bernard. After checking our papers, he invited us on board and we exchanged information. He told us that piracy had diminished and that he had not encountered any pirate ships lately. However, he did come across an abandoned Arab vessel with neither crew nor cargo. We concluded that pirates must have seized the cargo and detained the sailors, but left the ship in a hurry for fear of being found by British naval vessels. Captain Bernard offered us an excellent bottle of whisky after which we parted company.*

Sadleir's logbook was conspicuously empty for the rest of the voyage as he found little to record on his trip.

Indeed, with the exception of that meeting with the *Connoy*, the days were indistinguishable, blurring into an interminably dreary and monotonous stretch of time.

On the eighteenth day of the journey, Sadleir was prepared for the polite but dull banter with the captain and his aide, the hours spent gazing at the horizon, and the rest of a daily routine that had grown so tiresome. He was therefore completely disconcerted by a sudden shout of dismay from one of the sailors. All eyes turned to where he was pointing: Sadleir squinted at two ships in the distance.

The captain of the *Thetis* reached for his telescope, blinked and snapped it shut seconds later. 'All hands on deck!' he roared. 'Change course! Heading south!'

'What is it, Captain?' urged Sadleir.

The captain was already at the helm, turning the wheel frantically. 'We're doomed if he catches us.'

'Who?' insisted Sadleir.

The captain's reply was barely louder than a whisper. 'The pirate Erhama bin Jaber.'

Sadleir shivered at the look of terror in the captain's eyes.

Chapter 7

The Indian Ocean

THE CREW OF HMS *Eden* was showing signs of extreme boredom and weariness. Mansen felt morale on board was low in part because the crew had not been informed of the purpose of the voyage. He expressed his concerns to the captain as they stood on deck, taking in the ominous black clouds in the distance.

'Yes,' agreed Loch. 'I think the time has come, old chap.' There were squalls coming their way from the east, so he added, 'Let's wait until after the storm. Then you can announce a meeting for the officers to explain our mission.' This also would allow him time to decide exactly what he was going to tell them.

As the winds picked up, the waves grew higher with foaming crests and soon the ship began to reel dangerously as though it were little more than an old tub. But Loch was a seasoned captain and knew that it would take a lot more than a storm to pose a threat to one of the navy's finest vessels. He gave orders for the ship to keep its current bearings, straight through the tempest, and almost casually retired to his quarters where he poured himself a drink.

'How can you drink at a time like this?' moaned Lady Jesse, who was feeling distinctly unwell as the ship rocked violently.

He laughed, toasted his wife, downed his drink and poured himself another and then another. Like his father before him, Loch for many years had struggled to control his drinking. While he had tried to set limits on his daily consumption, he spent much time alone and had found no better friend than the bottle.

He noticed Jesse looking at the glass in his hand. She waited a moment and then spoke. 'You've had five glasses since you came in.'

She returned to her sewing. He looked at her and wiped a drop that had trickled down the side of his mouth.

'Why are you always watching me? It's like you're monitoring everything I do.'

'I'm only trying to help you, dear. You must do something about the drinking. You're only ruining your health.'

'I'm sick and tired of listening to talk about my drinking. Just let me do as I please.'

Jesse spoke softly, as though addressing a child. 'You can't live in isolation from your family and crew. You're the captain of this ship and I'm your wife. I hope you don't forget that.'

He didn't answer and fell heavily on the bed. In a few minutes the sound of his snoring filled the room.

The storm died down in the middle of the night and by the next day the sea was as calm as a stretched sheet that seemed to go on forever. Loch asked his officers to join him in the wardroom for dinner that evening. The captain and his wife surprised them with a delicious feast on a candlelit table, a sign that the captain was in good spirits. At the end of the meal, the captain tapped the glass with a spoon, and the officers grew quiet and listened attentively. Loch looked at his wife as though asking her

48

opinion on a play in which he starred, and then turned to the officers.

'Gentlemen,' he began, 'I will try to be brief. I'm rather good at that, according to my wife.'

The joke was received with a few chuckles and, not for the first time, Williams found himself thinking that Lady Jesse deserved better.

'As some of you may already know, we are on our way to the Arabian Gulf – a veritable pirate-infested sea – that is currently under the control of Arab corsairs.' His eyes happened to settle on Williams. 'Now for the less well-travelled among you, I will explain that Arabs come from the most uninhabitable, godforsaken region of the world. They are irredeemably uncouth – barbarians to a man – worse even than the Portuguese.'

That caused more genuine laughter.

'Our mission, gentlemen, is to fight those pirates in every creek and bay. This will not be an easy battle – the buccaneers are ruthless and while most of them are backward Arabs, some are Persians and Europeans who have been trained in the art of war.'

This time Loch's gaze fell on the ship's doctor. 'Now some of you may wonder why His Majesty's Government is even interested in that part of the world when our sphere of influence extends over so many other, more interesting places. And I know that some of you were rather hoping we would be going to the Caribbean.

'But the real fight is in protecting our trade routes and the East India Company is suffering a great deal from raids by pirates. So let us be as ready as we can possibly be and remember that the eyes of the Empire are upon us now.'

Williams waited for the captain to finish before asking his question. 'How long will our mission be, sir?'

Loch raised his eyebrows almost imperceptibly as though irritated by a banal question. 'As long as it takes,' he replied simply.

The ship's doctor spoke out and asked, 'How will we know our enemies from our friends in the region?'

'An excellent question,' Loch said. 'I almost forgot that important detail. While we cannot expect many friends, we do have some allies in the region. Those ships that raise red flags or flags with red spots are to be considered our allies. All others will be treated as the enemy.' He glanced around the wardroom at his officers. 'Now if there are no further questions, let us set a course for Muscat and from there to the island of Bahrain and see if we can't stir up a hornets' nest.'

Chapter 8

The Arabian Sea

T HE SAILORS ON HMS *Thetis* scrambled to spread the additional sails. They could see the two pirate ships gaining on them and feared they faced certain death if the ferocious Erhama caught up with them.

The captain ordered the muskets to be distributed to the men in preparation for combat, but the Indian sailors held the weapons uncertainly. Most had never fired a gun before; some trembled with fear, while others felt sick. The captain soon realised that resistance would be short-lived and he looked around the deck for the right place to make his final stand.

Sadleir joined him at the stern and told him of the six-month truce with the pirates, as relayed to Bombay by the Governor of Bushehr. The captain of the *Thetis* was relieved to hear this and ordered the weapons to be collected and returned below decks, much to the relief of the Indian sailors.

The two ships came alongside the *Thetis*, one on either side.

It all happened in a flash. Two groups of men who had lain hidden on board each pirate ship emerged suddenly and hurled hooks onto the *Thetis*. Then, in a concerted move, they pulled on the ropes until all three ships were close together.

Erhama's men wasted no time in jumping on board the *Thetis* to the complete surprise of the Indian sailors; instinctively they raised their hands at the sight of all the guns, knives and swords that were being waved in their faces. Erhama's men herded everyone to the bow, tied their prisoners' hands and forced them to sit down. Only the captain, his aide and Sadleir were left at the stern, duly bound and under the supervision of a group of heavily armed ethnic Baluchis.

Once he was satisfied that his men were in complete control, Erhama climbed aboard the *Thetis*. He glanced at the Indian captives at the bow before making his way towards the British officers. He summoned one of his men who could speak English and asked him to translate his words. 'What are you carrying on board?' he demanded.

'We're traders,' replied the captain of the *Thetis*. 'We're carrying cargo from India to the port of Basra. We are not fighters.'

Erhama signalled to his men to start searching the ship thoroughly. There was something suspicious about it; it did not look like a commercial vessel – its beams seemed too thick as if designed to withstand cannon fire. But then, he wondered, if it was a warship, why had it been transformed into a merchantman?

He peered at the three men in the stern. There was also something odd about them. They certainly did not look like the usual traders who chewed tobacco all day and spat everywhere. From their demeanour and manner of speaking, they seemed more disciplined, more like military men.

A few minutes later, one of Erhama's men emerged with the sleek wooden box that had been stowed under Sadleir's bunk. Erhama examined it carefully and asked the captain about its missing contents. This was followed by a brief exchange between the three captives, which Erhama's interpreter was unable to understand. But from the body language and the tone, it was clear to Erhama that the captain of the ship was annoyed with the other man.

'Where is the sword that was in this box?' Erhama repeated his question.

When the interpreter had translated the question the first time, Sadleir thought he had misheard. But the pirate knew about the sword and Sadleir had no idea how. He panicked that his mission might be over before it had even started.

When they failed to answer, Erhama threatened, 'I shall have to keep you in this heat for a few hours until the sun melts your frozen tongues.'

It was Sadleir who spoke next. 'There is no sword,' he said quickly. 'It's a box I bought in Bombay. What makes you think there's a sword?'

'You're a liar as well as a fool,' said Erhama coldly. 'And you would do well to learn some Arabic.' He held the box and traced the ornate calligraphy with his finger as he read: '"This sword is a gift from the Governor of Bombay to Ibrahim Pasha, a token of our friendship in fighting a common enemy." So I will ask one last time: where is the sword?'

Sadleir had a passable knowledge of spoken Arabic; he made a mental note to learn to read it as well. He attempted to parry and said, 'You're in breach of the truce you made with Governor Bruce in Bushehr.'

Erhama waited for the translation and then retorted sharply, 'Nobody can force me to do anything I don't want to do.' He glared at the man with his one good eye. 'But how do you know of my meeting in Bushehr?'

'We were told about it in Bombay.'

'So that's why you didn't try to escape or fight.' He turned to address his men. 'Our flag is well-known to all British naval officers as well as to the employees of the East India Company.' This caused the pirates on board the *Thetis* to roar with laughter. Erhama turned to face the officers again as he added with little mirth, 'I don't like the red banners that you have agreed with your allies. My colours are mine alone.'

With those words, Erhama withdrew to a shaded part of the stern where he sat, rhythmically clicking his sword in its scabbard. He asked his men where his son Bashir was. Nobody answered for a while and when he raised his voice, Dirar told him that he was below decks on the *Ghatrousha*, looking after a sailor whose gangrenous foot had been amputated.

'What?' roared Erhama. 'He's been sitting down there while we've been fighting here?'

'It's a noble act, sir,' said Dirar placatingly. 'The poor man can't walk without help and is still in much pain.'

'Ach!' Erhama did not try to conceal his disdain. 'Have I raised a doctor? How will he command my ships and my men with such a bleeding heart?'

He returned to stare gloomily at his captives, clicking his sword in its scabbard for seconds that turned into minutes that turned into hours. It seemed clear that he could do this all day and never tire, whiling away the hours with his sword. Even when he was brought some tobacco and coffee, his good hand was never far from the hilt.

For the British officers time dragged painfully. The sun beat down on them relentlessly, a scorching heat that was made even crueller by the suffocating humidity. While they were in danger of sunstroke, Erhama ticked away the seconds with his sword, whose sound now reverberated in their heads like a multitude of hammers striking an equal number of anvils.

It was the captain's aide who was the first to snap.

'You're nothing but a petty criminal,' he yelled. 'You'll hang for this. Hell is too good for you.'

Erhama called for one of his men. He was known as the 'stitcher', a man with a small frame but with such strong fingers that his main role was to fix rips in the sails. 'You know what to do when someone upsets us, don't you,' Erhama stated as the man appeared.

The man nodded, left to fetch the tools of his trade and returned presently with a needle as long as a finger and some thread. Erhama instructed some of his men to hold the aide down, while the stitcher sat on his chest and, with a practised hand, trapped the man's head between his knees and began to sew his lips together.

The aide let out a bloodcurdling scream and struggled in vain to move his body. From their vantage point, the captain and Sadleir saw the blood gush every time the stitcher drove his needle in and they turned in horror to Erhama and begged him to stop. He looked unimpressed and kept clicking his sword at the same deadening rate as he urged his men to hurry up and finish.

When the aide's mouth was half stitched, Sadleir shouted, 'I'll give you the sword!'

Everyone froze.

'I'll give you the sword,' he repeated. 'Just stop this cruelty for heaven's sake!'

The stitcher looked at his master, waiting for his orders. As soon as Erhama gave the signal, the man got off the aide's chest and Sadleir was untied. He rose wearily to his feet and had to hold on to the bulwarks for support as his legs had gone numb from the hours spent crouching. He was escorted below decks to his cabin, where he overturned his bunk and retrieved the sword, still wrapped in the tattered piece of cloth.

Heading back to the stern, he handed the sword to Erhama, who gave him an evil grin.

He inspected the scabbard for a while and then, drawing the blade, he muttered with admiration, 'Now that is what I call a sword.' He touched the fine steel and scrutinised the inscription. Then, with a final nod, he bellowed to his men, 'Our work here is done, boys.' He ordered the crew of the *Thetis* to be untied and jumped nimbly onto the *Ghatrousha*.

Once aboard his ship again, all the hooks securing the *Thetis* to the other vessels were unfastened and the sails unfurled as Erhama's ships headed quickly eastwards, vanishing as suddenly as they had appeared.

The crew of the *Thetis* could hardly believe they had escaped unscathed from the most notorious pirate of the region. Sadleir came to stand by the captain, who was already instructing two men to take the aide below decks to unstitch his lips and tend to his wound. Then he turned and punched Sadleir hard in the face, throwing him onto the deck. 'Damn fool!' he shouted. 'How could you hide the sword and keep the box? You almost cost us our lives.'

'I needed the box,' Sadleir said lamely as he got up slowly. 'I couldn't very well offer the sword as a gift without a box.'

'Well, you can't offer anything now, can you?' said the captain, livid with rage. 'You can both go to hell – you and that damned sword.'

Sadleir turned to look at the horizon as the captain began shouting to the Indian sailors. They would resume their journey to Muscat, but what was the point now? he wondered, as he fingered the swelling on his face from the punch. All he had left were the letters from the Governor of Bombay in his inside pocket. His mission was already over, he thought dejectedly. He was an abject failure.

Chapter 9

A s soon as the *Eden* sailed into the harbour of Muscat, thirteen cannon were fired from the Sultan's fort in salute. In turn, the ship fired an equal number of cannon into the air. The *Eden* dropped anchor a little way off the coast in the late afternoon and Loch held on to the railing on the starboard side and stared down at the water, mesmerised. It was so clear and blue that he could see all the way down to the sea bed, even though the ship was anchored in water that was no less than twenty feet deep. He was entranced by the large number of fish, a cornucopia of colours that weaved in and out of the nooks and crannies below the still surface.

He looked up at the fort that had welcomed their arrival and then scanned the harbour. The port of Muscat was shaped like a horseshoe, bordered on three sides by rocky black mountains. The mountains absorbed the heat of the sun during the day and radiated it in the late afternoon and evening. Loch could already sense the heat and humidity that the concave topography seemed to direct towards them, giving the impression that he was inside a slow-cooking oven.

A small boat flying the Sultan's flag, with oarsmen in identical uniforms and a heavy-set man standing at the back, drew alongside the *Eden*. On seeing Loch peering at him from the ship's deck, the man yelled at the top of his voice, 'Oh Captain! The Sultan welcomes you to Muscat. His Majesty will receive you at his palace at noon tomorrow. I come bearing gifts from His Majesty.'

The crew lowered a basket to the small craft, and the man placed the gifts inside. The boat returned to shore, its oars playing a quiet, rhythmic tune.

The sailors brought the gifts to the captain's suite for his inspection. Lady Jesse could not wait for her husband to inspect the gifts so she unpacked them and removed the ones she thought might be useful to her, particularly the precious stones and perfumes. There was a small, silver-coloured knife with an ivory hilt, the type that men in the region usually placed around their waists. She was so fascinated by its decorative inscriptions that she decided to conceal it in a special place in her room. She waited for her husband's return.

The next day a small party from the *Eden* rowed to shore and was met by the representative of the East India Company in Muscat, an elegantly dressed Indian trader called Gulap. It was clear that the captain's visit was a formal occasion to him because he was in his best national dress: a yellow turban, a golden gown that reached to mid-calf, a pair of loose cotton trousers that gathered at the ankle and two red slippers decorated with gold inscriptions from the top of the foot to the curled toes.

Gulap bowed when he saw Loch and Mansen. He put his palms together and raised them to his face, and then he accepted the captain's hand and shook it politely.

'It's a great pleasure for me, sir, to see you here in Muscat.' He spoke English with a distinctively Indian accent. 'Sir Rupert, His Majesty's representative in Muscat, apologises that he could not meet you in person. He is unwell, but hopes to recover soon.' He bowed again. 'But I am at your service, sir, and if you would like to follow me I know the Sultan would be happy to see you.'

Loch nodded and followed the man through the main souk, wedged between the eastern wall of the Sultan's fort and the sea. They walked past stalls and shops on the seafront that sold dates, amber, spices, knives, tobacco, ivory, various animal hides and dried fish. There were men and women of different ethnicities in bright colours milling around and weaving in and out of the stalls. They reminded Loch of the shoals of fish in the clear blue water.

A particular group of men caught his eye. They were each dressed in a single piece of cloth, wrapped around their waists and reaching down to their knees. Their shoulder-length hair had been plaited and their eyes were wide, dark and lined with kohl. They carried swords in scabbards slung over their shoulders and wooden shields decorated with large iron nails. They went barefoot, not caring much where they stepped.

Gulap noticed the newcomer's curiosity and said, 'These are Bedouins from the interior, sir. They are illiterate and backward and usually live in total isolation, completely cut off from the world. They are forced to come to Muscat to barter for the supplies they need.' He added, 'But don't be afraid of them, for they know that they are now in the Sultan's city and are peaceful and threaten no one.'

They moved on and entered a small yard covered with mats, which was the slave market where the live merchandise stood in the blistering heat. Slaves were brought from the coasts of Africa, particularly Zanzibar and Mozambique, and young men, women and children were displayed like any other commodity. Loch saw traders opening the mouths of slaves to check for healthy teeth; others felt their muscles to make sure that they were fit for hard labour.

The land began to rise a little higher as Gulap led them on to the merchant district. This part of town was neater and more organised. Trees lined the sides of the streets, providing shade to pedestrians, and people were better dressed, in white cotton gowns and colourful turbans; all the men in the area also wore ornamental gold or silver daggers. Gulap told the visitors that these were the original inhabitants of Muscat.

'They look haughty,' commented Mansen as he took in the stares of disdain from several men.

'They are a proud people,' Gulap said. 'We are the outsiders. Many Omanis regard the British as criminals and killers.' He flashed them a sudden smile, revealing his sparkling white teeth.

When the group arrived at the main gate of the Sultan's palace, they were stopped by the guards and asked to wait until the minister could be notified. Presently, he welcomed them with a disingenuous smile and, in turn, led them to the hall where the Sultan sat.

The breezy room overlooked the port, offering a panoramic view that allowed the guests to see every ship moored or anchored there; Loch and Mansen immediately glanced at the *Eden* in the distance. The floor of the hall was covered with luxurious Persian carpets, and the drapes swayed gently in the sea breeze. All the chairs had been arranged to face the Sultan's seat.

The Sultan was a young man who wore light cotton clothes and an unadorned white turban. On one of his fingers was a ring with a large diamond that refracted light into a miniature rainbow every time he moved his right hand, as it did now when he shook hands with each visitor and gestured genially for them to take a seat.

Sherbet, tea and baskets of fruit and various desserts were served. With a gentle smile, the Sultan invited his guests to eat and drink, sometimes recommending a particular date or dessert.

Loch complimented his host on his gracious hospitality and, after some pleasantries, he broached the subject of his mission. 'Your Highness,' he began, 'as you are no doubt aware, His Majesty's Government has been concerned for some time about the pirates who threaten our mutual interests. I have been given the honour of working with you to rid us of this common enemy.'

Loch paused when he saw the minister whisper something to the Sultan and then resumed. 'As part of our military pact, my first task is to seek the overthrow and arrest of the Wahhabi leader Ibrahim bin Ofaisan in Bahrain, and return the island to its rightful rulers, the Al-Khalifas. As you may also be aware, the Shah of Persia has agreed to assist us in this endeavour and will send troops from the port of Bushehr.' Loch grew more emphatic. 'We will not fail, Your Highness, for we have a solid alliance, a clear plan and the troops to make it happen.'

The Sultan smiled, nodded and exchanged a few quick words with his minister. The minister, who would be in charge of the whole military operation, then asked to have a meeting with the captain and his commanders in two days so that they would have enough time to coordinate the plan of attack.

Taking their leave from the Sultan, the ship's officers departed and reached the main gate where a platoon of guards in blue turbans was waiting to escort them back to the harbour. Gulap explained that this was the traditional treatment reserved for very important guests.

The guards held aloft their lances, each with the Sultan's emblem fluttering in the breeze as they marched smartly in two lines, flanking the guests on either side.

As soon as they reached the harbour, a boy who worked for Gulap came running over to them with a dispatch that had just arrived from Bombay. He handed the sealed paper to Loch. 'It's addressed to you, sir,' he said. 'It's from the Governor of Bombay.'

Loch broke the seal and read the short message from Sir Evan Nepean:

> *I hope you are well after your long trip from England. I am sending Major George Forster Sadleir with some specific instructions for you. He is due to arrive in Muscat from Bombay on HMS Thetis. Good luck.*

Back on board the ship, Lady Jesse summoned Williams to her room. He entered hesitantly, and she offered him the ivory knife as a token of future friendship. She asked him to tell no one about the gift, and then said, 'I will be staying in Muscat until my husband's long mission is over. Don't forget to drop by for tea whenever you're in the port.'

Williams smiled, and kissed her hand. 'Of course. It wouldn't be proper for someone like me to refuse a beautiful lady's request.'

Chapter 10

Muscat

A FEW DAYS LATER, HMS *Thetis* sailed into Muscat's harbour and dropped anchor. It was not flying the Union Jack and therefore was not greeted with the ceremonial thirteen-gun salute. Checking that the Governor of Bombay's letters were still in his inside pocket, Sadleir boarded a small boat to be rowed to shore, along with the captain of the *Thetis* and his aide.

No one uttered a word.

The aide had congealed blood on his lips and a wound that caused him intense pain whenever he tried to speak or eat or drink.

Sadleir's and the captain's injuries were not as obvious. But they were almost as raw, since, in the case of both officers, they related to a sense of dishonour. The captain could not forgive himself for the complete lack of resistance – despite the reassurances of that damned fool Sadleir – since he was ultimately to blame for losing control of his ship to the pirate. He had simply not acted in a way befitting an officer and gentleman of the Royal Navy.

Sadleir, too, had begun to doubt his mettle. As an officer in His Majesty's army, he should never have relinquished the sword. He had sworn to protect it with his life and yet had surrendered it at the first sign of torture. It seemed immaterial now whether or not Erhama had agreed to a truce, as the Governor of Bombay had claimed, and whether the pirate had therefore violated the agreement. He should simply never have yielded to the barbarian, and it depressed him to the core to think that he had.

No one had come to meet them at the docks and the crestfallen group walked in silence to the headquarters of the British government's representative in Muscat.

Sir Rupert had recovered from his illness and was in the middle of a meeting with Loch when the men from the *Thetis* were announced.

Sir Rupert instructed his servant to serve them tea and ask them to wait when Loch requested that they might join them instead. 'I have been expecting Major Sadleir,' he said. 'I believe he should join our discussion on the impending war as I believe he is involved in the mission.'

When the three men were admitted, Sir Rupert and Loch stared at the aide. 'Good heavens, man,' exclaimed Sir Rupert, after the perfunctory introductions. 'What on earth happened to your face?'

The captain of the *Thetis* answered for him and described in detail the events that had led to the disfigurement of his aide and the theft of the sword.

'Well, that's rather inconvenient, isn't it?' said Loch sarcastically. He knew how important the sword was to the mission and turned to frown at the major. 'Poor show.'

'We've lost the sword?' repeated Sir Rupert, not quite believing it. 'The second part of the campaign depends entirely on that damned sword.'

'I'm sorry, sir,' said Sadleir, speaking resolutely. Gesturing toward the aide, he said, 'I had to make an instant decision to save a life.'

Sir Rupert did not appear convinced.

'We have to do everything in our power to recover it now,' said Loch 'I think we should meet the Sultan to explain this new situation.'

Sadleir reached for the two letters in his inside pocket, deposited the first on Sir Rupert's desk and held out the second for Loch, making sure he had the naval officer's full attention as he handed it to him. 'These messages are from the governor in Bombay.'

The two men broke the seals of their respective dispatches and Sir Rupert was the first to speak. 'Captain,' he said, addressing Loch, 'we are all aware of the first thrust of the attack, namely, to fight the pirates in the Gulf and to liberate Bahrain.' He paused as he reread the directives from Bombay. 'But it is the second, wider strategy that has been fleshed out. You are to facilitate Major Sadleir's mission to reach Ibrahim Pasha by land, starting from the Al-Ahsa coast, and until such time as he returns to Muscat.' He looked up. 'I presume these orders match those contained in your letter.'

Loch nodded. In the first phase, he was to head for Bahrain backed by Omani and Persian forces to capture the Wahhabi leader Ibrahim bin Ofaisan, who would later be exiled to Persia. His second mission was to implement the agreement that Sadleir would sign with Ibrahim Pasha. But the key to the success of this second stage was the priceless sword that the major was supposed to have brought with him in order to entice Ibrahim Pasha to join in the fight.

'So much for the ingenious plan,' said Loch soberly. With Ibrahim Pasha in the pact, the Egyptian army would have moved from Diriyah to Al-Ahsa and on to Ras al-Khaimah where it would have joined up with the Sultan's forces in a pincer movement. Together they would have formed a colossal army unlike any the Gulf region had ever seen. This would have marked the end of the Wahhabis and the pirates, and their villages and hideouts would have been razed to the ground. 'Without the sword, we've lost that rather valuable carrot to bring in Ibrahim Pasha.' He contemplated their options.

'Well, Captain,' said Sir Rupert. 'You have been designated overall commander for this operation. What are your intentions now?'

'I see no other way,' he replied slowly. 'We must devote all our efforts to finding the damn sword so that we can return to the plan.'

'And how do you suggest we do that?'

'We must convince the Sultan to send his troops with us to look for Erhama.' He turned to the captain of the *Thetis* and asked him if the pirate had given any indication or had let slip any information about where he was heading.

'No, sir, I'm afraid not. His bearing was due west when he accosted us in the Arabian Sea. But that was ten days ago and he could be anywhere by now.'

Sir Rupert stroked his beard pensively. 'Throughout the long years I've spent here,' he said, 'I have gathered some intelligence on Erhama's activities in the region. Although he is of course often at sea, he does have three main hideouts: the north of Qatar, Ras al-Khaimah and his fort in Dammam. I think it is safe to assume that he is either already in one of these places or will be in the near future.'

'Ah well, that is already more promising,' said Loch, pleased. 'We should send spies immediately to these three locations and plan a raid on Ras al-Khaimah, since it is the closest.'

Loch was happiest when devising a strategy and he was already working out the details that would require the Sultan to agree to send a special force to cut off any escape from Ras al-Khaimah by land. 'We will possess the element of surprise, gentlemen,' he said enthusiastically, 'as we strike them simultaneously from land and sea.'

He turned his attention to Sadleir. 'As for you, Major, you will join us on the *Eden*. As soon as we lay our hands on the sword, I'll take you to the coast of Al-Ahsa to complete your mission.' He paused. 'Once we recover that sword, if you lose it again I will personally disembowel you – is that clear?'

'Yes, sir.'

Sir Rupert seemed less convinced by the new arrangement. 'While I salute your ability to come up with a plan so quickly, Captain,' he said, 'let me remind you that the removal of Bin Ofaisan from Bahrain is at the top of the Sultan's priorities.' That particular plan had been drawn up a long time ago with the Persian Prince of Shiraz and they could not change it now. It had nothing to do with the pirate or the lost sword. 'Let's implement the Bahrain plan and then turn our attention to Erhama.'

Chapter 11

Muharraq, Bahrain

S HEIKH SALMAN AL-KHALIFA, BAHRAIN'S ruler, sat drinking coffee in his *majlis* in Muharraq, smiling broadly at all the well-wishers who had gathered at his palace. Indeed, there were so many visitors scrambling over each other to offer their congratulations to him that carpets had been laid out in the outer courtyards to accommodate everyone. Sherbet and dates were offered and cattle were slaughtered to feed the guests. The smell of barbecued meat attracted everyone in the vicinity of the palace.

Sheikh Salman was celebrating the mysterious and sudden departure of Ibrahim bin Ofaisan and the consequent return to power of the Al-Khalifas.

Away from the celebrations and the shouts of joy, a worried young man was sprinting from the harbour, with one hand on his head scarf to keep it from slipping off and the other hand clutching the bottom of his thobe so that he could run faster. He covered the distance to the palace in record time and was stopped at the main courtyard by the guards. Panting and sweating profusely, he made them understand that something momentous was happening and that he needed an immediate audience with the sheikh.

When he was eventually admitted, he spoke in a highly agitated manner: 'My lord, there are seven ships with cannon ready to fire on Muharraq.'

'What?' said Sheikh Salman with disbelief. 'Are you sure?'

'Please see for yourself.'

Sheikh Salman hurried out, followed by the guests at his *majlis,* who were so numerous they formed an almost uninterrupted line stretching from the palace to the harbour. The sheikh asked for a telescope and saw Persian banners on three ships, Omani flags on three others and a Union Jack on the seventh. He shouted to everyone to evacuate the port area and take cover, and then summoned his closest advisers to board a small boat and row to the ship with the British flag.

Sure enough, the ships were facing Muharraq, their cannon visible through the portholes. Sheikh Salman ordered a servant to remove his white turban and attach it to the tip of an oar as a makeshift white flag.

The small boat moved among the men-of-war like a tiny child among giants and finally came to rest by the *Eden.* A rope ladder was lowered to them and once the sheikh had climbed aboard he came face to face with three officers who stared at him warily.

'I am Captain Loch,' said one of them, 'chief naval officer of the Gulf expeditionary force. And who might you be, sir?'

His expression softened slightly when Sheikh Salman told him.

'Then you are welcome here,' he said.

Sheikh Salman frowned and, indicating the flotilla of warships, asked, 'But what are you doing here, Captain?'

'We have come to arrest our mutual enemy,' replied Loch evenly. 'We are here for the outlaw, Ibrahim bin Ofaisan. He is wanted dead or alive, though I would prefer him alive, if only to enjoy breaking his legendary wilfulness.'

'But he's no longer in Bahrain, Captain,' Sheikh Salman said with a grin. 'Bahrain has returned to us, the Al-Khalifas.'

This was unexpected. Loch led the way to the wardroom and, once inside, he demanded, 'How did this happen?'

'We don't really know,' admitted Sheikh Salman. 'Ibrahim bin Ofaisan commanded his regiment from his palace, which was not far from mine. He controlled Bahrain with his troops and using his supply line from Al-Ahsa.' He started to explain how his grandfather had liberated Bahrain from the Persians through a bloody revolt and how, subsequently, his uncles had been forced into exile by the perfidious Ibrahim bin Ofaisan.

'Yes, but what happened to Bin Ofaisan?' asked Loch impatiently. He was not interested in a history lesson about Bahrain. 'Was he warned of our arrival?'

'I was supposed to have a meeting with him yesterday,' answered Sheikh Salman. 'Bin Ofaisan made me have coffee with him every morning in his palace, just to make sure I wasn't doing anything to undermine him. But yesterday when I arrived for the meeting, his palace was deserted. The only person there was an elderly slave who maintained that Bin Ofaisan had left on a boat in the middle of the night after having secretly sent his men to Al-Ahsa a few hours earlier.

'Naturally, I couldn't quite believe it, so I had the slave whipped – but even when the blood gushed from his wounds, he didn't change his story.' Sheikh Salman's smile broadened. 'That is why today we are celebrating our freedom from them.'

Loch did not share the sheikh's jubilation. 'Someone warned him of our arrival,' he said soberly. 'His escape is no cause for celebration.'

Once again, a neat plan had been blown apart by unforeseen events. There was now little point in remaining in Bahrain; but at least one element of the plan had been accomplished, namely, to reinstate the Al-Khalifas as rulers of the island.

Loch asked the sheikh for some fresh water to fill their barrels for the return journey to Muscat.

Sheikh Salman called one of his crewmen and asked him to fetch a goatskin water bottle from the boat. He poured a glass for the captain and asked him to taste the water. The captain drank the water, which was clear and sweetly fresh, unlike the water he had been drinking since his arrival in the Gulf. Most of the water he had tried until then had been so salty that it was good for neither cooking nor slaking thirst.

The captain eyed the sheikh with admiration.

'If this water is good enough we'll bring you more,' Sheikh Salman said and asked his servant to bring another bottle filled with fresh water. The crewmen of the *Eden* were amazed to see the man strip off his clothes, dive smoothly into the sea and return, a few minutes later, with the bottle full of water.

His mates helped pull him over the side of the boat, taking the bottle and handing it over to the sheikh, who poured another glass of water for the captain. The captain was astonished to taste the same sweet, fresh water once again.

'We have many fresh water springs at the bottom of the sea. Our men dive with their water bottles and put the mouth of the bottle on top of the spring. We'll fill your tanks with enough water to last your whole journey to Muscat,' the sheikh said. 'But we will not do the same for the Shah's boat. We fought them a few years ago and have no problem with fighting them again.'

Loch ordered the ships carrying the Persian troops to return to Bushehr.

After filling the barrels and watching the sheikh's delegation leave, Loch's mind returned to the mission at hand. He turned to Sadleir and said, 'It seems we have a spy in our midst, working for the Wahhabis. I'm afraid your mission has been delayed once more, Major.'

Chapter 12

Off the Coast of Qatar

T HE *GHATROUSHA* WAS MOORED off the northern tip of the
Qatar peninsula. Erhama bin Jaber sat on deck, smoking
and drinking coffee with his friend Bin Ofaisan and talking
about the ornate Indian sword the corsair had taken from the
British.

Bin Ofaisan held the sword with admiration, his fingers
trailing over the engraved inscriptions on the blade. He was
particularly taken by the image of a serpent coiled around the
base of the sword, extending its body along the blade. At the
tip, the snake's head appeared to strike at an invisible prey, its
forked tongue lashing out to the very point of the sword. The
hilt was inlaid with five red precious stones on either side,
along with a large gemstone at the base. Despite all the adorn-
ments, the sword had been designed to be light, lethal and easy
to wield.

'This is worthy of a king, Erhama,' marvelled Bin Ofaisan as
he continued to examine the sword. 'It would be dangerous for
you to keep it on board the ship.'

'I know that, brother,' replied Erhama. He gestured toward
the box that housed the sword, with the words of friendship to
Ibrahim Pasha emblazoned on the lid. 'The British are up to
something big and Ibrahim Pasha is somehow involved.'

Bin Ofaisan nodded. 'These are dangerous times.' He looked at the sword one last time, weighed it for balance and then handed it back to Erhama, who returned it to its case. 'We've lost Bahrain and Ibrahim Pasha could well move to occupy Nejd. We no longer have any allies except for the Qawasimis. I think we will have to join them in their fight against the infidels.'

'*You* will.' Erhama inhaled deeply then watched the swirling plumes of smoke as he exhaled. 'But I have some unfinished business with the Al-Khalifas.'

'That is ancient history, my friend,' Bin Ofaisan said gently. 'Isn't it time you focused on the bigger threats?'

Erhama's gaze followed a curl of smoke. 'I've never told you my story.'

'I know you've always felt betrayed by the Al-Khalifas because they didn't give you the booty you had expected.'

'The story is far more complex than that.' Erhama smiled mirthlessly. 'We are both fugitives with nothing but time, our ships and our swords.' As though reminded of its presence, he reached for his sword beneath him and began to move it rhythmically, a metronome with a melancholic beat to accompany his tale.

The pirate had been born in Al-Qurain, in Kuwait, to a destitute family that relied on charity for survival. His father had decided to emigrate to Qatar, to the north specifically, where the family had eked out a living in trade and diving for pearls. During their long stay there, Erhama had come to know the Al-Khalifas who had settled in Qatar after escaping from the Persian occupation of their island. They were related by blood since both families were descended from the Utub tribe, and Erhama considered them his kinsmen.

Having made some money from diving, he had bought a thoroughbred horse that he later sold to his cousins, the Al-Khalifas. This was a time when there was a lull in tribal conflicts, and everyone wanted to keep the best horses and weapons in case of sudden war. Trade had flourished during that period, especially with the arrival of the British and the establishment of the East India Company, whose ships began to import goods from India and China, and export pearls and horses from the Gulf region. In those days, Erhama's business had prospered as he began to buy horses from their owners, particularly thoroughbreds, and sell them to the British for their officers stationed in India and Basra.

He had married a cousin from the Utubs and his firstborn, Bashir, had been a baby when the tribe declared war on the Persians. Erhama had joined them to liberate Bahrain and proved instrumental in that war, constantly leading the attacks and putting himself in harm's way. But when they had finally driven the Persians out, the land and farms had been redistributed among the people and all he had received was a small orchard with a few palm trees. He had returned to the north of Qatar, having lost his eye and the use of a hand. Nursing his wounds and his rage, he had tried to revive the trade that he had put on hold during the campaign in Bahrain.

But after his return to Qatar, the Al-Khalifas had feared that he might pose a threat to them, so they had convinced the tribe not to buy his horses any longer and ordered their ships to stop transporting them to Bushehr or Basra. Erhama had begun to lose his wealth little by little and became burdened with debt. He could not sleep at night, afraid that he would wake up the next day begging for charity. His entire life had been on the verge of collapse and everything he had painstakingly built was slowly disintegrating like sugar in tepid water.

'One day Bashir was sitting at home with a crust of bread his mother had just baked,' Erhama recalled. 'Wishing to tease him, I snuck up behind him and pulled the piece of bread from his hand. Furious that it had been taken from him, Bashir began screaming and pounced on me with all his strength. I was forced to return his piece of bread to him. It was then that I realised I had to act like Bashir and reclaim what was mine.'

Soon after, Erhama had bought a small boat and gathered together a number of Arabs and ethnic Baluchis who had their own axe to grind with the Al-Khalifas. Erhama the pirate was born, and he had begun to attack and plunder the vessels owned by the Al-Khalifas.

'This revenge business is a complex thing,' said Erhama. 'As soon as people's hearts are filled with anger, they stop beating with tenderness and become as hard as stone. I became a monster, my friend, a beast that is only satisfied with scenes of blood and death. They killed everything human in my heart. I was no longer the man who played with his son Bashir, nor the man who cleaned his horses, fed them and looked after them. I became a different man.'

'I had no idea of that side of your life, brother,' said Bin Ofaisan.

'I have lost many of my best men over the years – and they, too, have lost much,' Erhama continued. 'But revenge keeps us going, like a poison that enters the heart and makes it as dark as night and as lethal as venom. Both the Al-Khalifas and I have entered the circle of vengeance and, in that spirit, they befriended the British while I became an ally of the Wahhabis.'

Bin Ofaisan laughed so heartily that his decaying teeth showed. 'I thought we were true friends, Erhama!'

'We are – you and I – but I don't like your people,' he said with brutal honesty. 'I'm not a pious man like you. I fight for my own cause and for that of others. I see that the wars in our region are nothing more than a conflict of interest among the powerful. To get a part of the booty you have to be strong. That's why I took the side of your people, although they may kill me one day as a heretic.'

Bin Ofaisan laughed even harder. 'The Wahhabis regard you as an ally and all your work benefits them,' he said. 'Some people see you as striving to promote God's message because you're attacking their infidel enemies and the interests of their allies. But I see you as a friend, Erhama, regardless of everything.'

Erhama peered at his companion and asked him directly, 'What do you get out of your alliance with the Wahhabis?'

'Nothing,' Bin Ofaisan said, serious. 'I lost my power in Bahrain. When I return I will be nothing more than a soldier in their army. Who knows, they might even label me a heretic because I listened to your advice and fled instead of fighting the British.'

'Then join me,' Erhama declared. 'Life is wide open and the sea always hurls a new ship our way that we can take as booty. That can be your new command: fight for yourself rather than for others.'

Bin Ofaisan shook his head sadly. 'You know that I come from Nejd. I can't abandon my family and friends there.' He glanced at the box on the deck between them that contained the priceless sword. 'Ibrahim Pasha is wreaking havoc in our territory and I can't stand idly by while my people are being killed and kicked out of their homes every single day.'

'Well, you'd better go back to them then,' Erhama retorted a bit testily. 'But I'm sure you won't be with them for long. They'll call you for other battles and you'll find yourself involved in the Hejaz, the Levant or Iraq. You may even die without anybody hearing about it or recognising you, destitute and with nothing to bequeath but a sword that somebody may find after your death.'

Bin Ofaisan was about to object, but Erhama continued, 'Your Wahhabis are like everybody else, including the British and the Persians. Piety is only skin deep. Underneath, everyone is the same: we all love money, women and power. Religion is only a means to an end, but others use different means to achieve the same end.'

Erhama waited for that to sink in and then added in a more conciliatory tone, 'At least promise you'll consider joining me.'

Bin Ofaisan consented with a brief nod.

Later, once everyone else had retired for the night, Erhama called Dirar and told him to set sail and to keep their destination a secret. At dawn, the *Ghatrousha* sailed towards Dammam at the eastern edge of the Al-Ahsa oasis. Erhama sat at the stern with the wooden box cradled in his arms like a baby.

Chapter 13

Muscat

THE *EDEN* AND THE three ships belonging to the Sultan of Oman arrived in Muscat from Bahrain. Loch was keen to finish the task of finding the sword as soon as possible so he ordered his crew to remain on board with the exception of two small parties. The first party went ashore to fetch provisions of food, water, wood and coal, as well as other supplies needed for the forthcoming military operation.

Loch, accompanied by Sadleir, led the second party and headed straight to the offices of the representative of the East India Company.

As was his custom, Gulap bowed when he saw them and brought his palms together as a sign of respect.

'Let's forget about formalities, Gulap. I need your assistance in an important secret mission,' Loch said directly.

The two visitors sat down without waiting for Gulap's invitation.

'How can I help you, sir?' enquired the Indian genially. 'Tell me what you need and I'm sure I'll be able to help.'

'Close the door and make sure that nobody can hear what I have to say. Then come and sit down here.'

Gulap did as he was ordered and looked at the captain, awaiting instructions.

'We've lost a priceless sword which was a gift from the Governor of Bombay to Ibrahim Pasha,' began Loch. 'It was stolen by the pirate Erhama bin Jaber from Major Sadleir during his journey from India. We absolutely must retrieve that sword regardless of the cost. Do you understand?'

Gulap nodded again. 'How can I help you, sir?' he repeated.

'I've been told you know everyone here,' explained Loch. 'I need you to find a man who can tell us the whereabouts of Erhama bin Jaber. But you must have absolute faith in him. He mustn't talk to anyone about this. Do you know anybody who fits the bill?'

Gulap gave it some thought.

'Well?' asked Loch impatiently.

'Perhaps,' replied the Indian. 'I may be able to find someone with information, sir, but I will need some time.'

'We're in a state of war and time is against us,' Loch said. 'I can give you until tomorrow morning.'

Without further ado, the officers rose to their feet and left the room. Gulap remained in his seat for a while as though hypnotised, and then he too left the office, heading in the opposite direction, towards an outlying part of town.

The following morning, a small boat came alongside HMS *Eden* with Gulap and a dark-skinned young man on board. Loch ordered his men to lower the ladder for them and, once they had climbed aboard, he led them straight to the wardroom.

'Is this our man?' he asked Gulap as he peered at the Arab. He seemed to be in his twenties and could clearly not understand English.

'My agents and I were very busy last night, sir,' said Gulap. 'And I believe we could not have found a more suitable man for you.' Nodding at the Arab, he added, 'This is Ali. He's a close friend of Erhama's son Bashir. They grew up together and he keeps many of Bashir's secrets. He may be able to answer some of your questions.'

Loch nodded and, focusing on the young man, asked Gulap to translate for him. 'Where does he expect Erhama bin Jaber to be now?'

The captain had to wait for Gulap to translate the reply. 'Do you really expect anyone to know where Erhama lives?' said Ali. 'He keeps his movements a closely-guarded secret even from his sailors. Nobody will be able to answer your question.'

'I need to find Erhama bin Jaber as soon as possible. Can he help us or not?' Loch followed Ali's movements and was hopeful when he detected a slight nod.

Ali spoke quickly and the captain was impressed by Gulap's fluent translation. 'Erhama has three hideouts. The first is in Ras al-Khaimah with the Qawasimis. The second is in the north of Qatar where he conceals his ship between Ruwais and the small island facing it. When he's moored there, Erhama never leaves his ship and usually stays only for a few days to get supplies. The third is his fort in Dammam. But he doesn't like to stay too long in Dammam because the fort is often subject to attacks from several sides even though it is located in difficult terrain.'

Ali paused for Gulap to catch up. 'Of the three, Ras al-Khaimah is the best place to hide for a long time without being discovered.'

'Ask him, Gulap, whether he can come with us as a guide. We'll pay him handsomely.'

Gulap relayed the question and turned once again to the captain. 'He can't. If Erhama knew Ali was helping you with this information, he would make his life hell. He says he likes the pirate's son and considers him his only friend. But he hates the father because of his cruelty. He says even Bashir complains about Erhama's treatment. He can't do any more than this.'

Loch nodded. 'Pay him and let him go,' he said. 'At least he has confirmed the information we already have on Erhama's hideouts.'

Ali seized Gulap's hand and started talking to him.

'There is something more, sir,' said Gulap. 'It may be important.'

'Yes?'

'Ali says that Bashir is in love with a girl who lives in a small village called Zubara on the coast of Qatar. But since her family is from the Utub tribe – his father's arch-enemies – Erhama has vowed he will never allow the marriage. But Bashir visits the village every now and then, giving various excuses in order to see her.'

Loch considered the information. He could already imagine another scenario whereby they would ambush the pirate's son and offer to exchange him for the sword. 'But that would take us further away from our mission,' he found himself saying aloud.

Gulap continued, undeterred. 'Ali believes that if you can get in touch with Bashir, he will cooperate with you. Unlike his father, who gave up trade and devoted himself to piracy, Bashir wishes to become a trader. Through him you can get to the father.'

'This information is valuable, Gulap. But I can't use it now. At another time, it may be worth gold, but not at the moment. My focus is on the sword, Gulap, do you understand?' Leading them to the door, he added to Gulap, 'Keep an ear out for any fresh information about Erhama. And do keep this man close as we may need him again.'

On their way out, they bumped into Sadleir, who had just returned from the Sultan's palace and wished to have a private meeting with the captain.

Loch nodded. 'Let's hope you have some good news.'

Mansen took care of escorting Gulap and the Arab back to their boat while Loch and Sadleir settled in the wardroom.

'I was at a meeting with the Sultan's minister and some of his senior officers, sir,' began Sadleir. 'The Sultan has agreed to send seven ships carrying five hundred men, in addition to two ships with a hundred horses. They propose that we sail along the coast as far as Khor Fakkan and drop a contingent of three hundred of the Sultan's infantry and cavalry there.'

Loch unfurled a nautical map on the table and trailed his finger along the Omani coast until it reached the creek of Khor Fakkan. 'Good,' he said as his finger moved on to the stronghold of the Qawasimis. 'They would travel on by land to Ras al-Khaimah, correct?'

Sadleir nodded. 'We would continue on our way by sea and then arrive at the same time as them since we will need to circumnavigate the land to get there.'

Loch made a quick calculation: in addition to his own soldiers, he would have four hundred infantrymen and a cavalry of one hundred under his command. 'That should be enough to look under each and every rock on the shore for that damned pirate,' he said, delighted. 'When will the Sultan's men be ready to leave?'

'Day after tomorrow, sir,' said Sadleir.

Chapter 14

Dammam, Eastern Arabia

I T WAS HIGH TIDE when Erhama's ships arrived at Dammam, on the eastern coast of the Arabian Peninsula.

When the sea flowed in, the whole area became a salty lake and anyone unfamiliar with the terrain or foolish enough to be caught in the high tide would sink in the resulting quicksand.

Erhama disembarked carrying the box with the Indian sword on his head and a bundle of valuables in his hand. With the exception of a few guards who remained on board ship, his crew followed him, wading in water up to their waists until they reached a familiar spot where the water level dropped down to their knees. They picked their way through well-trodden paths, walking in single file. The merciless heat of the sun beat down on them, making their long trek all the more excruciating and exhausting.

A few hours later they saw some palm trees and a small fort surrounded by a wall made of dry clay. Erhama dipped his hand in the sea water and wiped his forehead and face in an attempt to soothe the pain from the scorching heat.

'We arrived at the wrong time, sir,' said Dirar. 'We should have stayed on the *Ghatrousha* until low tide. It would have made our walk much easier.'

'You may be right,' answered Erhama, 'but I had to reach the fort as soon as possible.'

He stared at his fort, his refuge, which he had built years earlier. It looked like a mirage because of the heat that radiated from the ground and caused everything to shift into visions of lakes and shimmering apparitions.

No sooner had they got close to the fort than a few men appeared on its walls, raising their muskets against the phantoms coming from the sea. The procession was stopped by a warning shot fired into the air.

Erhama turned to his son and told him to give the men the agreed signal.

Bashir took a yellow handkerchief out of his pocket and tied it to a stick. He raised the stick, waved the yellow flag seven times and then lowered it again.

The guards fired three more shots into the air in acknowledgement.

Erhama and his company advanced to the fort whose main door was immediately flung open. Inside were four emaciated and dishevelled men wearing little more than loincloths and carrying various weapons around their waists and on their shoulders. They were already lined up as Erhama crossed the threshold, waiting to rub noses with Erhama as a sign of deep respect.

'How are you, Abu Misfer?' Erhama said to the leader of the group.

'I'm fine, my sheikh,' replied Abu Misfer reverently and he lowered his gaze. 'But I hope you have brought some food for us, master, since we've been surviving on dates and water for a month. We would like to eat something more nourishing.'

'You'll get plenty of that, don't worry,' answered Erhama with a smile. 'Our ship is full of mouth-watering food. When the tide goes out, go to the ship with the other men. But watch your step when you wade in the water.'

One night a few months earlier, Abu Misfer had fallen into a water-filled hole. As the water had risen to his waist and then to his chest, he had screamed like a man staring death in the face. He was dragged out of the hole after the water had reached his ears, and after that he shied away from the sea. Abu Misfer had grown up in the desert surrounding Al-Ahsa, living on dried dates, desert reptiles and camel milk.

'We'll go when the water ebbs, my sheikh,' Abu Misfer said.

Erhama then introduced the man standing to his right. 'This is my friend Bin Ofaisan,' he said. 'He will enjoy our hospitality for a long time, God willing.'

Abu Misfer advanced to kiss Bin Ofaisan's nose. 'Greetings to you, Sheikh bin Ofaisan. I've heard so much about you from sailors. Your presence at the fort is a great honour. We'll finally have someone capable of reciting the Qur'an properly during prayers.'

Erhama laughed. 'Don't say that, Abu Misfer. Bin Ofaisan is a politician and a warrior, not an imam at the mosque. You might scare him away with that kind of talk.'

'Don't listen to him, Abu Misfer,' said Bin Ofaisan. 'We'll recite the Qur'an together if you wish. But let's get some rest and eat first.'

In the evening, Abu Misfer's men went to the ship to fetch the food while everyone else took their positions around the fires that had been lit to bring life to the place. Abu Misfer's men were back at the fort before night prayers, lugging sacks of food such as rice, flour and butter.

A meal was cooked, its aroma filling the air, and the older men told stories to their younger counterparts about strange events they had witnessed during their travels, tales of monsters on land and at sea, tales of ghosts and devils.

Having eaten to their hearts' content for the first time in a month, they all went to bed and fell asleep almost at once.

Bashir was awakened by a kick in the foot. He sat up and saw his father.

'Bring a lamp and follow me, son,' directed Erhama.

'But where are we going?'

'I have no time to explain.'

Bashir did as he was told and, holding a lamp, he followed his father to the main gate and out of the fort. Once outside, Erhama asked his son to put out the lamp and walk behind him. They headed north for a while and then turned west, walking in silence the whole time.

Bashir's shoes felt damp and he heard the sound of water, so he realised that they were going through marshland. After a steep incline, he felt hot sand underfoot and they continued in that direction until they came to a solitary rock in the middle of a sea of sand.

Erhama took the box containing the Indian sword out of his cloak and wrapped it several times in a large piece of cloth. Near the rock, they dug a hole big enough for the box. After placing it in the hole, they covered it with sand and rolled the rock on top of it.

Satisfied that the job was done, Erhama turned to his son and said, 'This sword is priceless, so priceless that it will allow you and your children to live in prosperity. Never forget where it is buried or tell anybody about its hiding place, even if they tear you to pieces. Do you understand?'

'Yes, Father, I do. But why have we buried it?'

'Because I couldn't find a safer place than this,' said Erhama. 'Even your closest friends will sometimes betray you and steal from you. But the ground is man's most faithful ally.'

As they started back, Erhama gave his son a warning. 'This is our secret, boy,' he said. 'If you ever tell anybody about the sword or where it is hidden, I'll have to kill you and the person you tell. Do you understand, Bashir?'

Bashir was shocked. 'Yes,' he managed to say. 'Yes, I understand, Father.'

On the return to the fort, Bashir began to count their steps and ascertain the directions in case he ever needed to go back to retrieve the sword. It was pitch dark and there were few discernible landmarks, so he walked at a steady pace and started counting again every time they changed direction.

Chapter 15

Khor Fakkan, Eastern Arabia

K HOR FAKKAN WAS A small creek surrounded on three sides by bare, rocky mountains. Given its dramatic topography, it had long been used as a hideout by pirates and fugitives running away from enemies and bloody feuds. On its coast a small community of fishermen lived in houses made of stone or palm leaves, bringing water on camelback from springs hidden in the small valleys and ravines between the mountains.

The people of Khor Fakkan lived in absolute poverty and were completely powerless. They were accustomed to strangers who arrived unexpectedly, who often brought nothing but trouble to their land and who were to be avoided. Too many of their people had been killed in their own homes under mysterious circumstances or had been kidnapped in the dead of night and taken aboard the ships anchored out at sea. They had witnessed far too many battles between ships without understanding why they were fighting or what had come from the battles.

When HMS *Eden* first appeared in the bay and dropped anchor, the people of Khor Fakkan did their best to ignore the most magnificent ship they had ever seen.

Over the course of two days, a total of three hundred infantrymen, and one hundred cavalrymen and their mounts, came ashore on small fishing boats. Loch noticed the discipline of the Omani troops – a spit and polish he had never observed before in non-European armies. The Omani ships lowered their sails faster than the *Eden*, and their crew did not speak much and followed their orders to the letter.

After the troops had landed, they stood in neat lines for inspection. Once their number and equipment had been checked, the squadron leaders waited for the captain's command to begin their march across country to Ras al-Khaimah.

The ships continued their journey up the coast of pristine beaches and inlets and on through the Strait of Hormuz to reach Ras al-Khaimah on the other side. News of the expeditionary force travelled even faster by word of mouth up the same coastline, passing through a string of poor villages and hamlets, which in turn relayed the report to people who lived closer to the town until it reached the residents of Ras al-Khaimah.

Sheikh Hassan al-Qasmi did not understand the motive behind the campaign. He was the ruler of Ras al-Khaimah and an ally of the Wahhabis whose troops had arrived at the Buraimi oasis at the edge of the Empty Quarter. All the battle fronts that the Wahhabis had ignited were still blazing the length of the coast to Iraq.

Sheikh Hassan was a tribal leader whose alliance with the Wahhabis had imbued him with a religious streak that led him to see the invaders as evil infidels who, as such, should be eliminated. He was not prepared to negotiate or make concessions. All he wanted was to urge people to resist and repel the aggressors at all costs.

With his own followers armed and ready, Sheikh Hassan called on his allies all along the coast to prepare for battle and to send fighters as soon as possible. He reminded them of the atrocities committed by the Portuguese in past centuries, when those infidels had attacked their forebears' women, killed their children and cut off the ears of the faithful. The memory of those crimes was sufficient to arouse the passions of the region's inhabitants and convince them to fight the new wave of infidels who would run amok on this earth, killing, corrupting and laying waste to everything they came across.

The flotilla under the command of Captain Loch arrived near the coast of Ras al-Khaimah a few days later. He waited until darkness to dispatch some Omani scouts to establish whether the land force from Khor Fakkan had prepared the ground for the siege on Ras al-Khaimah as planned.

The group of five armed scouts rowed to shore in a small, inconspicuous boat. They were dressed in civilian clothes and soon vanished from sight into the adjacent farmland where they mingled with people in order to gain information. Some hours later, a sound could be heard coming from the spot where the men had disappeared – a combination of rustling leaves and muffled screams.

On the morning of the following day, Loch looked from the deck of the *Eden* to the shore where his scouts had landed. They had not returned yet and he was growing impatient.

Although they were late, very late to report back, he waited a few more hours. But before midday, he started to suspect the worst and sent another group of scouts to find out what had happened to the first party.

This second group landed at the same spot and, as they entered the farmland near the shore, they found the corpses of their colleagues, who had been torn apart by swords and spears.

They had been left there to rot in the sun; their limbs had been partly devoured by dogs and vermin.

They rushed back to the *Eden* with the news.

In a moment of rage, the captain decided to launch the attack. He ordered his men to prepare their arms for landing.

Sadleir, too, was getting ready to board a boat with the men when Loch held him back and instructed him to stay on the *Eden* and not to leave it under any circumstances.

Once on land, the soldiers lined up in two long rows and began to march along the shore, led by the captain and the Sultan's army officers.

They had not got far when they were attacked from the rear. All of a sudden the air was filled with the sound of gunfire and Loch rushed to the rear to find that a number of soldiers had been killed by snipers hidden in farms. He barked orders for the men to take rapid defensive positions when he heard gunfire coming from the front of the line.

He ordered a retreat to the beach to allow the force to regroup and confront the enemy.

With the sea at their backs, the soldiers lined up again in time to fire a volley into a group of horsemen that came galloping from the south. Horses and their riders fell, their screams mingled with the din of muskets being fired; the smell of gunpowder was now everywhere. The remaining horsemen regrouped and charged again. They were met with further volleys and more of them ended up lifeless on the sandy shore. The horsemen were forced to retreat, but the expeditionary force was not given a moment's respite.

From all along the shore, a bloodcurdling battle cry was heard and a sea of bare-chested armed men came out of hiding, opening fire and running at them in a frenzy, with raised swords and spears.

The two armies collided in a jumbled mass of flesh and steel. It was no longer possible to make out individual sounds as roars of rage and screams of pain mingled with pounding gunfire and clashing swords.

The battle was lost almost from the start. Hemmed in and outflanked, Loch's soldiers could do little more than fall back into progressively smaller circles, gathering together to protect each other's backs, like isolated pockets of land being swallowed up by the sea.

Eventually, the same bloodcurdling cry rang out and the attackers withdrew and vanished into the adjoining farmland as suddenly as they had appeared.

In the eerie calm that followed, Loch ordered a body count. They had lost almost one hundred men, who, along with the wounded, were ferried to the ships.

Even more catastrophically, they soon realised from some of the surviving horsemen that they had been firing at their own men. The Sultan's cavalry, which had been dropped off at Khor Fakkan, had arrived at the coast of Ras al-Khaimah and had camped not very far from the agreed spot to wait for the ships.

When the horsemen had heard the sound of gunfire, they had rightly assumed that a confrontation was taking place between the soldiers of the expeditionary force and local fighters. They had rushed to the battlefield to help their comrades who had mistaken them for enemy fighters and shot at them.

It was a humiliating defeat. Long after the flotilla had weighed anchor and returned to Muscat, people would relate the events of the battle, which only strengthened the influence of the Wahhabis in the region and increased the number of their supporters.

The campaign had suffered a huge setback and Loch expected the Admiralty to reprimand him severely for his blunder.

Chapter 16

Dammam

I N HIS HIDEOUT IN Dammam, Erhama reclined in his chair and, grinning at Bin Ofaisan, asked his guest whether he had heard the news from Ras al-Khaimah.

When Bin Ofaisan looked at him blankly, he said in a booming voice, 'The news of a magnificent victory. The news of a battle that will make your heart dance with joy, my friend. Who knows, we might even have to re-examine the whole situation.'

'Tell me, I'm very eager to hear what has happened,' said Bin Ofaisan as he edged closer to Erhama.

This time, as Erhama clicked his sword in its scabbard, it sounded like an uplifting beat. He related the events of the battle as they had been described to him by one of his agents. Bin Ofaisan whooped with delight when he heard that a third of the invading force of Omanis, British and Indians had perished.

'Is this true? You're not joking, are you?'

'It's true. The British captain went back to Muscat with his tail between his legs like the cur that he is.' He nodded and laughed as he added, 'He was outwitted by the tribesmen. He fell straight into their ambush.'

Bin Ofaisan began making a strange noise, something between a laugh and a shout for joy.

'Things are changing now,' said Erhama, 'and I believe this is the moment to strike. They're at their weakest. We must put out to sea to make some money – you will need money to return to your village in Nejd.'

'I'm ready any time you wish, Erhama. I haven't seen my village in years, or my orchard, which I left in the care of my son.'

'So let's get some money, old friend, before you lose what's left of your teeth. This way you'll die peacefully at home with your elderly wife.' Erhama found that so amusing that he started to laugh again.

'We have all aged, Erhama,' Bin Ofaisan said seriously. 'We ask God to grant us a blessed ending to our life. So in whose home will you die?'

'Me?' He shrugged. 'I hope I'll die fighting at sea.'

But Bin Ofaisan was still being serious. 'We ask God to grant us a blessed ending to our lives. But since the defeat of the English has given you such joy today, I would like to ask a small favour.'

'Of course.'

'I went for a walk with Bashir, who told me about his love for a girl from Zubara. He asked me to intercede on his behalf and ask you to allow him to marry her. So would you accept my mediation, brother?'

Erhama's mood changed abruptly, his face turning pale and his eyes narrowing. 'That's not a small favour, my friend,' he said soberly and then fell silent. Even his sword stopped clicking.

Bin Ofaisan tried again, saying gently, 'I know she's an Utub, but hasn't enough blood been shed, Erhama? This feud must end.'

Erhama lowered his gaze momentarily as though the trail of vengeance had turned and twisted to end at his feet. Then he lifted his head and said darkly, 'I've vowed revenge till death. They have ruined my life and I have to ruin theirs.'

'But what has Bashir and his marriage got to do with your feud?' Bin Ofaisan argued. 'He has his own life to live. He shouldn't have to sail with you from one place to the next, hiding out in one stinking hole and another.'

But Erhama was resolute. Desire for revenge had taken complete hold of him and he saw everything through its prism. 'And how do you suppose I could be the grandfather of his children when I'm trying to kill their uncles? Wouldn't that mean betrayal and hypocrisy?'

Bin Ofaisan struck his forehead with his right hand as though Erhama had gone completely mad. 'You, too, are losing your teeth, my friend. You're almost seventy – you may not survive another year. Isn't it time for a change of heart? Doesn't your old age tell you something?'

Erhama gave a wry smile. 'My age tells me to hurry up and be avenged before I die.'

Bin Ofaisan would not relent and tried a different tack. 'After death we will be judged and punished. What will you say to God then? Will you tell Him that you spent all your life seeking revenge and murder? That you prevented your son from marrying because of your hatred? Isn't this madness? Doesn't it show little faith in God's mercy?'

'You know very well that I'm not a pious man. What you say means nothing to me. Besides, who knows, God may forgive me because He knows what's inside my heart.'

'Your heart?' That caused Bin Ofaisan to snigger. 'So what's inside your heart, then? Even a lion doesn't attack its prey if it isn't hungry, but you – you fill that heart of yours with spite for your enemies and deprive all those around you of happiness just so that you might satisfy your lust for blood. You've always been stubborn, but until this moment I had no idea that you were as hard as rock. I pray to God to protect me from what is inside your heart, my friend.'

Bin Ofaisan walked away as if to save the rest of his sanity after this fruitless discussion. He sat at a distance from Erhama to show his displeasure.

Erhama smiled to himself at the thought of the precious sword that was buried not far from the fort and which he was saving for his son. It occurred to him that he might die soon, leaving the sword to Bashir, who would then be free to marry his girl. Why should he mind? Bashir could do as he pleased after Erhama's death.

Erhama looked at his friend, trying to pacify him. 'Let's prepare ourselves for the sea,' he said. 'The weather is better now and there will be many ships with enough cargo to make us rich men before we die.'

Bin Ofaisan joined him and, spotting Bashir in the distance, gave a short, apologetic shake of the head to signify that his attempt at mediation had failed.

Bashir looked at his father with simmering resentment.

The *Ghatrousha* set sail the following morning. Having grown weary and bored with their stay in the remote fort, the crew were in high spirits and keen for a new adventure. They were used to a life of challenges at sea which was also lucrative for them.

Everyone left with the exception of the guards under Abu Misfer and Bashir, who had woken with a severe stomach ache and asked his father for permission to remain in Dammam.

Bashir said goodbye to his father from his bedside as the excruciating pain prevented him from getting up. Having felt his son's forehead and taken his pulse, Erhama decided there was no fever and that Bashir was perhaps suffering from mild food poisoning or a stomach cold.

Abu Misfer, who was standing in the room next to his master, reassured him that he could treat any illness with his herbs and that he knew the right combination of leaves that, once boiled into a tisane and ingested, would work their magic on Bashir's stomach.

'That's fine,' said Erhama. 'Just don't poison him with your concoctions.'

With that, Erhama turned on his heel and went to join his men on the *Ghatrousha*.

Bashir was not remotely ill, but he stayed in bed the whole day, writhing dramatically whenever someone came to check on him, which caused Abu Misfer to prepare even more herbal tea for him.

He waited until night and then, believing the garrison had retired, he crept out of bed and made his way outside. But at the gate, a guard called to him from above. 'Where are you going, Bashir? Is your stomach pain better? Have my herbs cured you?'

Bashir looked up at the wall and could just make out Abu Misfer's silhouette.

'Almost, Abu Misfer,' he said. 'I feel much better now than I did this morning.'

'So where are you going?' repeated the guard.

Bashir had to think quickly. 'I must relieve myself of all that herbal tea you made me drink.'

'But we have latrines for that in the fort, as you know,' insisted Abu Misfer.

'Trust me,' said Bashir. 'My stomach has been rumbling all day. What will come out will only ruin your night if I do it in the latrines.'

Abu Misfer laughed. 'Then go,' he told him. 'The smell of my own body is enough for me!' As Bashir opened the gate, he added, 'But don't go far – it's a dark and moonless night.'

Once outside the fort, Bashir retraced the steps he had taken with his father, counting his paces, starting over each time he changed direction.

He reached the place where he believed they had buried the sword. But it was so dark that he could not see the rock at first and had to move his arms and legs in long, sweeping arcs, working his way methodically over the area.

His left foot struck the rock and he cursed everything from the moonless night to the stone for the sharp jabbing pain in his toes.

Then he bent down, rolled the rock out of the way and began to dig at the loose sand until his fingers felt the box.

He pulled out the box and embraced it as though it were a lost love. He gripped it to his chest and walked back to the fort. As he drew near to the gate, Abu Misfer's voice called out from his lofty sentry post. 'Is that you, Bashir? I thought you would never come back.'

Bashir shuddered with fear; he had assumed Abu Misfer would be asleep as he normally was at this hour. 'Why Abu Misfer? Do you hate me that much?'

'You know how dear you are to me. But I thought your soul had gone out of your body along with the food.'

Abu Misfer spotted the box Bashir was carrying but could

not make out what it was. 'What are you carrying? Have you married and produced children during your outing? I had no idea my herbs had that magical effect.'

Bashir tried to hide the tension that changed his voice. He was worried lest Abu Misfer should discover his secret. 'You're certainly very jolly this evening, Abu Misfer. What are you up to?'

'You haven't answered me. What are you carrying?'

'It's a bundle of wood I found on the way. I wrapped it in a piece of cloth that I had on me. I brought it because I thought we might need some wood for tomorrow.' Bashir muttered to himself, 'Damn you, fool. Why are you sleepless tonight of all nights? You used to sleep like a log every night.'

Bashir simply wanted to bring the conversation to a peaceful close, and go on his way. 'Let me in, Abu Misfer, you've cross-examined me enough.'

Abu Misfer ordered the gate to be opened. Bashir entered under the cloak of darkness, and rushed to his quarters. He closed the door, hid the box in a safe place and began planning his next move, all the while cursing Abu Misfer for nearly exposing him.

Chapter 17

Muscat

As soon as the flotilla dropped anchor at Muscat, Loch made sure that his officers did their duty towards the injured and dead and, asking Sadleir to join him, he went ashore in a small boat.

Loch knew that the shamefaced return to Oman meant he had to do something to boost his military standing: some elements in the Admiralty would doubtless use his defeat at Ras al-Khaimah to try and shunt him out of the navy. He would be forced to retire to his family estate, where he would command the respect of nobody but his servants and gardeners.

Loch stared down into the clear water, watching the teeming schools of fish that the local population ate with relish after drying and grinding them to a pulp and adding spices. The shoals were so abundant that Loch imagined they were following their craft. He noticed that the small fry, in particular, often changed direction suddenly to ward off any potential attacker.

He thought to himself, 'I'll follow your example.'

When the boat reached the shore, the two officers disembarked and walked through the narrow paths and stalls to get to Gulap's office.

The representative of the East India Company stood up from behind his desk and bowed in greeting. 'What happened to you, sir, was extremely unfortunate,' he said once he had straightened up. 'I thank the gods that you are well.'

Loch nodded impatiently and did not wait to be offered a seat. 'Listen, Gulap,' he said urgently. 'I want you to listen to me.'

'I'm listening to everything you say, sir,' Gulap replied.

Loch stood up suddenly as if he had been bitten by a snake. 'The sword, Gulap! The damned sword! We must have it back or I'm finished. Do you understand?'

Gulap had dealt with all sorts of people in Muscat, and sought to calm the captain. 'I understand, sir. But what is required of me?'

'I need to see that young Arab you brought to me, Bashir's friend – Ali,' he said, remembering the name. 'I need you to bring Ali to me now.'

Gulap was taken aback by this brusque request and did little to conceal his surprise. 'I'll do my best, sir. I just hope he's still in Muscat. Those people never stay in one place for long.'

'Go and fetch him now,' ordered Loch. 'I'll await your return with Major Sadleir.'

Gulap hesitated and his smile disappeared; he was not accustomed to taking orders like that, and could do without the rudeness. He had thought that the captain had got all the information he needed of Ali, but here he was again, with his arrogance and endless demands.

Gulap bowed before he left, swearing to himself that he would give an offering to the gods if that man left Muscat for good; he could already picture himself getting a sacrificial chicken or even a goat if Loch could be made to disappear.

In the office, Loch lit his pipe and explained his strategy to Sadleir. 'Ali could play a role in helping us find the sword you lost.'

Sadleir, bristling at the comment and remembering the captain's own recent defeat, said, 'We've had several painful losses, sir. But how can this Ali character help us?'

Loch blew out some smoke. 'Love. He told us that the pirate opposes his son's choice of girl. So we'll get Ali to take us to the son, and we'll offer Bashir all the moral and financial support he needs to marry that girl of his.'

'So long as he brings us the sword from his father – is that it?'

'Plain *quid pro quo.*'

'Do you think that will work, sir?'

'Both our reputations depend on it, Major,' the captain replied tersely. Without the sword, Ibrahim Pasha would refuse to join the alliance. With the sword, his army could crush the Wahhabis in the Arabian Peninsula and, by joining the Sultan of Oman's men and the regiments from Persia in a pincer movement, could eradicate the Qawasimis along with the pirate ships in the Gulf. 'I will have that final overwhelming victory and the minor hiccups along the way will be all but forgotten. The Admiralty will know who to thank for taming the Gulf.'

Not for the first time, Sadleir found himself thinking that the captain was one of the most self-centred men he had come across. The confrontation in Ras al-Khaimah that had resulted in so many dead and injured had hardly been a 'minor hiccup'. He was tempted to remind the captain that any victory depended on his own dangerous mission as he sought out Ibrahim Pasha to hand him the sword.

But he held his tongue and decided his own report to the regiment would ensure that, if they proved successful, he too would get his fair share of the glory.

They sat in silence. Sadleir opened a book on Arabic

grammar while Loch refilled his pipe and checked his pocket watch with growing frequency.

Eventually, Gulap entered accompanied by Ali. They were both sweating profusely and the Indian started to describe the pains he had gone to in order to track down the young man. Loch interrupted him with an outstretched palm and asked him to act as interpreter. 'Do you know where Bashir bin Erhama is, Ali?' Loch asked.

Ali was astonished that the man was asking the same questions he had already answered at their previous meeting. He found Westerners extremely perplexing. 'No, sir. I don't know.'

'Can you at least tell us the places where he might be?' Loch asked.

Ali smiled, wondering if the man were drunk. 'I told you about the places before, but I can't guarantee he's in any of them.'

The anger in Loch's voice was rising. 'You mentioned that Bashir was in love with a girl from Zubara and that his father objected to their marriage.'

Loch waited for the man to nod. 'I'll pay you a good wage for every day you spend with us while we look for Bashir. Do you agree?'

Ali wanted to know how much.

'I'll pay you ten rupees a day.'

Even Gulap was impressed by the amount and raised his eyebrows.

Ali considered the offer briefly and then nodded in agreement. He asked that it be made in writing, with the other two men signing it as witnesses.

'You're a trader, Ali, not a sailor,' said Loch with a thin smile.

To Gulap, he said, 'He's one of yours.' Loch held out his hand for a sheet of paper to write the agreement.

'When will you set sail, sir?' asked Gulap.

'We can't waste any time. We'll go at once to Zubara and hope Bashir will be there.'

'May the gods will it,' the Indian said formally, with a bow.

Chapter 18

Dammam

THE DAY AFTER HIS feigned stomach illness, Bashir stuffed the box with the sword into a bag of his belongings, put on a colourful turban and tied a belt made of cloth around his waist in the manner of sailors. He bid the guards at the fort farewell, climbed onto a donkey and left for the desert.

Abu Misfer was in his quarters and saw Bashir through the window. By the time he had rushed down to the gate, Bashir was already receding into the distance and gave him a little wave.

Abu Misfer turned to the guards and asked them where Bashir was heading.

'To Qatif,' answered one of them.

'Qatif?' he repeated with astonishment. The town was just a short distance by sea, so why was Bashir going by land? Abu Misfer stuck out his lower lip and raised his hands as if to declare that he understood nothing.

From a distance, Qatif seemed like a black dot in a sea of sand. The closer Bashir drew to that dot, the bigger and blacker it became. He arrived at a valley full of palm trees, springs and waterwheels. He spent the night in Qatif, wandering through its markets to buy provisions.

He headed back to Dammam the next day, the town itself, that is – the port not the fort. He steered clear of the main roads between the two towns in order to circumvent his father's fort and avoid meeting any of Erhama's men.

While the port of Dammam was not as big as Muharraq in Bahrain or Muscat in Oman, it nevertheless was a supply point on the shipping route linking the Gulf to Basra. There were many pedlars selling fresh water at inflated prices to the crews of those ships – unlike wood, spices, amber and perfume, it was one commodity the men could not do without. The water was brought from Bahrain's ground-water springs, from Shatt al-Arab or from the springs of the port of Bushehr.

Bashir walked around the docks, taking in the ships and their captains, masters with absolute power over their vessels.

He was particularly interested in the flags that fluttered from the masts of the various ships. The British Government had agreed with the tribal leaders of the region that their ships would fly red ensigns in order to set them apart from pirate vessels. The tribal leaders had taken it upon themselves to devise various flags according to their own particular whims, while keeping them predominantly red. Consequently, the motif as well as the shape of a flag – rather than its colour – generally indicated a ship's provenance or affiliations.

Bashir did not want to board a ship that flew the Utub emblem because, if his identity was discovered, he could be arrested and used as a bargaining chip with his father or be killed in revenge. Moreover, his father never passed up an opportunity to pursue ships that carried the Utub flag and might attack the vessel Bashir was on. For those reasons, Bashir preferred to take his time examining the ships and their captains, especially given that he had taken the circuitous route from Qatif precisely in order to cover his tracks as he set off on his trip to visit his sweetheart in Zubara.

After some time, Bashir settled on a medium-sized ship with a deep bilge – known in the Gulf as a *boom* – whose ensign bore two stripes, red and white, which marked it as either a Bahraini or Qatari vessel given the similarity of the flags used in those two locations.

'Peace be upon you, sir,' Bashir said as he approached the captain by the docked ship. 'Where are you from? Where are you bound?'

'Peace be upon you, my son. We're from Qatar and we're going to Bahrain to buy some goods. From there we'll sail home.'

'Where do you dock in Qatar?'

'Zubara,' said the man simply.

Bashir could not believe his luck. His heart started to beat faster simply on hearing the name of the town where his sweetheart lived – almost as though the captain had uttered her name.

'Would you allow me to come with you?' he asked. 'I'll pay, sir. I have enough money for the passage.'

The captain peered at him for a moment. 'All right, lad. We sail this evening, God willing.'

Bashir jumped on board and found a spot where he put his belongings. He asked for a drink of water and sat watching the sailors and the ship that would be his home for the next few days.

Once they had set sail, the captain called him over to the stern, offered him a cup of tea and asked his name.

'It's Bashir bin Abdallah, sir. I'm from Dammam.'

The captain seemed to be waiting for more but the young man remained quiet. 'And what takes you to Qatar?'

'I'm going to Zubara to see my uncles,' replied Bashir, falling silent again.

The captain handed him his tea along with a lump of sugar. 'Every human being has a story, lad, a tale you tell about yourself.'

Bashir looked at him quizzically.

'Please,' said the captain genially, 'have your tea.'

Bashir popped the lump of sugar in his mouth, held it between his teeth and proceeded to sip the tea, swirling it in his mouth so that it would be sweetened by the sugar. When Bashir's cup was still half full, the captain poured some more as a sign of hospitality and esteem for his guest.

'A human being is a life, Bashir, and every life tells a story,' the man said. 'If somebody asks you to introduce yourself, you have to offer something, tell them a bit about yourself.' He sighed with contentment as he finished his tea. 'Never claim that you don't have anything to say about yourself – that is one thing you should never say. Do you see?'

With a grin Bashir introduced himself again. 'My name is Bashir bin Abdallah. I live in Dammam and my father is Abdallah bin Mohammed al-Shamali, a horse-trader. I'm going to visit my maternal uncles in Zubara for a few days. Is that enough?'

The captain laughed. 'Yes, that's far better, Bashir bin Abdallah of the horse-traders in Dammam.' He gestured toward Bashir's bag of belongings. 'But tell me, why are you so careful with your bag? You can leave it on the deck. But you seem to feel you need to have it with you at all times.'

Bashir said quickly, 'Yes, I'm taking a gift from my father to my uncles. He would kill me if I lost it.'

The captain pointed to a small room at the back of the ship. 'You can always store it in my cabin. It will be safe there.'

'No, there's no need for that. I'll keep it with me. I'll be careful with it and will not lose sight of it.'

'As you wish, my young friend,' said the captain kindly. 'Men have such interesting stories to tell. Perhaps one day on our voyage you'll tell me yours.'

Chapter 19

The Arabian Gulf

ERHAMA STOOD AT THE bow of the *Ghatrousha* and scanned the sea. Several days had passed without a single ship appearing on the horizon and the sailors were getting restless. They were an unruly bunch who needed the thrill of the chase and the prospect of booty to keep them happy. Without that unifying drive, disputes among the crew -- from different backgrounds and competing tribes – often erupted.

Bin Ofaisan placed his hand on Erhama's shoulder and pointed to a ship on the leeward side in the distance that was sailing in the opposite direction and seemed about the same size as the *Ghatrousha*.

Erhama grinned slyly at Bin Ofaisan. 'Your eyesight is still sharp, my friend,' he said, reaching for his telescope.

'Yes, I'm not like those who have lost their teeth and their eyesight and cannot see beyond their noses.'

Erhama laughed and trained the telescope on the hull to get a sense of the weight, on the deck to estimate the size of the crew and on the mast to focus on her colours. 'You may be right, Bin Ofaisan. But I'm still the Erhama bin Jaber who fills people's hearts with terror.'

'Let's see what kind of ship she is and what we might take from her,' Bin Ofaisan said.

Erhama said nothing for a while, but Bin Ofaisan could see the muscles in his friend's jaw clench tight.

Erhama breathed darkly. 'The ship is from Bahrain.' He spun round and roared suddenly, 'Get ready, men! Today we fight the Al-Khalifas!'

The pirates knew that a rich trophy was in the offing and shouted with excitement. This was what they lived for, waiting weeks and sometimes months to experience the rush of a raid and the promise of wealth. They moved as a united fighting force again: hands turned the wheel, spread the sails and reached for weapons and grappling hooks.

The *Ghatrousha* headed in the direction of the other ship, increasing her speed, and the crew poured water on her sails to make them respond more effectively to the wind. The *Ghatrousha* gradually closed on her quarry.

When the ships were barely more than a few yards apart, the sailors threw the hooks and pulled on the ropes, trying to drag the Bahraini vessel closer so that they could jump on board.

The sailors of the other ship dashed to pull the hooks out or cut the ropes. But every time they succeeded in severing one line between the vessels, two more grappling hooks would come flying over the top, sinking their iron tips deep into the bulwarks. The crew prepared to be boarded, with their muskets and spears primed.

The battle erupted with a deafening volley of gunfire and sailors on both sides collapsed where they stood or fell into the sea. With the muskets fired, the spears came next, in long, sweeping arcs that often struck their intended targets, who screamed with the sudden pain of iron buried deep in their flesh.

Then came the clash of swords and daggers as both decks turned red with blood. Some of the fighters were even down to their bare fists and ducked and swiped and kicked at their foe relentlessly.

As the battle raged on, the numbers on the Bahraini vessel began to dwindle and the crew retreated to encircle a young man in his twenties who wielded a sword and a pistol. He looked particularly horrified by all the blood on the deck from the dead and injured.

Once the pirates had completely surrounded the group, Erhama called a ceasefire in his booming voice and, stepping casually over an inert body, he approached the band of resisters and told them to lay down their arms.

His pirates were veterans and so, while he had lost some men in the fight, most of the casualties were from the Bahraini ship.

Erhama was joined by Bin Ofaisan as he repeated his ultimatum to the survivors. 'You've fought bravely,' he told them. 'Now you must surrender or die.'

Gradually, they all dropped their weapons and fell to their knees, until only the young man and two sturdy slaves remained standing.

'Surrender, lad,' Erhama ordered. 'This is your last chance.'

At first, the young man did not say anything and just stared at Erhama with deep resentment. 'So you are Erhama bin Jaber, are you?' His voice cracked with emotion. 'I've heard a lot about you.'

'I don't harbour any ill will towards you, lad. You're still young, so surrender – I only want the cargo you have on board.'

'Over my dead body,' retorted the young man, holding his sword firmly. 'My father warned me about you. You're nothing but a thief who should be killed.'

There was something about the youth that reminded Erhama of Bashir. 'If your father were here he would want you to surrender. What's your name, son?'

'Ahmed bin Salman al-Khalifa.'

There before Erhama stood the son of his arch-enemy – Sheikh Salman's own flesh and blood. 'The hostility between your father and me can only end in death,' he uttered slowly. 'But you are not my enemy. Drop that sword and order your slaves to surrender for we have not come here to kill you.'

Erhama had attacked their ships before and appropriated their cargo, but he had never killed any of his cousins.

Bin Ofaisan intervened at that point to try to defuse the situation; the young man was after all immature and unaware of the possible consequences. Bin Ofaisan stepped between Erhama and the two slaves, extending his hand to stop an attack by either side. Mistaking the gesture, one of the slaves lashed out with his knife, injuring Bin Ofaisan in the arm. Bin Ofaisan reeled back in surprise and sudden pain, and tried to stem the flow of blood with his other arm.

Erhama did not hesitate for a second; he promptly aimed his pistol at the slave and shot him dead on the spot. The other slave raised his knife and, with a thunderous scream, lunged at the pirate. With his pistol spent, Erhama deftly parried with his sword and thrust straight into the man's abdomen. For a second, the man stood perfectly still, transfixed by the steel blade that had pierced his body to emerge on the other side. He slipped off the sword and was dead by the time he landed near his friend.

Erhama's sword swung next to press against the young man's chest. He yelled at him to surrender.

But, feeling the tip of the sword, the young Al-Khalifa took a few steps back until he reached the end of the ship. His feet had become entangled in the coiled hawser on the deck and, as he took one more step backwards, he tripped over the cable and fell over the side.

Erhama was not fast enough to stop the young man, who suddenly disappeared from view. Rushing to the side, he found him dangling by one foot, still attached to the heavy rope; his head had crashed violently against the hull and he had died from the force of the impact.

This was not the victory Erhama had intended.

Erhama's enmity with his cousins, the Al-Khalifas, had just entered a new phase. The Al-Khalifas were certain to pursue him relentlessly now and strive to kill him. From that day on, there would be no safe haven for him anywhere.

Erhama ordered the Bahraini ship to be looted and all her cargo to be transferred to the *Ghatrousha*, and got the stitcher to help with the injured. He directed the survivors of the enemy vessel to return home with the young man's corpse. He also asked them to relay the story truthfully so that the family of the young Al-Khalifa might know that his death had not been intentional.

Suddenly, one of Erhama's sailors shouted, 'Ship to starboard!'

'Let it go,' replied Erhama. 'We've seen enough blood for one day.' Turning to his men, he said, 'Untie the hooks and throw the corpses into the sea. Transfer our wounded to the *Ghatrousha* and set a course for our fort in Dammam.'

From a distance, Bashir and the Qatari captain watched the scene. 'One of the ships belongs to the Utubs of Bahrain,' the captain said as he looked through his telescope. 'The other has her flag coiled around the mast so I can't make it out.'

'What do you think is happening there?' asked Bashir.

'I don't know, lad, but I can see corpses floating on the water.'

'Are they fighting?'

'I don't see any clashes now. The fight might be over. But I can see a group of men talking to one another.'

He raised a hand to the sky as he declared, 'May God protect us from the evils of the sea.'

The sailors repeated 'Amen' after him.

Chapter 20

Zubara, Qatar

THE *EDEN* AND A smaller vessel, HMS *Mercury*, set sail from Muscat to Zubara to look for the lost sword.

According to the revised plan, the *Eden* would remain at Zubara for two days. If the search took longer than that, Loch would return to Muscat with his ship, leaving the *Mercury* behind until such time as Sadleir was able to retrieve the sword.

Though the passage to the Qatari coast was uneventful, Sadleir woke up anxiously every morning, afraid that time was running out. He had received news from Gulap that fierce skirmishes had broken out between the Wahhabis and Ibrahim Pasha's troops. According to recent dispatches from Nejd, Ibrahim Pasha had attacked some areas, leaving nothing behind; merchants and travellers spoke of the murder of women and children in cold blood. If Sadleir did not complete his mission quickly, Ibrahim Pasha's scorched-earth policy would probably alienate the Sultan of Oman, and the pact that the British were working towards would be dead in the water.

If anything, the ongoing battles in the Arabian Peninsula would make Sadleir's task harder because the local population, including their Arab allies, would come to regard him with suspicion as the man in cahoots with a criminal and murderer of innocent civilians.

In a matter of days, the two ships arrived at Zubara, which was very much like any of the small ports studded along the Gulf. It had no more than a few commercial vessels and fishing boats, with a small fort on the shore and a village made of mud houses.

It was Ali's idea that Sadleir should pose as an English merchant in the pearl business and that he would act as his assistant. 'It might take us a few days to look for Bashir bin Erhama.'

His words had been translated by a bilingual crew member, and Sadleir was gratified to realise that he had understood most of the Arabic.

Loch turned to Ali. 'A few days?' he grumbled. 'I thought you knew a great deal about him.'

'We can't just turn up at the house of his sweetheart and ask her if Bashir has been there,' replied Ali. 'That's not how things are done here. We need to make enquiries in a way that won't draw attention to us. You have to be patient.'

Loch didn't like the idea of leaving without having any information concerning the sword. But even if he did leave before, the *Mercury* could take Sadleir to Qatif if he managed to find the sword.

'The *Eden* will remain here for two days,' he said. 'It would be good if you had some information for me by then.'

Sadleir and Ali left on a small boat that took them to shore. Once on dry land, children gathered around them to stare curiously at Sadleir's strange clothes. Their arrival also attracted the attention of some men sitting on wooden chairs who sent a servant to invite the newcomers over.

Ali recognised one of the men and rushed to kiss his head and nose, and, out of respect, addressed him as 'uncle'. 'So glad to see you again, uncle,' he said warmly. 'I hope you're well.'

The man, who was called Abu Matar, looked at Ali with avuncular affection. 'We've missed you, Ali. I've always seen you in the company of Bashir. Where is he?' He peered at Sadleir.

'I would truly like to see Bashir,' answered Ali and, indicating Sadleir, he added, 'He's an English trader who wants to buy some pearls.'

Abu Matar kept his eye on the stranger.

'His name is Sadleir and he's a new trader in the pearl market. He asked me to introduce him to the merchants in the area and this is our first stop since we met in Muscat.'

Abu Matar nodded slowly. 'Well, Ali, go to my house and get some rest. I'll join you soon for lunch – you can tell me your news then.'

Still surrounded by the children of Zubara, Ali and Sadleir made their way to Abu Matar's house. They were admitted by a servant who recognised Ali and were led to the main living room where they were served refreshments.

Abu Matar came presently, accompanied by some of the men who had been with him at the harbour. They all ate, talked and laughed, and once his other guests had left, Abu Matar turned to Sadleir and handed him a pearl for him to evaluate.

Sadleir looked at the pearl, turned it over in his fingers a few times with little real enthusiasm and returned it to Abu Matar. 'It's pretty,' he said simply.

Abu Matar shrugged. Addressing Ali, he asked him directly, 'So who's your friend? If he's a pearl merchant, then I'm a king.'

Ali looked at him nervously, but did not reply.

'I gave your friend the best pearl I have,' continued Abu Matar. 'It has a dark tint and is perfectly round. This is one of the rarest pearls and would make the eyes of a real pearl merchant pop out. He looked at it as if I had shown him a pretty shell. So tell me, who is he?'

Ali decided to tell him the truth. 'I hope that what I say will remain a secret, uncle, because the situation is very dangerous. Sadleir here is a British officer and he wishes to meet Bashir. Can you help us?'

Abu Matar exhaled audibly. 'You know, Ali, how dear you are to me – as dear as Bashir himself. I've raised you both since you were young and I would never hurt Bashir.'

'We would never hurt Bashir,' Ali said immediately. 'Sadleir only wants to meet him to ask him about his father – and he's the only one who can help us.'

Abu Matar seemed satisfied. 'I haven't seen Bashir for ages. He usually comes here to stay, as you know, because of his amicable relations with Salwa's family.'

In the event, they did not have long to wait for Bashir.

The following day, the ship from Dammam sailed into the harbour and dropped anchor. The men of Zubara knew its identity and gathered to wait for the captain to appear. They greeted all the passengers, including one who held a box tucked under his arm.

Bashir waited at the end of the line of sailors to find out how things stood. He saw Abu Matar among the men welcoming the passengers and went to kiss his head and nose.

Abu Matar thumped his chest and laughed aloud as he teased, 'You're here to see Salwa, not this old man.'

'I'm dying to see her again, uncle,' Bashir admitted. 'But I'm always pleased to see you.'

Abu Matar patted him on the shoulder. 'Well, I have a surprise for you.'

In many respects, Abu Matar had been a true uncle to Bashir; with Erhama frequently absent, Abu Mater had often looked after him as a child. Bashir trusted him unreservedly and they held hands as they walked away from the docks.

When Abu Matar asked about Bashir's father, he detected some reticence and concluded that the relationship between father and son was strained. 'Let me tell you a little about your father, Bashir. I know there is some misunderstanding between you, but you must know that his heart is as strong as a lion's but also as compassionate as a father's.'

Abu Matar went on to tell him how, many years before, he had worked in the wood trade, importing from India and exporting to Basra and Bahrain. He had established a large network and things had been going well until disaster struck. One year, a terrible storm had hit the Arabian Sea, Oman and the Gulf, devastating everything in its path. His ships coming from India had sunk with all their cargo, leaving him with nothing. In addition to the lost merchandise, the families of the missing sailors had asked for compensation, which had made him bankrupt overnight. He had been so desperate that he had thought of committing suicide. 'But I put all my faith in God's grace,' he said. One night, he had heard a loud pounding on the door; his heart had sunk, as he had been convinced it was yet another creditor coming for money. However, it was Erhama bin Jaber who had stood there with a purse full of money which he handed to him, telling him it would see him through to better times.

'Your father saved my life,' said Abu Matar. 'I'll never forget his kindness.' As they reached his house, he waved grandly. 'Everything I own now actually belongs to him. And do you know that I have never repaid your father and he has never asked me to.'

Bashir had never heard this story and felt as if Abu Matar were describing the generous act of a man other than his father. He had never seen that side of Erhama. 'But I don't understand why he objects to my marriage, uncle.'

'Your father may be right to object, son.'

'He's only against it because they're Utubs and they're his enemies. But he seems to forget that he himself is an Utub. Isn't that ridiculous?'

Abu Matar laid his hand on Bashir's shoulder and said gently, 'Salwa's father was once your father's partner and they were very good friends. People even envied them their close friendship.'

He described how, in the course of a business trip to Bombay, Salwa's father had become acquainted with an Indian perfume trader who had agreed to send him a shipment every six months. Salwa's father had given the perfume merchant a substantial down payment as a guarantee, which he had disbursed from his own resources rather than from the common funds he had with his partner, Erhama.

A few months later, the cargo of poor-quality perfumes had arrived and no one had wanted to buy the stock, even those who had strong business links with Salwa's father. Wishing to minimise his loss, he had turned to Erhama and claimed he had struck the deal on their behalf as partners and that the funds paid to the Indian merchant had been communal. He had demanded Erhama cover half his losses.

Erhama had paid Salwa's father the money even though he had not been convinced, and he had tried to forget the whole matter and worked to rebuild the business once again. 'But it was clear that things did not go smoothly between the two men after that.'

Salwa's father had ended his partnership with Erhama and decided to settle in Oman. He had left his wife and little girl in Qatar and nothing had been heard of him after that.

Several years later, a small dark-skinned boy of ten had come to Erhama's ship while it was docked at Muscat and asked to work as a cabin boy. He carried a small bundle containing all his worldly possessions.

'That was Ali,' said Bashir.

'Yes, that's right,' confirmed Abu Matar. 'Taking pity on the lad, your father adopted him and brought him along to Zubara. During your father's repeated absences, I took Ali into my home and treated him as one of my own, especially because he was an orphan. Erhama asked me to look after both of you since you were too young to go to sea.'

Ali had left the bundle with Abu Matar's wife for safekeeping until he was fifteen. They had opened it on his birthday when Erhama happened to be in Zubara and found inside a dagger, some money, a little gold, a few silver bracelets and some papers. There were several messages that they had read together. 'We all froze,' recalled Abu Matar, 'as though we had been turned into stone.'

One of the sheets had been the last will and testament of Ali's father's, who, as it turned out, was Erhama's old partner – Salwa's father. In it, he testified to having defrauded Erhama, begged him for forgiveness and entreated Erhama to look after his wife and daughter in Zubara.

'Why didn't you ever tell me?' exclaimed Bashir. His head reeled at the revelation that his best friend was his sweetheart's half-brother. 'Why, uncle?'

'The tribe has never acknowledged him to this day,' Abu

Matar said slowly. 'Ali is the offspring of a mixed marriage between a man from the Utubs and a black African slave.'

'And?' Bashir asked.

'Everybody has lost in this situation. Ali remains unrecognised by his father's tribe and you –' he paused, 'and you, well, your father objects to your marriage for two reasons: because the girl's father betrayed his trust and because Ali would be the uncle of your children. That is unacceptable to Erhama. As you said yourself, he is also an Utub.'

'So that's why Ali went to Oman,' Bashir said with sudden clarity; he was beginning to see events in a new light.

'When Ali faced all those problems here, he decided to go back to Oman to sell the family home and settle there. I believe you met him every time he passed through here on business.'

'But does he know he's Salwa's brother?'

'Yes. Most people know. But nobody is ready to acknowledge anything.'

'But then why didn't Ali tell me that he was Salwa's brother? He knew I was in love with her and hoped to marry her. I told him all the details and he often carried my messages to her.'

'Don't forget that you grew up together,' explained Abu Matar. 'He's like a brother to you and hopes you will marry his sister. That way her mother might relent and acknowledge him, which might lead the whole tribe to recognise him.'

'Good God! I wish I could see Ali to tell him that I know. I hope I can help him.'

'Why don't you tell him in person then?' asked Abu Matar with a broad grin. 'He's in my living room waiting for you.'

The old man enjoyed Bashir's reaction as his look of incredulity turned slowly to elation. 'Really?' He hurried to the door. 'Excellent. I have something that will solve both our problems.'

'And what is that?' Abu Matar asked.

But Bashir had already stepped into the house with the priceless sword under his arm.

Chapter 21

Dammam

THE *GHATROUSHA* DROPPED ANCHOR at her usual hiding place some distance from the fort of Dammam. While the crew disembarked in a state of joy at the booty acquired from the Bahraini vessel, their captain seemed to walk with leaden feet.

Erhama was not at all happy at the turn of events. His back was hunched and his face gloomy. It was as though the battle had added ten years to his age.

He entered his fort and was welcomed by Abu Misfer, who tried as usual to lift his spirits with a few anecdotes he had heard from the Bedouins or the farmers in the area. Erhama remained silent as though he were not there.

After a while, he looked up and asked to see his son.

'Bashir has gone to Qatif,' Abu Misfer told him.

'Why did he leave for Qatif? When did he recover from his stomach ache?'

'He recovered the day you left. Thankfully he emptied his stomach outside the fort that very night – but I could swear there was still a smell. He even came back to the fort carrying a load of wood. The next morning, he took a donkey and travelled to Qatif to visit a friend of his.'

'Did you say that he left the fort at night?' Erhama asked with alarm.

'Yes, sir.' Abu Misfer could not understand his master's concern. 'He'll be back soon, I expect.'

Erhama jumped to his feet and, ordering everyone to stay in the fort, headed out to the secret location in the desert. Even from a distance he sensed that the rock had been moved. Running the last few feet, he stood and stared with disbelief at the traces of digging.

'No!' he screamed. Not Bashir. Not his own son. 'No!'

He fell to his knees and held his head as though trying to check the sudden onset of nauseating dizziness.

Even after several minutes, the land continued to spin vertiginously so he remained on the ground, with his back to the rock, as he considered what to do.

'Why?' he moaned miserably. Why had Bashir done this? Erhama had nothing good left in his life. He had even lost his son.

He was panting as though he was still running. He picked up a handful of sand and threw it. This was what his life had come to – he was as insubstantial as sand blowing in the wind.

He sat there for such a long time that his body went numb. He had to force himself up, fearing his muscles would seize up if he sat there any longer.

Erhama dragged his feet all the way back to the fort. He looked even older than when he had left and retired immediately to his room, closing the door behind him.

Everyone knew something terrible had happened. Erhama never went to his room upon returning from the sea, preferring to stay in the central courtyard, lying on a carpet by the stove, talking and drinking coffee with his men.

Bin Ofaisan knocked several times on Erhama's door. He decided to open it even though there was no answer.

He found Erhama lying on his bed, his back to the door and his scarf covering his head and face entirely as though he were dead.

'What's happened, Erhama?' Bin Ofaisan asked quietly.

Erhama did not turn to face him. 'Nothing,' he said curtly. 'I'm tired. I need some rest now.'

'You can tell that to everyone else,' Bin Ofaisan countered, 'but not to me. What is it, old friend?'

Erhama remained motionless.

'I will really leave you if that's what you want.'

'Yes,' said the reclining figure. Bin Ofaisan was about to turn away when Erhama spoke. 'There isn't a single part of my body, Bin Ofaisan, that has not known pain. In my long life I've felt the steel from swords and lead from bullets.' He turned to his friend and uncovered his face to reveal the tears in his eyes. 'Only my heart has remained intact all these years. But it was stabbed today with a poisonous knife. I don't think it will beat for much longer.'

Bin Ofaisan was stunned. He had never seen Erhama like this.

'God is great, old man,' he said, trying to sound reassuring. 'Tell me what happened so I can share some of your pain.'

'Bashir took the Indian sword.' Erhama winced; it pained him even to talk about it. 'Maybe he'll give it to his sweetheart's family or sell it to somebody in return for money. He has betrayed me. Why am I always being betrayed? This is not the first time, but it is by far the worst and most painful.'

'Then let's look for him, Erhama,' encouraged Bin Ofaisan. 'He will have a reason for what he did – I know it.'

'And what reason can a son have for betraying his father?'

retorted Erhama bitterly. 'Yes, I will find him. I'll leave tomorrow. But you won't want to come with me as I'll kill him with my bare hands when I find him.'

He tried to lift his arm and found it would not move. He tried again and failed. 'Poison!' he cried with grief. 'My son's poisonous act has paralysed my right side!'

Abu Misfer was called and, sitting near his master, he held the numb arm and began to massage it. He asked his patient to open his mouth so that he could examine his tongue.

'You're treating me the way you treat your camels when they fall ill,' Erhama snapped. 'But camels don't become paralysed out of sorrow.'

'But they do. They fall ill just like human beings. You'll heal, God willing.'

Abu Misfer told the men outside to light the stove.

'Will you burn me again with your hot irons, Abu Misfer? They've caused me great pain in the past and I doubt you'll find a single spot on my body that will be fit for burning.'

Bin Ofaisan and Abu Misfer carried him down and laid him on the carpet in the courtyard to wait for the iron rods to become red hot.

'May God protect us from your fire, Abu Misfer. You enjoy burning and torturing people as if you were the guardian of hell,' Erhama complained.

Unperturbed, Abu Misfer told them a story about how his father used to treat the sick camels in the desert. The Bedouins would bring their camels to him to cure them of many complaints: a snake bite, a thorn in the throat, the bite of another camel, an abscess of the tongue or even a psychological trauma that prevented the animal from eating.

One day a Bedouin had brought Abu Misfer's father a camel whose female companion had just died. 'Camels also have feelings, you know,' Abu Misfer said when everyone around him started to laugh. 'Camels do grieve.'

The camel had refused to eat or drink, so Abu Misfer's father had patted it and talked to it, wet his hand with water and wiped its face and mouth. But the camel would not budge. So he had decided to treat it by burning.

The camel had screamed so loudly when the hot iron made contact that froth had gushed out of its mouth and Abu Misfer had been worried it might attack them. But the following day, the camel had begun to eat and drink a little, and a little more the day after that. On the third day after treatment, it had grazed with the herd and found a new female that was prettier than its former mate.

'In fact the camel outlived my father,' said Abu Misfer, provoking more laughter. He ignored them and, checking to see if the iron had turned red hot, added, 'I'll do to you what my father did to the camel. That way you'll find a woman to marry instead of spending all your time with Bin Ofaisan.'

Several men held Erhama down as Abu Misfer began by placing the hot iron on a shoulder and then on his neck. Erhama screamed and the smell of burnt flesh filled the air.

Abu Misfer heated the irons one more time and focused on various other parts of the body that sizzled briefly upon contact.

Eventually, they carried him back to his room, spread some fat on all the sores and left him to rest and shiver in bed all night under a quilt.

Three days later, as Abu Misfer had anticipated, Erhama began to feel his right side again. By the fourth day, he was back to normal and barking orders on the deck of the *Ghatrousha*. As they weighed anchor and spread sails, Dirar came to ask him for the bearing.

'Southeast,' Erhama told him. 'Set our course for Zubara.'

Chapter 22

Muharraq

THE GUARDS MANNING THE entrance to Sheikh Salman al-Khalifa's palace stopped a man who, with tears welling up in his eyes and repeatedly wiping his face with his sleeve, asked to see the sheikh.

The head guard was summoned, heard the man's tragic news and rushed inside the palace. He returned shortly afterwards with Sheikh Salman himself, who listened with growing horror as the man repeated his story.

They all left for the harbour where the vessel that had been attacked by Erhama was moored. Sailors and workers had gathered around it to carry the dead and wounded from the ship.

The sheikh's son was solemnly brought to where his father stood and was lowered gently to the ground. Sheikh Salman sat by his son's head, ran his hand over the cold forehead and whispered a few words. Then he hid his face in his headscarf so that he could weep in private.

His men stood behind respectfully, waiting for him to give his orders.

Wiping his face with the drenched scarf, Sheikh Salman asked them to bury his son without the ritual washing since he was – in his father's eyes – a martyr. Like all martyrs, he would be laid to rest in the same condition that he died.

More tellingly, Sheikh Salman did not accept condolences for his son, a sign that he planned to avenge his death. His *majlis* in the palace remained open as usual, as though tragedy had not struck; the men who came to sit with the sheikh drank their coffee in mournful silence without daring to ask about his plans.

A few days later, Sheikh Salman instructed the head guard to arrange a meeting with a select group of Sunni and Shia religious leaders, along with a successful pearl merchant called Abu Saleh, one of his closest acquaintances.

The guests arrived on the appointed day and Sheikh Salman received them. 'As you know, Erhama bin Jaber killed my son. I buried him in his bloodstained clothes and didn't accept condolences. I asked the sailors who were on the ship with him for details of the battle against Erhama bin Jaber and I believe they told me the truth.'

Sheikh Salman was able to describe the circumstances that had led to the tragic death dispassionately, as though describing the fate of someone else's son. 'Erhama didn't kill him with his actual sword, but he was the direct cause of his death. He knew he was my son.' He stopped and asked the guests for their opinions on the matter.

The religious leaders were the first to speak and they urged him to be forgiving and merciful. Revenge, they told him, would bring only evil and should therefore be avoided.

Sheikh Salman turned to the pearl merchant.

'Your son was like a brother to my boys,' Abu Saleh said pensively. 'He occupies a special place in my heart. This is not an easy matter, but if you allow me a little time I will come up with a plan to help you get your revenge.'

'What do you have in mind, my friend?' Sheikh Salman asked.

'Leave it all to me, my sheikh. I promise it will make you happy.'

The religious leaders objected, but Sheikh Salman seemed satisfied. 'Very well,' he said, raising his hand to bring the conversation on the matter to a close. He knew Abu Saleh to be a shrewd man and trusted him to devise a suitably horrible and painful end for Erhama.

After Abu Saleh had returned to his shop in Muharraq, he called his Indian assistant, Sharma, and asked him, 'Are you still in touch with the representative of the East India Company in Muscat? What was his name now?'

'Gulap? Yes, sir,' he replied. 'We visited him last year while on our way to India. We still correspond from time to time.'

'Good. I want you to send him a message on the first ship to Muscat telling him that we are on our way to meet him for some important business.'

A few weeks later, Abu Saleh and Sharma disembarked at the port of Muscat and headed straight for Gulap's office. Gulap received them with much bowing and a shower of compliments. He offered them some cold sherbet and they exchanged pleasantries.

Abu Saleh quickly got to the point. 'Mr Gulap, you are well aware of the long-running conflict between Erhama bin Jaber and the Al-Khalifas. The latest victim of this conflict is the son of Sheikh Salman, our ruler and my friend.' He paused. 'We're here because we need a favour from you, a special favour that must remain absolutely secret.'

Abu Saleh opened a bag and brought out two purses that he tossed on Gulap's desk. The Indian picked up one of them, opened it and emptied the contents into the palm of his hand.

He held a cluster of large, round pearls. Having dabbled in the gems, Gulap knew what they were worth on the market and whistled appreciatively.

He dropped the pearls back in the bag, left both bags on his desk and, with his fingers clasped together, asked, 'What can I do for you, sir?'

Abu Saleh knew he would have to pay a high price for what he had in mind. He reached across the desk to grasp Gulap's hands in a gesture that suggested both friendliness and secrecy. 'I want you to do something to make Erhama disappear from the face of the earth. We don't want to see him ever again. He has caused far too much trouble.' He squeezed Gulap's hands. 'I know that you work for the British and that they are the only ones who can put an end to all this and bring peace to the Gulf. Do you understand, Gulap? If you succeed in solving this problem for us, you will receive two more purses of pearls that are even more valuable.'

'Leave it to me, sir,' said Gulap with a firm nod. Abu Saleh withdrew his hands and the Indian slipped the two bags of pearls into his pocket.

Chapter 23

Zubara

W HEN BASHIR ENTERED ABU Matar's living room, Ali jumped to his feet. They hugged each other warmly and asked after each other's health and well-being. Bashir's smile faded when he spotted Sadleir; he was always uncomfortable around strangers – and a foreigner to boot.

Ali introduced his friend simply as Bashir bin Erhama, and Sadleir as an English pearl merchant who had come with him from Oman. They shook hands politely.

Abu Matar looked at Ali after this brief introduction and smiled to himself. He was curious to see what would transpire from the meeting.

Sadleir's attention was drawn to the wrapped box under Bashir's arm. It was the same size as the case that had contained the sword and that Erhama had taken from him at sea. But now was not the right time to broach the subject, so he decided to wait to tell Ali about it.

As darkness fell, Bashir realised that he had to talk to Ali about his plan. He asked him if Sadleir spoke Arabic, to which Ali replied with a noncommittal wave.

'I think I have a way to solve all our problems, Ali,' Bashir said, running his hand over the bundle next to him. 'I have a very valuable sword that we could sell. With that money, I will be able to marry Salwa and you will be able to build your life and ask your tribe to recognise you.'

His expression told Ali that he knew about his past. 'You will have enough money to sway even the most stubborn minds.'

Ali looked at the box. 'What are you saying, brother?'

'I have a sword that is worth a fortune. If we use the money well, we will be able to change our situation.'

Bashir unwrapped the package to reveal the wooden box.

Sadleir's heart was pounding so loudly he felt sure the others could hear it.

Bashir opened the box and took out the jewel-studded sword. Ali and Abu Matar stared at it incredulously, while Sadleir itched to reach over and snatch it and run off with it as fast as possible.

Bashir held the sword in both hands as he told them how it had been found aboard a British vessel. He did not know that Sadleir had a working knowledge of Arabic, the reason he had been singled out for the mission in the first place. He did not know that Sadleir had been entrusted with the sword as a gift to Ibrahim Pasha. And he certainly did not know that Sadleir had been aboard that British vessel.

The sword went from Abu Matar to Ali, who gave it to Sadleir so that he could see it again at close range. Sadleir handed it back reluctantly to Bashir, who returned it to its box and wrapped it up again.

Sadleir was keen to speak to Ali privately and ask him what was going through his mind. He needed him to steal the sword from Bashir so that they could go back to the *Mercury*, which was waiting for them at the harbour.

He thought he would have his chance when Abu Matar called it a day and retired to his room. But when the old man left, Bashir and Ali began conversing quietly; Sadleir could not help but notice how Ali's face brightened when Bashir spoke.

Ali was conscious of Sadleir's gaze and found himself wishing he were alone with Bashir. He wanted to explain to Bashir that Sadleir had come along precisely for the sword and that they had to devise a plan to rid themselves of him before they could discuss what to do with it.

Sadleir wanted to remind Ali that he had to keep his word to Loch, who was waiting for them impatiently. Bashir, in turn, wished to elaborate his plan for their futures without the stranger's presence.

The three men looked at one another, each wishing to speak without the presence of the third.

Finally, the men retired to different corners of the room and tried to sleep.

In the dead of night, Sadleir crept to where Ali was sleeping and woke him with a hand on his mouth.

'We have to take the sword,' Sadleir whispered urgently.

Ali whispered back that the time was not right and told him to go back to sleep.

In another corner of the room, Bashir eavesdropped on the conversation, his eyes shut.

Sadleir awoke the next morning with the tip of the sword pressed against his chest.

'Get dressed,' Bashir ordered, prodding Sadleir with the blade. 'Go back to Muscat. You're not wanted here.'

But with the sword pinning him down, Sadleir was unable to sit up, let alone get dressed and leave. He turned his head to look at Ali questioningly.

'You should do as he says,' Ali said.

Sadleir realised that Ali was a passionate and emotional man who would not agree to Bashir's action unless compelled to. With the sword still pressing down on him, he tried to be calm and said in his broken Arabic, 'But I'll help you, Ali, as much as I can. I'll be with you. I'll make sure you get the money you need.'

Ali turned to Bashir and asked him to wait until they had heard all that Sadleir had to say. Bashir moved the sword away from Sadleir's chest, but watched him warily.

Sadleir sat up. 'I know that both of you need money to solve your problems. I also need the sword to solve my own problem. So let's find a solution that will satisfy all of us.'

Ali nodded and Bashir waited to hear more.

'You could hand me the sword,' said Sadleir, gaining confidence, 'and I would give you the money you need after you help me complete my mission.'

Bashir and Ali stared at each other in amazement. 'What mission?' Bashir asked suspiciously.

Sadleir explained the salient points of his quest to find Ibrahim Pasha in the Hejaz. 'Your role would be to accompany me there and guarantee my safe return. You can have all the money you need to solve your problems.'

'We could have all the money we need without risking our lives,' countered Bashir. 'We could just sell the sword like I said.'

'Yes,' agreed Sadleir, 'but that sword was stolen. You would be living off dirty money.' Remembering the distinction that Ali had made between Bashir and his father, Sadleir said pointedly, 'You would be no better than a thief or a pirate.'

Ali did not relish the thought of British men-of-war pursuing them for the rest of their lives and said as much.

'If you help me,' continued Sadleir persuasively, 'you would essentially be paid for your services. No one would question where you got the money.'

'But how much would we get in return for such a dangerous undertaking?' Bashir wanted to know.

Sadleir knew he had a winning hand; all he had to do now was to establish trust, particularly if these young men were to become his companions. 'I don't know,' he said honestly. 'But let's go to Captain Loch and discuss the whole thing. He will decide the sum of money you deserve in return for your services. But for heaven's sake, let's hurry – I just hope the captain hasn't already left for Muscat.'

Bashir agreed but wanted to leave the sword behind, hidden in a secret place, until he knew the specifics of any agreement. Sadleir appealed to him not to do this because time was running out. Bashir had the word of an officer and a gentleman that this was not a trick of any kind, and could simply walk away with the sword if he was not happy with the deal.

Bashir looked Ali in the eye and said, half jokingly, 'You know that I'll sever that little head of yours from your body if I ever find out that you cheated me with the help of this man.'

Ali laughed. 'Don't worry – I need my head no matter how little it is. Besides, who else would do the thinking for us?'

They collected their belongings and told Abu Matar's servant that they were leaving and that he should pass on to his master their apologies for their hasty departure.

On the way to the harbour, Bashir wanted to call on Salwa briefly, but Sadleir pressed him on so that they could meet Loch and conclude the deal before the *Eden* sailed for Muscat.

Bashir hesitated for a moment and then decided to go with them.

In the event, they soon discovered that Loch had already left, forcing them to hire a small boat to take them to the *Mercury*, which was waiting for them. As soon as they boarded, Sadleir ordered the captain of the vessel to set a course for Muscat.

Though disappointed the *Eden* had already gone, Sadleir could not believe his luck: not only had he retrieved the Indian sword but he also now had two men who could serve as guides on his hazardous journey to the Hejaz.

The ship had to sail north before swinging southeast in order to circumvent the peninsula of Qatar. They arrived at the north-ernmost point by nightfall and the captain lit a small lamp hanging on the mast and lowered one of the sails in order to reduce the ship's speed.

Sadleir and Ali stood on deck looking at the Qatari coast. Narrowing his eyes as though he had caught sight of something, Ali asked Sadleir whether he had seen a brief flashing light. He thought nothing more of it when Sadleir said he had not.

In the early morning before the light of day, the crew woke up to find that a heavy blanket of fog had descended. The captain had no choice but to drop all the sails and cast anchor as they waited for the fog to lift. He hung several lamps on the ship's bow and stern as a warning to any other ships in the vicinity.

It took a few hours for the sun to chase away the fog; gradually, the sea around them became visible again. As the captain ordered the anchor to be weighed and the sails to be spread, one of the sailors shouted suddenly, 'Ship to starboard! She's approaching quickly.'

Sadleir took hold of a telescope and squinted at the blotches of mist to the right of the ship. He certainly did not want a repeat of his experience on the voyage from Bombay. But he was not unduly concerned; he expected a commercial vessel had also been caught out by the fog.

The mist began to form small low-lying clouds that skimmed the surface of the sea. For a fleeting moment, a ship became visible and then was hidden again by another pocket of fog, as though they were playing hide and seek.

'It's a ghost ship,' said one of the sailors with dread as the silhouette reappeared briefly, only to be concealed once more.

Most of the crew had gathered around Sadleir to stare into the fog and point their finger at anything that moved.

The *Mercury* entered a wall of fog and the captain was again forced to reduce the ship's speed and lower her sails. One of the sailors was about to light the lamp and hang it on the mast when Sadleir ordered him not to. 'One can never be too sure,' he said darkly.

'What do you mean?' Bashir asked.

Sadleir waved his hands toward the starboard. 'More likely to be a ship full of pirates than phantoms,' he said. 'But you should be all right if it's one of your father's vessels.'

Bashir shuddered at the thought. He had been so careful to cover his tracks from Dammam that he kicked himself for not having taken similar precautions now. How would he face his father if he met him at sea?

Bashir did not have to wait long to find out.

All of a sudden, the *Mercury* shook violently as the other ship collided with her, causing everyone on deck to lose their balance. When they looked up, they saw the other vessel had struck their starboard side.

It was Bashir's worst nightmare. He saw his father at the helm waving his sword, with Bin Ofaisan and Dirar standing beside him.

There was hardly any resistance as the pirates boarded the *Mercury*; if Erhama was surprised at seeing his son on board he showed no sign of it. He ordered his men to tie up all the prisoners without exception, though Bashir and Ali were separated from the others. Erhama quickly found the familiar bundle containing the sword.

He had spotted and recognised the British officer, but he began with the other members of the ship's crew, asking them whether any of them had played any part in smuggling the Indian sword.

Eventually he came to stand in front of Sadleir. 'We meet again,' he said. 'And again I must take that sword from you.'

Sadleir's jaws clenched tight.

Erhama then took hold of him and drew him closer to Bashir and Ali. 'Do you have any children?' When the Englishman did not respond, Erhama continued, dangerously calm, 'I used to have a son. But that son pretended to be ill and then stole from his father.'

Erhama glared at Bashir, then turned to Sadleir again. 'What is the punishment in England for a son who betrays his father like that?'

Erhama now moved to stand next to Ali. 'Like father like son, eh?' he said bitterly. He spun round and seemed to address everyone. 'His father was once my friend – and he betrayed me. But for the sake of that friendship, I took this boy in as a son and look how he too chooses to repay my kindness.'

He stepped brusquely away from them. 'As I said before, I have no sons left.' He turned to Bin Ofaisan and gave his verdict: 'Throw these two rats overboard and make sure their hands are tied firmly. May God forgive them for their sins because I cannot.'

Erhama proceeded to order his men to carry away from the ship everything they could lay their hands on.

Bin Ofaisan tried to intercede to stop the death sentence. 'Have you gone mad, Erhama? You can't kill them just because you're angry with them.'

Erhama glared at Bin Ofaisan. 'Don't argue with me. I'm tired of your constant blabber.'

'But you simply can't do that,' Bin Ofaisan appealed to the pirate, his eyes turning red with emotion.

This was not lost on Bashir, who now spoke out, in a shout almost as loud as any pirate. 'Leave him, uncle. When he decides on something he never backs down. May God help us all.'

Bin Ofaisan sat in front of the two young men and put his hands together as though he had decided to pray for them before their death. Then he patted them on the shoulder, his face filled with compassion and pity.

Erhama's men did as they were told. Dragging both Bashir and Ali by the hands, they made them stand on a plank that had been placed over the side of the ship. Ali screamed for mercy while Bashir looked resigned to his fate, waiting to be pushed into the water.

If Erhama was at all hesitant, he did not show it; without looking at the victims, he gave the signal for his men to carry out the sentence and the two fell into the water. Then he approached Dirar and told him they were to head for Muscat.

When they hit the water, Bashir screamed at Ali, trying to tell him how to float with his hands tied. Bashir managed to stay afloat on his back by filling his lungs with air and breathing briefly and intermittently. Ali was having more trouble controlling his body in the water, spinning repeatedly on his back and then on his front.

'Listen to me, Ali.' Bashir gasped for air. 'Turn on your back. Don't panic or you'll die.'

He repeated the instruction in an attempt to encourage his friend. But Ali was facing the terror of death and fighting a losing battle against it.

From a distance the crew of the *Ghatrousha* watched the thrashing of the water as the two young men struggled to stay afloat.

Ali kept disappearing then reappearing, gasping and spluttering as his lungs filled slowly with sea water.

'Save me, Bashir,' he screamed. 'I don't want to die!'

With his own hands bound firmly, all Bashir could do was shout instructions and words of encouragement, even as he was gasping for air and losing the strength to speak.

Ali gradually sank deeper and resurfaced less often.

After several final attempts to remain afloat, Ali vanished in a brief cluster of bubbles. He never resurfaced.

Bashir, fighting for his own life, found the energy to curse his father.

Several hours passed and Bashir remained on the surface like discarded flotsam. But he was able to use his legs to paddle roughly where he thought the coast would be. Every so often, he forced his body to twist briefly so that he could cool his face from the scorching heat of the sun.

When night fell, he started to think of the sharks that tore their victims limb from limb, and reduced his splashing in order not to attract attention to himself.

When the sun rose, he was reassured to find that he had not drifted off course during the night, so he continued to move his legs and turn his body in the water from time to time to cool off. He tried desperately not to think of his raging thirst.

By the evening of that day he noticed some rocks jutting out of the water and paddled with renewed hope. He was surely just a short distance away from land now and he fought the deep fatigue that pervaded every inch of his body. Hours later his feet hit the rocky bottom of the sea. When he tried to stand up, his legs were too numb and weak to carry him.

He managed to float over to a dry rock and began rubbing the rope tying his hands against the rough surface. The rope frayed and then snapped.

He used his hands, now free, to crawl out of the sea.

Chapter 24

Muscat

THE *GHATROUSHA* AND THE *Mercury* arrived at the port of Muscat at the same time. Port officials did not see the pirate ship because she had lowered her flag and had kept very close to the *Mercury* as though they belonged together. They dropped anchor near other ships and Erhama, accompanied by Bin Ofaisan and Sadleir, headed straight for the British representative's office where they expected to find Loch. Erhama held the box with the Indian sword under his arm, still wrapped in the cloth Bashir had used.

The three men entered the office where they found the captain of the *Eden*.

The pirate was the last person Loch expected to see in Muscat. His mouth hung open in astonishment as he took in the group; even Sadleir, dressed in an Arab sailor's loose slacks, looked completely out of place.

'I've come to solve a mutual problem,' Erhama said directly. 'You and I are like birds of prey that hover around their victims. I'm here to hand your prey over to you so that you may give me mine.'

Loch glanced at Sadleir and, finding no clues in his face, turned back to the corsair.

Erhama unwrapped the piece of cloth around the box and Loch shifted in his seat uncomfortably. 'This has caused me to lose two sons,' Erhama said, 'one of my own flesh and blood and the other by adoption.' He opened the box and extracted the sword. 'This sword has become a burden and I'm willing to get rid of it for something in return.'

'How much did you have in mind?' Loch asked.

'Will money bring back my son?' Erhama said angrily. He paused and then resumed more evenly, 'I want you to leave my enemies to me and not interfere in the conflict between us. You should not support either of us.'

'You mean your tribe, the Utubs?'

'Yes,' said Erhama. 'A long feud continues between us, particularly with the Al-Khalifas, the rulers of Bahrain.' He gestured toward Bin Ofaisan. 'He will return to rule Bahrain and if you interfere I will turn the sea upside down on your heads again.'

'I don't give in to threats,' said Loch coldly.

'And yet threats are all you seem to understand. You British sign agreements with all the rulers of the Gulf but you breach them when you find they conflict with your interests.' He thumped his chest. 'You know that I'm different from them, for I own the sea and I have men who will fight with me till their last drop of blood. If you violate our agreement, I will destroy your trade. You will wish you were fighting the Qawasimis instead of me.'

'Well, Erhama,' Loch said at length. 'We couldn't possibly put any agreement in writing – it would have to remain strictly between ourselves. But you propose to give me the Indian sword in return for my allowing you to confront the Al-Khalifas without any interference from His Majesty's Government? If you manage to win your war with them, you would return the Wahhabis to Bahrain and you don't want us to intervene. Is that what you propose?'

'Yes, that's right. But you need to know that Bin Ofaisan has become one of my men and no longer works with the Wahhabis since you turned against him in Bahrain.'

'Very well,' said Loch slowly. 'However, in addition I would ask that Bin Ofaisan agree never to become our enemy if he does take power again in Bahrain. That's my condition.'

Erhama and Bin Ofaisan exchanged a few words and then they both signalled their agreement.

Loch asked to see the sword. Sadleir came to stand beside him when Erhama complied.

Loch unsheathed the blade and watched it sparkle as it reflected a beam of sunlight. He smiled and relaxed as he thought of their plan: the time for rallying the forces against the Wahhabis had come. He turned to Sadleir and handed him the sword: 'It's in your safekeeping now. Protect it with your life. If you lose it again, know that I will cut you up into little pieces. Now go and complete your mission, Major.'

Turning to Erhama, Loch held out his hand and said, 'You have my consent to the deal. It's not something I like but I will honour this agreement with you.'

Erhama shook his hand. 'In this part of the world, the British are not known for honouring their agreements. I hope you will keep your word.'

Bin Ofaisan did not like Loch's attitude. 'Ever since your ships appeared in the Gulf, you have been deciding who rules and who is overthrown,' Bin Ofaisan said to him. 'The day will come when you will be sent packing. I just hope that you will not leave any of your friends behind when that happens.'

Loch took a cigar out of a box on the desk and lit it before responding. 'Our interests dictate that we avoid power being concentrated in the hands of a single party. Your Wahhabi friends may sweep over the whole area if we're not here. They have already declared their enmity to us and their allies are attacking our ships at will. Aren't the Qawasimis your allies?'

Bin Ofaisan answered, 'But Captain Loch, what you see here is nothing but political change hiding behind the cover of religion. You know that political conflicts usually begin with religious or ethnic slogans, but over time their nature becomes clear.'

Wanting to put an end to the conversation, Erhama and Bin Ofaisan left the office. Sadleir emerged a few minutes later – reunited with the sword that he had lost twice since Bombay. He returned to the harbour where he had to prepare for his trip to Qatif. From there he would make contact with the Ottoman troops stationed in Al-Ahsa who, he hoped, would then arrange to guide him to Ibrahim Pasha's camp. He had held on to the dispatches from the Governor of Bombay, including a letter to Sheikh Bani Khaled, who would help him on the next leg of his mission.

Chapter 25

Muscat

LOCH HAD NO IDEA that Gulap had a plan that could destroy his dreams of promotion in the Royal Navy. While Loch basked in his seat after his successful negotiations with the pirate, the Indian emerged from his own clandestine meeting with Abu Saleh and Sharma.

Gulap walked through the narrow streets of Muscat thinking of the best way to implement their agreement. He strode the length of the town with his hands behind his back, oblivious to his surroundings.

Abu Saleh had been clear in his demand: he wanted the British drawn into the feud between Erhama and the Al-Khalifas. Gulap's role was to find a pretext that would nudge His Majesty's Government into taking sides and helping the Al-Khalifas to get rid of Erhama.

Gulap had accepted because of the fortune that Abu Saleh had placed on his desk and because of the promise of even greater wealth upon completion of the task. Gulap had worked for years for the East India Company in Muscat. He had built strong relations with British merchants and officers as well as with the ruling family in Muscat. But he was still only an employee who depended on the stipend he received from his superiors. His employment could end at any time and, therefore, he needed something to fall back on, he told himself. Abu Saleh's pearls would provide that safety net.

He knew he risked losing everything if anyone ever found out about his secret meeting. So he focused instead on a successful outcome and tried to come up with the best strategy.

He was so preoccupied that he ignored the greetings of people he passed or gave them only curt replies. He eventually ended up in the port area by way of the slave market. He was acquainted with many sailors, merchants and workers, and he was forced into several conversations as a group of merchants gathered around him.

As they were talking, he turned to glance at a Royal Navy ship in the harbour, where British and Indian women and their children were on board. When he enquired about the ship, he was told it was a British vessel travelling from India to Basra, and that the women and children were the families of British officers and Indian military men living there – ships often called at Muscat en route to Basra and back.

The captain of the ship, who was being addressed by an Englishwoman, turned to the men on the docks and beckoned over the best-dressed among them.

'Yes, sir?' said Gulap. He approached the ship and greeted the captain formally, introducing himself to him.

'I say, I'm very happy to meet you,' the captain said a bit too keenly. Gesturing at the woman standing beside him, he said, 'This kind lady here wishes to go to town to do some shopping. I'm reluctant to allow her to go alone as she might lose her way. I wonder if you might be decent enough to escort her and return as soon as possible?'

'Of course, sir,' Gulap said genially. 'I'll accompany her and bring her back in a few hours.'

The Englishwoman thanked him and smiled when she heard that she would have someone to take her and her teenage daughter to the souk. Then she signalled to a group of women who promptly joined her. When Gulap realised that he was going to be responsible for the woman and her daughter, plus another Englishwoman and two Indian women, he raised his eyebrows and looked helplessly at the captain.

The captain just smiled as if saying, 'You'll be with them for a few hours, but I'll be with them for weeks,' and asked Gulap to return by noon at the latest.

Gulap led the women to the souk, asked them what they wanted to buy and promptly wished he had not enquired.

The women all started to talk at once about what they were each looking for and about how hot the day was but how good it was to stretch one's legs after a long sea passage. The first Englishwoman was particularly chatty. 'Let me introduce my friends here,' she began. 'I'm by the way the wife of an English officer living in Basra and this is my daughter. The ladies here are also the wives of officers in Basra and Baghdad. We're going to see our husbands. How I hate ships! They're moving prisons. Do you know how terrible the food is? How I hate the sea! You should see how we suffer when the wind blows. My God! It's tragic! And the husband of the good Indian lady here was shot in Baghdad. You should have seen how she wept!'

There was no way for Gulap to stop her. 'But wait, I haven't told you about the British lady who has suffered constant stomach pain. She has lost so much weight because she has had no appetite. But in the end I suppose it's better for her, because she was rather plump. Her husband may prefer her this way! And wait! I must tell you the story of the sailor who fell for one of the girls here with us! You can't imagine how he suffered just to talk to her! But the captain was on the lookout and ordered him to stay in the crow's nest for an entire day. Can you imagine? Isn't that suffering? I wanted to tell you that I'll buy some dried fruits for my husband. I'm told that the price of a rhinoceros is quite low. Is this true? Do I have enough money?'

She turned to consult with another woman, and Gulap found himself feeling pity for the man who had to live with such non-stop prattling. But his thoughts were interrupted.

'Are you married, Mr Gupal?' she asked.

'It's Gulap, Ma'am,' he said.

'I'm so sorry. My servant in India has a very strange, long name, so I just call him George. So much easier,' she said.

'I can imagine,' he said.

'Are you happy in this part of the world, Mr Gualap?'

'It's Gulap, and yes, I'm happy here.'

'But you haven't answered my previous question, Mr Golop. Are you married? Your wife must be happy here, though it's dreadfully stuffy and hot during summertime, isn't it?'

Finally Gulap said, 'Yes, I'm married, Ma'am. The gods have offered me a beautiful woman who doesn't talk much.'

After several interminable hours of shopping and small talk, Gulap accompanied the women back to the ship, followed by a group of porters carrying their purchases.

When the captain saw the group approaching, he grinned at Gulap and called out, 'You really were a godsend. Thanks for bringing them back on time.'

Gulap smiled and waved, thinking to himself: may the gods send you their curses for such a tedious experience. Turning to the women, he said, 'I'm delighted to have made your acquaintance and to have been your guide today. I wish you a pleasant, safe trip.'

'Thank you, Mr Gulp.'

Gulap left the harbour feeling resentful of providence, which had thrown these women in his path and wasted his time. He thought of making an offering to the gods so that these women might be kidnapped and sold at a slave market for their utter foolishness.

That was when it hit him.

He had found the perfect tactic to draw the British into the feud between the Al-Khalifas and Erhama.

Chapter 26

The Coast of Qatar

BASHIR TOUCHED THE SANDY beach with his hands. Stepping onto land, he was briefly elated to feel the dry sand beneath his feet. He was certain he had been washed ashore on the northern tip of Qatar since that had been the closest area of coast when he and Ali had been thrown overboard. Thoughts of Ali dominated his mood.

He realised he was completely alone. There was not the slightest movement or glimmer of light in the dark night. No matter how loudly he might shout, nobody would come to his aid. He collapsed on the sand and, closing his eyes, was overcome by a deep fatigue; his mind and legs ached from the trauma of the last few days.

He woke up the next morning with a jolt. The blazing sun was beating down on him and his feet were sore from the sharp pebbles and rocks that he had stepped on the previous night. Although his wrists were tender where they had been bound, he did not worry about them as the sea water would heal them.

Looking behind him, he found a hill between the sea and the desert. He decided to climb to the top to see where exactly he had made landfall.

From the top of the hill, he saw a village in the distance and boats on a small creek that ran through it. He could make out children playing on the beach and men busy mending nets and removing seaweed from the hulls of their fishing boats.

He began to walk towards the village with lumbering steps. Once on the beach, a dog picked up his scent and began to bark, which drew the attention of the children. They came running up to him and Bashir stopped and fell to his knees to alleviate the agony in his feet. The worst was over and he had survived.

In the afternoon, Bashir ate fish and dried dates at the house of one of the elders of the village. His feet and wrists were bandaged after a paste of herbal painkillers had been applied to the wounds. These had been brought by the imam of the mosque, who, in addition to providing religious services, was the area's barber, healer and teacher.

As Bashir ate the food, his host held out a large pan containing some milk. According to tradition the host would not eat with the guest but would serve him until he had finished his meal.

The old man asked Bashir why he had been alone on the beach.

'I fell off a ship that was sailing from Bahrain to Oman,' he answered.

'I saw traces of rope on your wrists,' said the old man. 'Are you a slave running away from your master?'

When Bashir raised his hand to look at the bandage, it was as if he were seeing it for the first time. He felt more comfortable telling a partial truth than a complete lie.

'My hands were tied,' he admitted. 'Our ship was captured by pirates – they threw me into the sea and killed my father.'

Tears welled up in his eyes – genuine tears, since the pain of Ali's murder was still so raw. It occurred to him that, in another sense, he was not exactly lying since his father was dead to him.

The man nodded sadly. 'These things happen too often now. Many homes in this village have no adult men – they have been killed at sea either by British gunfire or pirates attacking their boats.'

Bashir felt the bandages on his feet. 'I need to go home tomorrow because I have a lot to do.'

'It's up to you, son, but I advise you not to walk because your feet need time to heal. Where do you live?'

'I have an uncle in Zubara. From there I'll go to Bahrain where my family –' His voice trailed off.

'Don't worry,' his host said kindly. 'Zubara is not very far from here. I'll lend you a donkey to take you there and my son can go with you to look after you.'

After the brutal treatment by his own father, Bashir was overwhelmed by the generosity and compassion of a stranger. 'I don't know how I can ever repay you for your kindness,' he said.

Bashir and the man's son reached Zubara after a full day of travelling. They went straight to Abu Matar's house as Bashir did not wish anyone else to see him in that state. Once there, Bashir invited the boy to stay the night and leave the following day, but the boy preferred to head back to his village straight away.

Bashir entered Abu Matar's living room and waited for him to return from the souk.

Abu Matar was surprised to see him again so soon after his hasty departure, and he frowned at the bandages around his wrists and feet. Bashir described everything that had happened to him over the past few days until he came to the moment when they were thrown off the ship.

Abu Matar closed his eyes at the news of Ali's death.

'You made a serious mistake, Bashir,' said Abu Matar finally.

Bashir looked down, shamefaced.

'You broke your ties with your father the moment you decided to steal the sword from him. And now you'll have to fend for yourself.' He paused. 'But your father has a lot of property. All the ships that he owns, as well as the fort in Dammam and the valuable waterwell within it, will be yours one day. You shouldn't give all that up.'

Bashir had not considered this. 'So maybe I should stay as close as possible to the Dammam fort.' Erhama was an old man obsessed with revenge and surrounded by enemies. He probably did not have much longer to live, Bashir thought, and all his property would be snapped up by his men if the rightful heir was not around to claim his inheritance.

'Yes, you have to be close to the fort of Dammam. Keep an ear out for any news of your father, so that you can act if anything happens to him.'

'I'll leave tomorrow, God willing.' Bashir's expression changed abruptly as he added less sombrely, 'May I ask a special favour of you, uncle?'

'Yes, son, what is it?'

'Could you help me meet Salwa before I leave? Who knows, it may be the last time I see her.'

'Do you really love her?'

'She's with me all the time,' Bashir said. 'I think of her all day long. She wakes up with me, eats and sleeps with me. Without her, my life is as dry as the desert.'

'It's love then, Bashir. I expect it is this love that helped you to overcome your ordeal at sea.' Abu Matar called his wife and asked her to invite Salwa to their home on some pretext.

Bashir folded his arms over his chest and waited. After what felt like hours, he heard a familiar woman's voice calling Abu Matar from inside the house.

'Salwa is here,' Abu Matar said as he got up to join his wife in another room. 'I'll leave you two alone.'

Bashir tried to kiss Abu Matar's hand out of respect and appreciation, but the older man quickly withdrew it. 'May God forgive us all, my son.'

Salwa entered the living room and her look of joy at seeing Bashir was soon replaced with concern as she noticed his bandages. 'Bashir,' she said, 'are you alright?'

'I am now.' He felt whole again just by seeing her. His heart began to beat faster; his love for her was the only thing that gave him the strength to endure life's miseries.

With a lock of hair that kept slipping out of her veil, Salwa seemed more beautiful than ever. She was well-spoken, good-humoured and fully aware of the difficulties Bashir had with his father. But they never talked about that or about the problems Erhama had had with Salwa's own father.

'Every time I pass through this town I do my best to see you, Salwa.'

Their eyes met.

'I'm always happy to see you, Bashir,' she said coyly. 'You know that I live only in the hope of seeing you.' She looked at his wounds again with concern. 'But what happened to you?'

'That's nothing,' he said, shrugging it off. He looked into her eyes again and loved the way they flitted from one bandage to another. 'I will never have peace until you become my wife.'

Her eyes left his wrists to focus on his face again. 'I hope we will be together, Bashir. But please don't take risks for me. If God wills it then we will marry. Otherwise, it will never happen.'

'God has created you for me and me for you. I have no doubt about that. So let me do what I can to fulfil our dream.'

'I'll pray to God that He may protect you, Bashir.'

They talked for a while longer until Salwa felt she had to leave in case anyone saw them alone together.

'May I ask a small favour, Salwa?'

'Yes. I'd be happy to do anything you ask.'

'May I kiss your hand? Would you allow me to do that?'

Timidly, Salwa extended her hand to him. He took it and placed her palm on his mouth, kissing it passionately as if he were kissing her lips. Then he put her palm on his cheek and eye.

Bashir left Zubara to go to Qatif, which was where Abu Misfer and the other guards at his father's fort bought provisions once a month. There he would hear the latest news about Erhama.

With a few possessions provided by Abu Matar, Bashir arrived at the port of Qatif. He immediately set about looking for work to earn his living. He did not know how long he would stay or who he might meet. He had no idea how to plan his life, but he knew that finding a job at the harbour was of paramount importance.

He noticed a large number of ships anchored at the entrance and sides of the harbour. By looking at their flags, he could tell that most had arrived from India and Basra, while others had come from Bahrain; only a few were from Oman.

He enquired about the harbour master and found him in a shed. In the manner of the men of the region, he was wearing a piece of cloth on his head that was fixed in place by a second, differently-coloured cloth. He was smoking and had a long white beard and shifty eyes that inspired little trust.

With his bundle of possessions, Bashir stood in front of the old man. He greeted him and received little more than a glance of disdain. Bashir repeated the greeting in a louder voice and another man sitting near the harbour master asked what he wanted.

'I need a job,' said Bashir. 'I'm a traveller stranded here. So could you help me?'

'Where are you from?'

Bashir realised that it would not be easy for him to find employment without a credible story; harbour masters were notoriously cautious about hiring strangers, to avoid falling foul of the authorities. Officials at ports across the region generally worked for the benefit of one party or another, and they were the ones who usually exposed smuggling operations. They sometimes even decided the value of the tax to be paid for merchandise. Their work was humble and unrewarding but it was of great value to the authorities as it enabled them to control trade and trafficking.

'I'm from Zubara in Qatar, sir,' said Bashir. 'I'm on my way to visit my uncles in Nejd, but I've lost all my money and need work to pay for my trip.'

The harbour master was still smoking quietly and it was the other man who answered. 'Do you know anybody in this area?'

'No, sir, I don't.'

The man grew impatient and said irritably, 'Then get lost, boy. Don't waste our time.'

Desperate and with nowhere to go, Bashir stayed put and insisted, 'I speak English and Hindi, sir. I can also read and write. I may be more useful to you than you can imagine. I will stay here only for a short while and then will be on my way to Nejd.'

The man glared at him. 'I told you to –'

He was suddenly interrupted by the harbour master. 'Did you say you speak English and Hindi?'

'That's right, sir.'

'Can you calculate as well?'

'Yes, I know how to add, subtract, find percentages and calculate taxes, if that's what you need.'

The harbour master held a brief conference with the other man and then, turning once again to Bashir, said, 'Alright, I'll give you a job. I want you to be one of my men and do exactly as I ask, without questions. But if I suspect for a second that you have betrayed me in any way, I will know how to deal with you. Do you understand?'

'I do, sir. You'll find me of great assistance to you.'

The harbour master pointed to a seat with a large ledger on it. 'I want you to sit near me and look at these accounts. Calculate the taxes owed to us.'

Bashir calculated the taxes owed by the ships whose names and merchandise were recorded in the ledger. When he handed it to the harbour master, the old man looked at him and asked him to add a further ten per cent onto the taxes without recording the additional sums in the book.

Bashir was also required to tell the ships' captains of the total tax owed. After receiving the sum, he would subtract one-tenth and hand that over to the harbour master.

Under the harbour master's orders, Bashir soon realised that he had become an unwilling accessory to corruption. But he needed the work and so he kept his sense of disgust to himself.

As the days passed, Bashir managed to establish a few friendships. He learned how to help merchants evade the payment of the tax itself or the harbour master's extra percentage. He also began to have some authority over some of the porters who worked for the harbour master. They started to report directly to him on the details of the daily transactions at the harbour.

One morning, he saw a Turkish officer sitting with the harbour master. He learned that his name was Khalil Agha and that he was in charge of the Ottoman garrison in Qatif and Al-Ahsa.

He was struck by their conspiratorial looks and, since he was out of earshot, he stared hard at the two men and tried to discover what they were up to. They smiled slyly at each other and laughed, and then the harbour master turned to open a box. He brought out a purse of gold coins and handed it over to Khalil Agha, who counted the coins and then put them back in the purse and tucked it away inside his breast pocket.

The two men stood up and kissed each other like old friends, and Khalil Agha left with a grin on his face.

Chapter 27

Muscat

Gulap smiled smugly as he thought of his brilliant idea – though now he had to sell it. He forced himself to look miserable and worried as he strode to see Loch in Sir Rupert's office.

He knocked on the door and entered when he heard the captain's voice.

Loch was relaxing in his chair, mulling over in his mind the mission that was now back on course. Sadleir had the sword and Ibrahim Pasha would soon join in their alliance. He felt he had the whole world at his feet.

Loch looked up and saw Gulap's long face. 'You again?' he said with clear displeasure. 'I sometimes wonder if you're the reason for all the bad luck I've had since I came here. I do hope you've brought some good news for a change.'

Gulap shook his head. 'I have bad news, sir.' There was not the slightest hint in his voice of any guilt he might be feeling, but his knees were shaking and so he sat down without waiting for Loch's permission.

'I am a firm believer in the science of astrology,' said Loch. 'And I suspect my stars are never at their best whenever I see you. Go on, give me the bad news.'

Gulap cleared his throat. 'I've just received information that a ship belonging to the East India Company has been attacked by Erhama bin Jaber. An Englishwoman and her fifteen-year-old daughter have been taken by the pirates, sir.'

Loch almost fell off his seat. 'What?' he roared. 'There's some mistake. Erhama has never dared to take hostages before.' He could not believe it, especially not after their clandestine meeting and agreement. 'What on earth would make him do something like that?'

Gulap tried to think of the saddest thing he could possibly imagine so that he would appear visibly affected. 'I don't know, sir. I'm merely relaying the information. It happened in the waters just off Muscat.'

'When?'

Gulap explained how the ship had called in at the port on its way to Basra and how it was full of families of British soldiers and officers. 'They were attacked as they were leaving Muscat.'

The timing was right, Loch realised with growing frustration; the ship's departure from Muscat certainly coincided with Erhama's own exit.

'Just imagine, sir,' said Gulap in a faltering voice. 'Imagine that fifteen-year-old girl in the hands of a seventy-year-old monster. I shudder to think of it. He'll surely sell them to the highest bidder.'

'Gulap, are you sure of this information?'

He nodded dejectedly.

'I won't hesitate to kill you with my own hands if this news is not accurate.'

'Do you think I would trouble you with it if I wasn't completely sure?'

Loch hesitated for a moment and then decided that the serious turn of events warranted the disclosure of his secret arrangement with the corsair. He told Gulap of their verbal deal and added, 'His demand was simple and straightforward. Neither we nor he would interfere in each other's business. So what happened? Why would he break his word?'

'Sir, you are a naval officer with much experience,' Gulap said flatteringly. 'You know better than most that pirates never keep their word. They are not officers and gentlemen – they have no sense of honour. He has stabbed you in the back and kidnapped an unarmed woman and child – subjects of His Majesty's Empire. I shouldn't be surprised if he was rushing as we speak to sell them at one of the slave markets.

'Even the gallows are too good for the likes of Erhama. I suggest you kill him as soon as you find him without investigation for the liar and criminal that he is. We need to do that for the sake of those two unfortunate souls.'

Gulap had overstepped the mark and Loch narrowed his eyes at him. 'Your suggestions are not welcome,' he said icily. 'You work for the East India Company and you report to me – is that clear?' He pointed to the door. 'Now go and find out more about this incident. And keep me informed.'

Gulap nodded and left the office considerably more worried than when he had entered it. He had thought Loch would simply swallow his story and order his ships out to track down and kill the pirate. It seemed clear now that the captain would need more evidence before committing his men to this pursuit.

He hurried to his office and drafted a message to Sharma, the assistant of the Bahraini pearl merchant, telling him that their plan to involve the British was in hand and that he needed him to write a particular letter to the commander of the British armed forces in the Gulf, Captain Loch. He even took the liberty of drafting Sharma's letter so that nothing could go wrong. Then he sealed his message and hurried to the harbour to find the first ship to Bahrain.

A week later, Loch received an anonymous letter. Written in English, it informed him that two British subjects, a mother and daughter, were being sold at the slave market in Bahrain and that many traders were enthusiastically bidding for them. The writer of the letter was certain that their price would be high in view of the scarcity of similar high-quality goods on the market.

Loch read the message, repeating the words 'high-quality goods' to himself in disgust. He did not need any more encouragement; he jumped to his feet and called his lieutenants.

A few days later, the *Eden* with all her crew and weapons sailed into the harbour at Muharraq in Bahrain and a party landed and demanded that the Bahraini authorities hand over the two British hostages immediately.

Sheikh Salman could not believe what he was hearing and he followed the party back to the *Eden*. The discussion between the sheikh and the captain went on for a long time, during which the sheikh swore that he knew nothing about the incident and denied that Bahrain even had a slave market. Several witnesses were brought forward and they all confirmed Sheikh Salman's assertions.

Loch did not wish to return to Muscat without being certain about the kidnapping. So he travelled on to Bushehr where he was met by Governor Bruce and his second-in-command, Matthews. They had not heard any news about a kidnapping and the East India Company, always very quick to inform its offices across the region of any conflict or loss, had not issued any warnings about abductions on the high seas.

'I received some information that the mother and daughter

were being sold in a slave market in Bahrain,' said Loch as he accepted a glass of Shirazi wine. 'But when I went there, everybody denied the report, including the sheikh himself.'

'Who supplied you with that information?' Bruce asked him.

Loch finished his drink in one gulp. 'The agent of the East India Company in Muscat,' he replied. 'His story was corroborated by an anonymous letter from Bahrain.'

'That is strange,' said Bruce pensively. 'We all have the interests of the Company at heart. We receive the same news and instructions as the office in Muscat. But we've heard nothing of the sort, have we?' he said, turning to Matthews.

'No, sir. This is a small region – this sort of news would have spread like wildfire,' Matthews said. 'Our merchantmen and men-of-war constantly sail through the area and we are on very good terms with many of the rulers here. I don't think an abduction could remain secret for long.'

The governor nodded. 'My dear Captain, you must be particularly on your guard,' he said. 'This region is full of conflicts and conspiracies. I shouldn't be surprised if this information were part of some scheme. But I can verify it if you give me a few days as we have ships that sail to Basra on a daily basis and they will surely confirm or deny the news.'

The captain flicked the glass with the tip of his finger, making a loud clinking noise.

'But then perhaps we should dispose of him anyway,' said Bruce slowly. 'Whether Erhama has kidnapped them or not is almost irrelevant. By removing him from the scene we would surely be getting rid of a constant headache.'

'Yes,' agreed Loch, 'but I have given my word to the pirate. I would need incontrovertible proof that he had broken the agreement before being released from my bond.'

'Agreement?' Bruce asked. 'What agreement?' It reminded him of his own attempt at getting Erhama to accept his terms.

Loch described the arrangement that he had with the pirate.

'But surely, my dear Captain, that should not prevent us from approaching a third party to do the job for us.'

'A third party?' enquired Loch with a frown.

'There is someone in Bushehr who could rid us of that corsair once and for all,' explained the governor, adding almost affably, 'Would you care to meet him?'

'Erhama could never know we were behind it.'

'Of course not, dear chap.' Bruce raised his voice to call his Persian guard, Abbas.

When Abbas appeared, Bruce told him to invite a man named Sadek to the coffee house for an important meeting with a visiting dignitary.

The governor watched him leave and sighed. 'I swear if he didn't know how to choose the best Shirazi wine, I would have got rid of him a long time ago.'

'Who is this Sadek character?' Loch wanted to know.

'Officially, he's the Deputy Governor of Bushehr – a local fellow we keep on to make him feel important. No real power as such.' Despite the title, Sadek did not report to Bruce; he was a Persian from an influential family who had been given the position simply to boost his prestige. Everyone in Bushehr knew that all the decisions were made by the British and, more specifically, by His Majesty's governor.

'But he knows all the scoundrels and blackguards in these parts,' Bruce said. 'Just don't fall for his charms.'

Chapter 28

Qatif, Eastern Arabia

SADLEIR SAT IN HIS cabin aboard the ship bound for Qatif and wrote his first report since the start of his difficult mission. He brushed some dust off the paper and, dipping the pen in an ink bottle, wrote: *'To His Excellency, the Governor of Bombay'.* He added the day's date, 20 June 1819, and described the events of the past months that had led him inexorably to the port of Qatif.

Qatif bay was some twenty miles wide and was bounded by a long spit of sand to the north and a desert plain to the south. At the heart of the bay, extending over ten miles from the northwest to the southeast, was the island of Tarut, covered with palm trees and full of freshwater springs.

At the northern approach to the bay, the water was deep and safe for navigation, though it lay at a distance from Qatif itself and compelled ships to stop near Tarut. At the southern end, which ran parallel to the desert plain, the sea was shallow and hazardous for ships. Further south stood the fort of Dammam, which was surrounded by water on all sides and had recently been restored by Erhama.

Sadleir left the ship and boarded a small craft that took him to Qatif. Once there, he hired a porter – from a crowd desperate for his business – to help him carry his belongings onto the wharf. A port official checked his identity and heard his request to be taken to the headquarters of the Ottoman garrison to see the commander, Khalil Agha. The official nodded, asked him to wait and headed straight for the shed to inform the harbour master.

The man sitting beside the harbour master looked up from his ledger in surprise when he heard Sadleir's name. The harbour master was intrigued by Sadleir's visit to Khalil Agha and asked that he be brought to him.

Bashir rose to his feet and took his leave on the pretext that he needed to finish some private business. Sadleir would almost certainly recognise him and greet him. A few minutes later, he saw the major coming to the shed to meet the harbour master. When Sadleir emerged he was accompanied by two workers he had employed to act as guides – for a fee that he had agreed with the harbour master. They brought some donkeys and, after they had tracked down another man, the group rode away from the harbour area to the souk. The last man in the group was a Persian called Mirza, who had been recommended to Sadleir by Gulap in Muscat.

Qatif's market was crowded and sold the usual array of goods – rice, wheat, barley, vegetables and dried and fresh fruit, much of which was grown on farms in the area. Sadleir needed to stock up on provisions but soon tired of bargaining with every seller for each item purchased – though it did give him the opportunity to practise his Arabic.

As he negotiated with a merchant to try to lower the price of some dates, a man came up behind him and whispered, 'Don't turn around. I'm Bashir bin Erhama.'

Sadleir was astounded but resisted the urge to look at Bashir. Was it possible that he had survived that terrible disaster on the

Mercury? He had been sure that both young men had drowned that day. Sadleir was happy to hear his voice, and pleased also to meet someone familiar in this alien place.

Bashir whispered, 'Let me do the bargaining for you – I know how to deal with these merchants.' Then he spoke loudly to the stallkeeper to agree a considerably reduced price.

Sadleir stepped back to allow Bashir to haggle, which completely perplexed Mirza.

The process of buying provisions lasted a couple of exhausting hours, after which Bashir vanished and all the purchases were placed on the backs of donkeys and tied securely. The group then started on their way out of Qatif.

As they left the town for the Ottoman base, heading southwest on the road to Al-Ahsa, Bashir appeared again from one of the farms. Now that they were out of town, they did not need to conceal their friendship: the two men shook hands and hugged, much to the surprise of the others in the group.

'Am I glad to see you!' exclaimed Sadleir. 'But why all the secrecy in the souk?'

Bashir grinned at him. 'It's a long story. But tell me, what are you doing here? I thought you'd be with Captain Loch.'

Sadleir laughed at the thought of Loch riding a donkey in that heat. 'It seems we still have a lot of unanswered questions. We've a long way to go and it's good to have someone to talk to.' He grew more serious as he asked Bashir how he had survived after his father had thrown him overboard.

Just recalling the events of that dark day reminded Bashir of his recurring nightmares. With some difficulty, he described how he had managed to paddle to safety after a full day and night at sea. He thought of Ali who had panicked and drowned.

'We could hear his screams,' Sadleir said. 'I thought you had both perished.'

'God rest his soul.'

'So what are you doing here?' Sadleir asked.

Bashir glanced behind him at the other members of the group to make sure they were far enough away not to overhear them. Then he explained that he needed to be close to the pirate's fort to claim his inheritance when Erhama died. 'And what about you?' he asked. 'Why are you in Qatif?'

'I have a difficult and confidential mission,' Sadleir replied. 'Truth is, I can't really tell you unless you promise to stay with me until it's over.'

Bashir looked at Sadleir to see if he was joking. But the major was quite serious.

'So, what do you say?' he said. 'Will you join me, Bashir?'

'But if I go with you, I may end up far away when my father dies and I would lose everything.'

Sadleir was silent, thinking of what he should say next. 'I can't promise you much, Bashir,' he said, 'but let me say this at least. You are totally different from your father. You will never be able to control his men, men who believe that you're dead anyway. And you don't have your father's cruel streak, so they won't fear you. They might even decide to kill you as soon as Erhama passes away, in order to get their hands on his money. They may even kill you believing that's what he would want.'

Bashir found himself nodding in agreement.

'Look,' Sadleir continued persuasively, 'I will pay you handsomely if you accompany me and I also promise to find you work in Bahrain, Oman or Bushehr as soon as we return. You're educated and speak several languages. You won't have trouble finding a job.'

'I've spent all my life on the high seas with my father,' Bashir said slowly. 'I never had a homeland or friends except for the sailors on his ships.' He remembered the sense of loss and loneliness he had felt after being washed up on the shore. 'It could be the beginning of a new life for me.'

Sadleir smiled and patted Bashir on the back. 'Now swear to be with me for the duration of my mission so I can give you all the details.'

'I promise you, Sadleir, that I'll be a brother to you on this trip until we return together or die together,' Bashir said formally, placing his hand on Sadleir's shoulder.

Satisfied, Sadleir described some of the finer points of his mission, especially the role that the priceless Indian sword would play in drawing Ibrahim Pasha into the tripartite pact with the British and Omanis against the Wahhabis.

'Do you have the sword with you?' Bashir asked in surprise.

'Of course. It's hidden in one of the boxes on the donkeys.'

As they rejoined the rest of the group, Bashir thought about how the entire region would change irrevocably. People were already talking about Ibrahim Pasha's siege of Diriyah and the famine in Nejd and Hejaz. They were worried about all the British ships that were trying to control trade in the Gulf and that had already brought so many new ideas that were altering the way they lived.

Bashir knew that his own life and everyone else's would soon change for ever.

Chapter 29

Bushehr

LOCH WAS TAKEN TO a popular coffee house overlooking the harbour of Bushehr, where traders met to smoke and make deals. Abbas found a good table and, removing his turban, he used it to dust the seats for the captain and the governor. Then he stood behind Bruce and shooed away the flies with the same piece of cloth.

'A very useful turban you have there,' commented Loch with a grin.

They were served tea and hookahs while they waited for Sadek, the Deputy Governor of Bushehr.

Loch took a long draw on the hookah and released the smoke through his nose, enjoying the sensation and finding that it went well with the tea.

Their conversation was interrupted by a loud commotion when the deputy governor strode into the coffee house escorted by several guards carrying swords and pistols. Their arrival was enough to drive away a number of customers; even those who had never met Sadek hated his very presence.

The man marched up to their table, shook hands with them and then made a show of sitting down on a rickety seat as though it were a throne. Sadek was a thin man and wore a flamboyant Persian outfit that harked back to a grander past. His narrow eyes darted around constantly and he had a long, sharply aquiline nose and thick eyebrows that met in the middle forming a coal-black line. He wore gold rings studded with the turquoise stones beloved by Persians, and around his neck hung a collection of charms tied randomly to protect him from evil spirits.

Loch had had to deal with all sorts of people in the course of his career, but he had never before met anyone quite so obviously sly.

One of Sadek's guards slapped the owner of the coffee house because he had been too slow to rise to his feet when their master walked in. They heard the man apologise lamely, asserting that he had not done it on purpose and that he had simply been caught unawares by the unexpected visit.

The slap was a warning signal to the waiters, who rushed to serve extra tea, cold water and the finest tobacco in well-lit hookahs.

'Thank you for coming at short notice,' said Bruce.

Sadek remained quiet while he sipped his tea and tasted the tobacco. He adjusted his position and looked directly at the governor. 'I was told by your servant Abbas that you have important guests. So would you please introduce them to me?'

'Of course.' Bruce gestured towards his companion and said, 'This is Captain Loch, the man responsible for fighting pirates in the Gulf. He's a very important figure in the Royal Navy.'

Sadek slowly turned his gaze on the officer as though he had expected a real dignitary. 'Captain Loch,' he said with the slightest nod and added sardonically, 'Your reputation precedes you, sir. What happened to you in Ras al-Khaimah was most unfortunate. It must be terrible to be beaten by a backward bunch of Bedouins.'

The blood rushed to Loch's face. He was about to get up, but he felt Bruce's hand grab him under the table.

'Hardly the time or place to talk about that, Sadek,' said Bruce with polite reproof. 'I thought it would be a good opportunity for both of you to become acquainted. I think you will need each other to fight the pirates.' Turning to Loch, he added, 'Our friend here is the nephew of the Prince of Shiraz and he is hugely fond of trade. But I wouldn't be lying if I said that he has many enemies.'

Sadek laughed heartily at that, breaking the tension. 'Most of whom are dead actually. And I expect the rest will follow soon enough.'

Bruce decided they had exchanged enough awkward pleasantries and went straight to the point. 'The captain is here because he heard that two British subjects – a woman and her child – had been kidnapped by pirates. Have you heard anything about this?'

'No. But those pirates are capable of such things.' He paused and then enquired, 'Is that what you've come to talk about? What is it you want? Why have you called this meeting?'

'Erhama bin Jaber,' said Bruce. 'We suspect him of being involved and we wish to get rid of him as soon as possible. I know he's your sworn enemy.'

'I see,' Sadek said. 'And so you would like me to eliminate him for you?'

'Yes.'

'Why?'

'Erhama is a vicious pirate who cannot be allowed to attack our merchantmen and abduct our people.'

'Yes, but why ask me?'

Loch stepped in. 'For political reasons, we cannot be seen to be involved. We can provide you with intelligence but no one can ever know that His Majesty's Government is supporting you in this. We would deny having had this meeting if you ever made it public.'

Sadek sniggered. 'Perhaps you should just wait for Erhama to come to Bushehr and then stab him in the back with a dagger.' He waved at the governor. 'God knows he comes here often enough to have private chats with our friend here.' Then, turning abruptly to Abbas, who was standing behind Bruce, he asked him, 'When was the last time Erhama was here? And remind me, what was it the governor said to him?'

Abbas's face turned pale. He could not understand why his real master – Sadek – had chosen to blow his cover as a spy on Bruce.

Bruce spun round in his seat with a stunned look on his face.

'Hmm?' prompted Sadek. 'Speak up, man.'

Abbas took two steps away from the governor and came to stand next to Sadek's guards. 'He was here many months ago, sir. The two men did not sign any agreement. Erhama left as suddenly as he had appeared.'

'You dog,' spat Bruce. 'You cowardly little cur.'

'Don't be too hard on yourself, my dear friend,' said Sadek with a chuckle. 'If you knew how many spies there were around you every day, you'd be astonished.' As the governor fumed, Sadek added, 'I'm at your service, gentlemen, if, that is, you can afford me.'

The governor was still too enraged to speak, so Loch asked him, 'How much do you want?'

'Now we are beginning to understand each other, my dear Captain. I'll get rid of Erhama for you without a problem and I'll keep your involvement a secret. But in return I want you to get rid of my uncle so that I may be named Prince of Shiraz.'

Chapter 30

Outside Qatif

S ADLEIR, BASHIR AND THEIR guides arrived at the Ottoman
base outside Qatif. Sadleir instructed Mirza and the other
two to wait outside while he and Bashir entered through the
main gate, past a dozing guard leaning on his rifle. Given the
stifling heat, the long working hours and the widespread corruption of their officers, the morale of the troops had hit an all-
time low.

Bribery was so prevalent that everyone on the base was aware
of the various tactics their officers employed, such as extorting
money from traders or sending their soldiers to seize merchandise on sham pretexts. The lower ranks were also very quick to
please their superiors.

Some of the soldiers considered apprehending the pair. But
Sadleir's presence gave them pause; they knew that their officers
were in contact with their British counterparts across the region.
The appearance of a foreigner at the base was proof of those
high-level communications with British officers and elicited
little more than mild curiosity.

Khalil Agha was eating at his desk when Sadleir and Bashir
were shown into his office. On seeing them, he stood up right
away with a piece of bread still in his mouth. As he could neither
swallow the food nor speak to them, he signalled to them to sit

down. He wiped his mouth with his cuff and proceeded to finish chewing the bread.

Sadleir introduced himself and extracted a letter from his breast pocket.

The Turkish officer took a handkerchief from his pocket, wiped his hand and reached over the desk for the sheet. He opened the letter and read:

> *To Whom It May Concern:*
> *From the undersigned, Sir Evan Nepean, Governor of His Britannic Majesty in Bombay.*
> *The bearer of this message is Major George Forster Sadleir, an officer in His Majesty's 47th Regiment. He is on an urgent mission to His Excellency Ibrahim Pasha and until such time as he completes this mission, he is to be treated as an ambassador of His Britannic Majesty. All who read this message are urged to help him and to remove any obstacles that may stand in his way.*

Khalil Agha finished reading the letter and returned it with a wry smile Sadleir could not quite understand. He extended his palm in a gesture to signify that Sadleir should now tell him what he wanted.

'I need to see His Excellency Ibrahim Pasha in the Hejaz,' he began. 'I wish to head from here to Al-Ahsa where I will meet the commander of the Turkish garrison so that he may arrange an armed escort to Ibrahim Pasha's camp. But the road from here to Al-Ahsa is hazardous, and I therefore kindly request that you provide me with protection.'

Khalil Agha scratched his chin. 'Who told you the road from here to Al-Ahsa is dangerous?' he said. 'It is quite safe and you can go at any time.'

'Sir,' Bashir interjected, 'you know better than anybody that the roads are unsafe in these parts.' The Turk would certainly be aware of the tribal conflicts, particularly between the supporters and opponents of Ibn Saud. 'All we want is a small group of soldiers to protect us until we arrive in Al-Ahsa.'

Khalil Agha looked sharply at Bashir and then turned back to Sadleir as he said, 'I don't have enough soldiers.'

Sadleir was tempted to mention all the bored and dozing soldiers he had just seen. Instead he said insistently, 'We need protection, sir. Any danger we may face will be your responsibility. I carry important information for Ibrahim Pasha, who would be most upset if it should become lost. And now, will you provide us with protection or not?'

The Turkish officer was visibly annoyed. He shook his head and, reaching for a rattan stick, he struck his palm impatiently as though he itched to use it on them. He made it known that the meeting was over and that they should leave.

Sadleir folded the paper, put it back inside his pocket and was about to rise to his feet when Bashir held on to his arm and whispered, 'He's just after some money. I saw him receive payment from the harbour master in Qatif. If you want him to do anything for you, you must pay him.'

'I don't see why I should,' Sadleir whispered back. He shot the Turk an angry look; Khalil Agha, by contrast, seemed amused by their hushed conversation. 'God damn him,' added Sadleir quietly. 'Just look at him. He didn't even care about the letter from the Governor of Bombay.'

It was Bashir's turn to be amused. 'And why should he care about your governor in Bombay? All these officers are interested in is accumulating as much money as possible before they go home. Pay him, Sadleir, unless you want to be at the mercy of angry Bedouin marauders.'

Sadleir cleared his throat and said to Khalil Agha, 'How much?'

The Ottoman officer put down his rattan stick.

After much negotiating by Bashir and many complaints from Sadleir, they finally agreed on a sum of fifty gold riyals.

Sadleir took out a purse and was about to count out the money. 'That will of course include horses for us.'

'No,' replied Khalil Agha. 'Only an armed escort of two riders. I don't have enough horses to lend you.'

'You can be sure I'll mention your name in my report, sir,' Sadleir said icily as he dropped the coins on the desk. He rose to his feet and added to Bashir, 'It's clear we won't get anything more out of this officer. Come, we've wasted enough time here.'

Once they had emerged from the base, they found Mirza in a heated argument with the other two men. They wanted to be paid and head back to the harbour because they feared that the road was dangerous and were not willing to risk their lives for nothing.

Mirza tried to convince them to stay, but they insisted on leaving. The discussion continued for a long time because the donkeys had also been hired. Sadleir and Bashir sat in the shade of a tree as they waited for Mirza to end the dispute and for the two Turkish cavalrymen who had been assigned to them to appear.

After a great deal of shouting and cursing, Mirza managed to buy the donkeys from them and paid their expenses from Qatif to the Ottoman base. By the afternoon, the Turkish officers emerged on their horses and the group resumed their journey towards Al-Ahsa, overwhelmed by the sense that the trip had not had an auspicious start.

They travelled in silence, the horsemen protecting the van and rear of the group, until they arrived at Sheikh Musharaf's camp at the edge of the desert.

Sheikh Musharaf was a local chieftain who tried not to get embroiled in the conflict between the Turks and the Wahhabis. He had benefited from a road tax imposed on travellers in return for his protection, which had kept his tribe free from hunger. But in the midst of all the clashes taking place between the different factions, Sheikh Musharaf could not remain isolated and he had many contacts with the Wahhabis as well as with the Turks and their allies.

His camp lay close to the only source of water available on the road from Qatif to Al-Ahsa. The site was made up of a number of tents that housed around two thousand people; in addition to his private army of three hundred fighters, he could count on the support of many Bedouins in the vicinity who swore allegiance to him.

Upon arriving at the camp, the group went to the sheikh's tent to obtain information about the road ahead and receive news of the skirmishes that were taking place in Diriyah and other places in Nejd between Ibrahim Pasha and the Wahhabis.

Sheikh Musharaf welcomed them warmly and offered them food and water. 'I hope you didn't encounter any trouble on the road,' he said, holding out a plate of dates.

'No, sir,' replied Bashir as he reached for a date. 'The road was fine and the only problem we had was with Khalil Agha, who refused to provide us with any horses.'

Sheikh Musharaf nudged the plate towards Sadleir. 'Horses

have become scarce in this area. They are in high demand in times of war.'

'What is the news on that front?'

'It's very bad, son,' he said grimly. 'Ibrahim Pasha has destroyed Diriyah and many people have left their farms and are now starving. Things have become much more difficult. Some people are forced to rob travellers out of hunger. You will find unpleasant scenes on your way. But where exactly are you going?'

Sadleir took the date stone delicately out of his mouth and answered vaguely, 'We're on our way to Al-Ahsa.'

Sheikh Musharaf seemed to suspect that they were going further. 'I would advise you to return to where you came from. But if you must go on, take as much water as you can carry as it is very hot in this area and this is the last spring before the desert. Wherever you go and whatever your purpose, I wish you a safe trip.'

The following morning they arrived in Al-Ahsa, an oasis with plenty of fresh water and groves of palm trees. The settlement was inhabited by a mixture of Bedouins and Shias who had been greatly affected by the latest events in the region. Some Bedouins subscribed to the Wahhabi ideology, even if they were less inclined to propagate it with the sword. The Shias, on the other hand, were particularly terrified by developments as they found themselves caught between two equally unappealing factions – they disliked the Wahhabis and distrusted the Turks.

Al-Ahsa had a relatively large garrison of Ottoman soldiers, totalling around a thousand horsemen, who maintained a fragile peace in the town as the surrounding districts burned. It was the main force that the Ottoman Porte depended on for controlling the eastern part of the Arabian Peninsula.

However, the garrison had been in the area for a long time and was frequently cut off from its command centre in distant Istanbul, which meant that salaries often arrived late. Without its commander, Mohammed Agha, at the helm, this force would have become an undisciplined and unruly unit. But Mohammed Agha played a major role in establishing security in the town, inspiring confidence in its inhabitants and working as a mediator between warring factions.

After arriving at Al-Ahsa, Sadleir's team proceeded as planned to the headquarters of the Turkish garrison to meet Mohammed Agha.

The Ottoman commander was a slightly overweight fifty-year-old man with a short white beard. He tried hard to preserve the military bearing of his youth. A pious Sufi, he was not corrupt – unlike other commanders on the periphery of the Ottoman Empire – and he concentrated all his energy on maintaining a disciplined and efficient garrison.

Sadleir presented his letter from the Governor of Bombay, the one he had shown to Khalil Agha outside Qatif. The Ottoman officer read the message and then folded it respectfully and returned it to Sadleir.

'Your timing is perfect,' he said. 'I've recently received instructions to vacate Al-Ahsa and proceed to an area near Diriyah to join Ibrahim Pasha's army. You may take this opportunity to join our caravan, which will leave within two days.'

Sadleir was delighted to hear the news as he had been worried about the reports of thieves everywhere and the threat of losing the Indian sword again. An armed Turkish caravan would provide him with the sense of security he needed.

Sadleir used the intervening period to rest and get supplies. Two days later, his party arrived at the Turkish camp outside town, at the edge of the vast expanse of desert. It was over-crowded with camels, horses, donkeys and men. There were about six hundred camels laden with crates, fully armoured horsemen, donkeys carrying water and food, a large number of accompanying Bedouins and some merchants taking advantage of the situation to sell their wares to the caravan.

Sadleir bought three camels for himself, Bashir and Mirza. He had to pay dearly for them as the Turkish garrison had bought most of the animals available on the market.

Mohammed Agha divided the caravan into groups, each consisting of fifty camels, such that each group would become a cohesive unit and be responsible for the elements within it in order to avoid losing lives or camels on the way. In case of an attack, the groups were instructed to move close together to create a stronger whole that would be capable of putting up a stiff defence.

The morale of the Turkish soldiers was high. Most were leaving a place where they had spent long years doing little but suffering from heat, flies and disease.

As was his custom in difficult situations, Mohammed Agha raised his eyes to the heavens and asked God for help. He gave the signal for departure and hoped they had enough water to last them the journey. The drought that had swept through the area, together with the outbreak of fighting, had almost dried up all the wells.

The verdant landscape of Al-Ahsa stood in sharp contrast to the desert beyond it. The caravan left Al-Ahsa behind and, after several hours of trudging through the barren desert landscape, they reached a salt plain where the animals' hooves sank in the fine powder. The layers of salt broke up under the feet of hundreds of animals and men, and were picked up by the wind to form eddies around the caravan.

The difficulty of walking through this sea of salt was compounded by the unbearable heat, which made breathing extremely difficult. The travellers were forced to cover their faces with scarves to protect them from the hot air and the salty dust that flew all around them.

'Where are you keeping the sword?' Bashir asked Sadleir.

'Don't worry. It's safe,' Sadleir answered, beckoning to Mirza, who had tied the donkeys together to keep them safe amid all the animals and men.

Chapter 31

Bushehr

WHEN BRUCE REALISED THE price for Sadek's cooperation, he looked around the coffee house to make sure nobody was listening. 'This is very serious,' he said, his voice little more than a whisper. 'We are on good terms with your uncle, the Prince of Shiraz. We've signed several agreements with him which allow us to trade freely.' Britain controlled Bushehr and collected the levies on merchantmen that docked at the harbour. If the Prince of Shiraz were to get wind of this, thought Bruce, trade in the region would suffer.

Sadek waved his hand as though chasing away a fly. 'Getting rid of the old man is the least of my concerns,' he said. 'The real issue, gentlemen, is how to maintain our cooperation after his overthrow.' He was worried that he might not be recognised by the Shah and, therefore, by the British as well. 'If you supported me and put pressure on the Shah to recognise me, the problem of getting rid of my uncle would be solved easily.'

Loch also surveyed the coffee house, his gaze resting on Sadek's guards all around their master. 'I'm not sure this is the best time to have this discussion. Why don't you give us a chance to think about your proposal?'

'Very well,' replied the Persian slowly. 'But remember, gentlemen, that I'm in a bit of a hurry and that favourable circumstances do not last for ever. I'll await your prompt response.'

He then gave them his usual disingenuous smile and, nodding to his escort, left with as much fanfare as he had arrived.

Abbas was about to leave when Loch called him back. 'Unless I'm much mistaken,' he told him, 'you haven't been dismissed by your employer, the governor.'

'But,' stammered Abbas helplessly, not daring to look at either Bruce or Matthews, 'I thought –'

'You're not paid to think,' Loch cut him off. 'You're paid to guard Government House. So why don't you run along and do your duty.'

Abbas nodded and ran off, relieved.

'He is not staying with us,' fumed Bruce. 'How long has that snake been a spy?'

'That's why you need to keep him, my dear chap,' countered Loch. 'Now that we know where his true allegiances lie, he may come in handy one day.'

'That dog,' said Bruce, unconvinced.

'Just keep him on a tight leash.'

The tension in the coffee house eased with Sadek's exit; customers began to filter back in and the sense of fear that had dominated the place while he was there evaporated as conversations picked up again around them.

Loch, Bruce and Matthews were quiet as each analysed the situation from his own perspective.

Matthews was the first to speak. 'I shouldn't be surprised if even his mother had no love for him. Sadek is impudent in every sense of the word.'

'It's a hefty price,' said Bruce thoughtfully, adding to Loch, 'What do you think? He'll eliminate that pirate for us once and for all – but are we ready to cooperate with him?'

Loch blew out some smoke and stared at the wispy formations it made. 'This meeting has taught me two things: first, never to leave my ship without men protecting my back.' He was thinking how they had been in a position of weakness with all of Sadek's guards swarming around them. 'Secondly, whenever I'm forced to deal with a scoundrel, I should always find a way to be rid of him as soon as he has served his purpose.'

The governor gave him a quizzical look. 'How so?'

'I sat with the corsair,' explained Loch. 'Erhama is a man I consider to be violent and heartless, and yet I was not as repulsed by that meeting with him as I am now. If we are to use Sadek to eliminate Erhama, we will have to get rid of him soon after. He would pose a threat to us if he ever became the Prince of Shiraz.'

'So what do you propose, Captain? You have two scoundrels and a single knife. Who will be first?'

Loch answered with questions of his own. 'How does one go about requesting a meeting with Erhama? When the Governor of Bombay asked you to propose the six-month truce with him how did you get him to come to you?'

It was Matthews who replied. 'I spread the word at the harbour that the governor wished to meet Erhama. News travels particularly quickly among sailors and the pirate graced us with his presence soon after.'

'Really?'

'Yes, Captain. Erhama knows how to get information while at sea and he has many agents in every port in the region. Those ships transport more than just cargo – they carry news and rumours.'

They left the café followed at a distance by Abbas, who did not dare draw any closer. Though he had been exposed as a spy for Sadek, Abbas still felt he needed the job, since it bestowed a kind of status on him at the harbour. And his closeness to Bruce afforded him protection and respect.

When they reached Bruce's home, Matthews signalled to Abbas to go on his way. They went inside and sat down at a table, while Bruce pulled out a bottle of vintage Shirazi wine.

After several glasses of wine, Loch knew what needed to be done. 'The priority is Erhama. If we leave him to fight his enemies, he will grow stronger and cause us problems in the future, especially if he wins major battles. We certainly cannot tolerate the return of Wahhabi rule in Bahrain. Their presence in Ras al-Khaimah and other ports is bad enough.' He enjoyed nothing more than devising strategies and clinked glasses with the other two as he added, 'So we'll use Sadek to remove Erhama and get out of my pact with him. That way we can concentrate on fighting the Wahhabis in Arabia without having our backs exposed or having to depend on a fragile agreement with a pirate like Erhama.'

He held out his glass for more wine. 'Matthews, you need to spread the word that the governor wishes to meet Erhama.' Then, turning to Bruce, he said, 'Meanwhile you inform Sadek that he has our support and that Erhama is coming to Bushehr. He has to devise a plan to eliminate him. Once he does, you must tell the Prince of Shiraz of his nephew's intention to usurp him. In this way, we'll get rid of both Erhama and Sadek.'

'Are you sure that's the best plan, Captain?' said Bruce. 'Why should the Prince believe his nephew is conspiring against him?'

'Subterfuge, dear chap – those at the top are always convinced that there are conspiracies about. You must remember that whoever spies *on* you can also be made to spy *for* you if you pay him enough. I'll leave Bushehr tomorrow. Let me know your news as soon as possible.'

'Tomorrow?' said Bruce with astonishment. 'Surely you're not suggesting that I execute this plan on my own, Loch?'

It was Loch's turn to look surprised. 'Why shouldn't you? Matthews here will help, won't you?'

'But my dear Captain,' Bruce said, trying to sound reasonable. 'I'm not used to such palace intrigues. If you intend to get rid of your enemies, please don't make it my responsibility.'

'His Majesty's enemies,' corrected Loch.

'Well, I'm just not sure I can manage a plot like this,' admitted the governor lamely.

Loch turned to the window so that he would not be seen, before rolling his eyes. In the distance, he could just make out the silhouette of the *Eden*, which seemed to call out to him like a siren.

After the wine and the events of the day, Loch was not in any condition to continue arguing or take decisions. He stood up sluggishly and asked Bruce to find him a bed because he was too tired to leave. Bruce pointed upstairs where the bedrooms were. Bruce and Matthews stayed at the table.

The next morning, Loch went down to find Bruce asleep in his chair with his head resting on the table, the sound of his snoring filling the house, an empty glass on the floor and flies buzzing around his open mouth. Matthews had dozed off in an armchair, his hands waving automatically to chase the flies.

Loch shouted at them to wake up. No sooner had Bruce opened his eyes than he called out to Abbas to bring him breakfast and tea. But he remembered that Abbas would not dare enter his house after the previous evening's discovery. Bruce went heavily to the kitchen to prepare breakfast for himself and his guests.

Over breakfast, Loch said, 'Let's talk about the plan we started yesterday, Bruce. I want your opinion so that we can get it over with because I may leave today.'

'I'm still of the same opinion, Captain. It would be hard for me to manage a plot like this. I'm no good at conspiracies and am surrounded by a bunch of untrustworthy spies. I'm about to retire. I just want a decent pension from a company that I've given more than thirty years of my life to. I'm not ready to make a mistake that the East India Company might hold me accountable for.'

Loch got up, and went to the door for a breath of fresh air. But he could not bear the heat that seemed to slap him in the face the moment he opened the door. He swiftly closed the door and returned to his chair, picking up the glass lying on the floor and putting it on the table. Bruce and Matthews followed Loch with their eyes.

Loch looked at the men and told Matthews, 'Bring me Erhama as soon as possible – use all the means of communication available to you. And then arrange another meeting for me with that odious Sadek.' He added to Bruce, 'I trust you won't mind if I direct things from your home, then.'

Chapter 32

Between Al-Ahsa and Diriyah

WHEN THE CARAVAN REACHED a well called Ma'a al-Meleha – Salty Water – Sadleir asked Bashir to look after the donkeys that were loaded with their baggage and Mirza to fill the water bottles.

A few hours later, Mirza came back with the bottles filled to the brim and tied them to their camels. Sadleir reached for his and took a swig. The water was brackish and tasted and smelled awful, but they had to make do with it as there was no other source for miles.

As it began to grow dark, Mohammed Agha ordered everybody to carry on. However, the Bedouins accompanying the caravan were angered by this, for they wished to light fires and enjoy their coffee as they always did when travelling.

Sadleir had noticed that the Bedouins seemed unconcerned about planning for the future, living instead from one moment to the next. If they had no money, they would ask others for some and if they had no coal to light their fires, they would take it from others. When they got hungry, they would sit and eat with other people. They never planned for their needs.

When darkness fell, the commander of each group lit a lamp and raised it on top of a pole tied to a camel, such that it was visible to all the members of the group. Seeing this array of lights swaying in the night with every step, Bashir said to Sadleir with amusement, 'That's why we call the camel the ship of the desert.'

Sadleir pulled on the reins of his mount and stopped for a moment to survey the landscape. 'What a wonderful sight,' he said with awe as he took in the long line of lights twinking like terrestrial constellations. 'Never imagined I would see anything like it in my life.'

The caravan had reached Khurais, halfway between Al-Ahsa and Diriyah, when the heavens opened and it began to pour. Though it was not the rainy season, the sudden torrential downpour was so heavy that Mohammed Agha ordered the whole caravan to stop. The camels were made to sit and the travellers began to cover their belongings and use any available clothes to protect themselves from the water.

So much rain fell that the valleys began to fill up and several members of the caravan, worried that they might be caught in the gushing streams, scrambled to find a foothold on adjacent mounds. In the resulting mayhem and poor visibility, some Bedouins managed to steal a number of camels and donkeys, along with whatever had been strapped to the animals' backs.

A few hours later, the rain stopped as suddenly as it had started. People emerged from beneath their covers like wraiths rising from their graves. Everything was soaking wet, including the camels, which had difficulty getting up because their loads had absorbed rainwater and were now much heavier. Their feet slipped or sank in the puddles, making it difficult for the caravan to move.

In the early morning, Mohammed Agha ordered part of his cavalry to pursue the Bedouins who had stolen the camels and donkeys in order to bring them back as soon as possible. The horsemen returned in the afternoon, with the stolen animals and the thieves tied with ropes. Once they reached the caravan, Mohammed Agha lined up the culprits and ordered them to be executed in public.

The executioner's sword fell on the thieves' necks in full view of the petrified spectators, and the bodies were carried without ceremony or respect to hastily-dug holes in the ground. A rumour spread around the caravan that the Turks were beheading Bedouins for no reason.

During the night, many of the Bedouins accompanying the caravan escaped, leaving even their personal belongings behind, out of fear they would be wrongly accused of stealing and summarily decapitated.

In the morning, a horseman arrived carrying a message from Ibrahim Pasha to Mohammed Agha, requesting him to camp in Khurais and to stay there until further notice because the road to Diriyah was too dangerous.

Bashir and Sadleir followed these events with keen interest. They realised that the loss of the Bedouins was not a good sign since they served essentially as guides, interpreters and scouts. Their absence would make the journey more hazardous.

Not all the Bedouins had run away, but those who remained felt weak and vulnerable. Some of them sought the protection of Turkish officers while others patiently bided their time before making an escape bid.

As Bashir and Sadleir sat drinking tea near their animals and talking about the reasons behind Mohammed Agha's decision to wait, a young Bedouin man approached them and asked if he could sit and share their refreshments.

Sadleir was taken aback by such forwardness but Bashir smiled kindly at the man and asked him his name.

'It's Met'ab, but don't ask me about my tribe. These days you can be killed just because someone has a vendetta against your tribe that you know nothing about.'

'Have you ever killed anyone?'

The Bedouin smiled wryly. 'Do I look like a killer? I once killed a lizard and a hedgehog that I found on the way and ate them because I was hungry.'

'But why did you join the caravan?'

'It's my bad luck and my mother's prayers to God to punish me,' he answered earnestly. 'I was a bad child who made her life a living hell, so she prayed to God that I should be punished. Every time a tragedy occurs, I remember her and pray to God for her, so that He may forgive me.'

Bashir repeated his question.

'I was starving. When I saw the caravan with so many people, I thought they would surely have something to eat. I thought that if I joined I wouldn't die of starvation. How I wish I hadn't come along!'

Sadleir was amused by the young man's honesty. 'Well, at least you haven't died of starvation yet,' he said cheerfully.

The young man shook his head. 'If you opened my stomach you wouldn't find anything there except the remains of that lizard. As for the hedgehog, it spent about two tortuous days in my stomach before it found its final resting place in a hole in the ground not too far from here. If you'd like I could show you the place.'

Sadleir raised a hand. 'I'd rather not, thank you.'

The Bedouin brought an atmosphere of jollity to their little group and they invited him to stay. He did everything they asked, collecting firewood, unloading the animals and tethering them, and preparing tea and coffee. More to the point, though, he was amusing and entertained them in the long hours as they waited.

The caravan stayed put for several days and Sadleir grew increasingly impatient. Although Bashir was in favour of waiting for the caravan to be given the order to carry on, Sadleir decided he had hung around long enough. He felt he was running out of time and did not want Ibrahim Pasha to leave for the Hejaz before he could meet him and put forward his proposition.

By dawn of the following day, their small group prepared to leave the caravan, packing up their belongings and filling their water bottles. Sadleir and Bashir rode their camels, followed by Mirza, who had tied the two donkeys behind his camel. Last was Met'ab, who preferred to be at the rear, explaining that those at the front often met their deaths first.

The group moved west towards Diriyah. But the area was teeming with thieves and assassins after Ibrahim Pasha had destroyed the farms and irrigation systems. To guarantee their safety until Diriyah, they would have to seek the protection of the tribes that had settled there.

It was fortunate that Met'ab could talk to the Bedouins they encountered on the way. When he asked for the name of the chieftain who could best provide them with protection, everybody agreed that Sheikh Arar was the one they should appeal to. His camp was not very far northwest of Khurais.

When the group arrived at the camp, Sheikh Arar welcomed them by offering them dates and milk and asking them where they were heading. On learning they were going to Diriyah, he lowered his head dejectedly and told them that the settlement had been completely destroyed by Ibrahim Pasha before his withdrawal in the direction of the Hejaz. He advised them to return to the Turkish caravan and remain with it until the situation became safer.

But Sadleir insisted on moving on to meet Ibrahim Pasha, so Sheikh Arar agreed to send his nephew, Jarbou, to be their guide and protector as long as they treated him as generously as possible. Sadleir agreed to this without specifying the sum that he would pay him.

Sheikh Arar summoned his nephew, a thin man with shifty eyes, a broad moustache that grew over his mouth and plaited hair that came down to his shoulders in the manner of the Bedouins. Sadleir took an instant dislike to him.

Jarbou shook hands with Sadleir and Bashir and sat down beside his uncle, listening to his prospective role on the journey. He nodded from time to time as a sign of understanding and acceptance. But when he turned to Sadleir during the conversation, the major could not help feeling that he was hiring a thug.

'When will you leave?' Jarbou asked his uncle's guests.

'At dawn,' answered Sadleir. 'You need to be ready by then.'

In the morning, they said goodbye to Sheikh Arar and set off on their animals. After a few steps, Jarbou came alongside Sadleir on his camel and asked him, 'How much will you pay me, Englishman? And how much will you pay for my camel?'

Sadleir tried to mask his irritation. 'Fifty riyals to Diriyah. As for your camel, I'm not responsible for it.'

Sadleir spurred his camel forward.

Bashir and Met'ab were also uncomfortable around Jarbou and tried to avoid talking to him. When he felt that he was alone, Jarbou began to raise his croaky voice and chanted to drive the camels, thus provoking the rest of the group to move even further away from him.

Two days after they had left Sheikh Arar's camp, Jarbou asked Sadleir for one hundred riyals or he would return home. They were, he said, his expenses for the journey and the camel.

Because Sadleir could not bear to be blackmailed, he called Bashir and Met'ab to ask them about the best way to deal with him.

Bashir suggested that they let the man go because he was no better than the bandits they might encounter along the way. Met'ab, on the other hand, advised Sadleir to pay him since anything could happen in the desert and they could vanish without a trace: if Jarbou left and collaborated with others, they would kill, rob and bury them in the desert.

After some discussion, Sadleir decided to pay Jarbou his money. He would be kept as a guide until they reached Diriyah where a complaint against him would be presented to Ibrahim Pasha, who would hopefully punish him.

The group continued on its way until it reached the camp of Sheikh Fallah, a distant cousin of Sheikh Arar and also distantly related by marriage to Jarbou.

Jarbou stepped forward proudly to greet Sheikh Fallah, who stood up and shook hands with each one of them. The sheikh then asked them to sit down and ordered coffee and dates to be brought to them.

The elders of the tribe sat listening to the conversation. Jarbou monopolised the talk and presented himself as the protector and leader of the group, telling them that he had been chosen because his name alone inspired fear in the hearts of bandits.

Bashir and Met'ab noticed that some of those present were poking fun at Jarbou, which made it clear that they knew only too well his propensity for boasting. After everybody had finished their coffee, Sheikh Fallah invited them to get some rest and then return for supper in the evening, insisting that they should stay even after Sadleir tried to turn down the invitation.

The members of the group filled their water bottles, and unloaded and fed their animals. Met'ab grabbed hold of Sadleir's hand and pulled him urgently to one side so that no one could overhear their conversation.

'Listen,' he said, 'this is your chance to shut Jarbou up and stop him from blackmailing you. Otherwise he might ask for more money as soon as we are on our own in the desert. It's not far to Diriyah and we can manage without him. So let's get even with him now.'

'But how?'

'Sheikh Fallah is clearly an honourable man,' said Met'ab, 'otherwise he would not have insisted that we should stay for dinner. Explain to him how you were blackmailed and ask him to be a fair judge in the matter.'

Sadleir followed Met'ab's instructions carefully and later, once the dishes were laid out, he addressed the chieftain and said, 'Before we can accept your fine food, Sheikh Fallah, I wish to complain to you about Jarbou.'

'May God forgive us all,' the sheikh exclaimed. 'What is it?'

Sadleir described his relative's behaviour during the trip and when he reached the point about the hundred riyals, all the guests shook their heads in disapproval.

Sheikh Fallah lowered his head and said nothing for a while. Then, speaking in a clear voice, he asked everyone to start eating in the name of God and promised that he would resolve the matter.

Everyone ate in silence, contrary to the custom at such gatherings.

Later, Sadleir and his companions were getting ready to retire for the night when Sheikh Fallah appeared together with Jarbou and some of the elders of the tribe.

Jarbou fell to his knees and begged Sadleir to forgive him for his misconduct. He promised to return all the money he had been given.

The sheikh and his entourage waited with stony expressions until Sadleir declared that he forgave Jarbou and that the money he had been given was his due. At that point, one of them patted Jarbou on the shoulder and took him away.

'My relative has shamed us,' Sheikh Fallah said. 'I'll punish him myself for his misbehaviour. I'll send two of my men to accompany you to Manfuhah – for I have heard that Diriyah has been destroyed.'

Sadleir tried to turn down the offer, particularly since Manfuhah was quite near by. But again the sheikh insisted. It was a matter of honour.

Chapter 33

Bushehr

TIME DRAGGED FOR LOCH in Bushehr. The town was boring and nothing moved in it except the flies that pestered people as they ate, slept or talked. Ten days had passed since Matthews had spread the word that the governor wished to meet Erhama on an important matter, and it might take the pirate anywhere up to three weeks to respond and sail to Bushehr.

Loch looked at Bruce and suggested, 'Let's go hunting with your friend Sadek. The climate in the mountains surrounding this miserable town will be a refreshing change.' He added, 'Maybe we'll find out what that bastard is planning.'

'Good idea,' agreed Bruce and, summoning Matthews, he ordered him to prepare the horses for a hunting trip and to organise servants to accompany them. Almost as an after-thought, he added, 'And send an invitation to Sadek to join us.'

'And make sure Abbas comes with us,' insisted Loch.

The next morning the horses and hounds were ready and the mules were loaded with food, water and rifles. Loch asked, 'Where shall we meet Sadek?'

'At a spring half a day from here,' replied Bruce. 'It's a particularly pleasant spot that I know he likes. He always spends time there enjoying the weather and the natural beauty of the place – his guard may be down.'

They rode off on horseback, leaving Matthews behind to manage the affairs of Government House. They made a great deal of noise as they left the quiet town and, heading east on a dusty road, they began the tiring ascent to the top of a mountain.

The weather was bearable in the early morning, but the heat of the sun soon became intolerable, especially as they climbed the mountain. Along the path, dusty at first, small bushes grew; by noon, trees began to appear, adding a touch of beauty to the scenery and providing some protection from the sun. Loch turned back to look at the sea, the harbour and the moored ships in the distance. He remembered that he had an appointment with Erhama bin Jaber. If his plan succeeded, it would set his mind at ease.

When the group reached a dense cluster of trees, Loch heard the sound of cascading water. Sadek emerged from the trees with his wan smile and opened his arms to them 'Gentlemen, the place and the food are waiting for you. I look after my friends in the same way I take care of my enemies.'

Loch tried to ignore the irritating snigger and the way Sadek laughed at things that were not remotely funny. He managed to return the smile, however, as he thought that Sadek's days were numbered.

After dismounting, Sadek led them to a courtyard where the branches of the trees intertwined to form a canopy. The ground had been covered with expensive carpets and there was a welcoming cool breeze. Cushions had been scattered everywhere for guests to lean against, while hookahs vied for space at the edges of the carpets. Plates full of desserts had been placed in the middle. Nearby was a stream of water filled with all kinds of fruit that had been put there to cool down.

Loch could not believe his eyes. He felt he had suddenly been transported from the hellish environment of the town below to something akin to paradise. Resting against the nearest cushion, he stretched out his legs and reached over for a hookah. He inhaled the smoke and then quietly exhaled from his nose, enjoying the taste of the tobacco to the full.

'Why do you go anywhere else,' he asked Sadek, 'when you have your own patch of heaven here?'

Sadek accepted the compliment and offered them a plate of desserts.

Loch could not resist sampling the subtly different sweets and accepted a glass of clear water from the nearby spring. After the heat of the road, he drank the water leisurely, smacking his lips after each sip.

Once his guests were refreshed, Sadek came straight to the point. 'Are we still in agreement, gentlemen?'

Bruce answered immediately, 'Of course. Why else would we be here in this little paradise of yours?'

Sadek knew that his plot to overthrow his uncle and become the new Prince of Shiraz would never succeed without the support of both Bruce and Loch. Sadek had always considered the governor as little more than a pen-pusher – a rather ineffectual employee of the East India Company with close ties to the Shah. But with Loch's participation, the financial and military sides would work together to convince the Shah to acknowledge his legitimacy.

Loch agreed with Bruce. 'Yes,' he said. 'I believe you will soon achieve your ambition.'

Sadek smiled. 'Let's talk about the details. You tell me what you wish me to do and I'll do likewise.'

Loch asked Abbas to bring him more water and then spoke. 'We've arranged for Erhama bin Jaber to come to Bushehr and we expect his ship to dock soon at the harbour. You will have to be discreet as he has a lot of loyal friends in the area as well as enemies. You should be particularly mindful of the Qawasimis and their agents who are in all the ports of the Gulf. And as we stated before, if the operation fails for any reason, we will deny any knowledge of it. So don't bet on our protection if Erhama survives.'

'Leave that to me,' said Sadek, cracking his fingers as though preparing for a wrestling match. 'As for my demands, I want you to apply pressure on the Shah to recognise me as the Prince of Shiraz after I get rid of my uncle. The Shah will never refuse a request by both a British governor and a commander of the navy. And besides,' he said a bit petulantly, 'who is he to refuse in the first place?'

'So we will put forward your name to the Shah, and you will do the rest, right?' verified Loch, as he asked Abbas to fix his hookah.

'That's right, Captain. As I told you, just leave things to me. Once you see Erhama's ships on the horizon, simply send word to me.'

Sadek called to his servants to bring the grilled meat and vintage wine.

It was time to celebrate.

They all returned from their camp in the mountains the following day. Matthews began to spend more time at the wharves, his telescope scanning the horizon. This made sailors and dock workers suspect that something significant was about to happen, though they were not exactly sure what that might be. At the coffee house, rumours circulated that the British were expecting the arrival of Erhama on an important matter, but explanations varied according to the speakers and circumstances.

Loch felt that he was wasting time waiting for the pirate, and his crew was beginning to grow restless; fights broke out and unruliness prevailed. In fact, his lieutenants were finding it difficult to impose their authority on the *Eden* while she was moored at Bushehr.

Loch decided to sail as soon as possible. He was having his last evening meal with Bruce and Matthews when suddenly, out of the blue, Erhama appeared with his raised sword and his dagger and pistols at his belt. Behind him and ready to react to the slightest provocation were Dirar and two Baluchi fighters similarly armed.

Everybody was stunned to see him. Abbas dropped the bottle of wine he had been carrying and froze in his place. All eyes were fixed on Erhama as though he were a phantom that had materialised from the depths of hell.

One of the Baluchis closed the door and stood guard outside.

Erhama smiled at them drily. 'Why do you look so stunned?' he asked them. 'Have I changed that much? I never imagined I was that horrible to look at.' He indicated their plates and added genially, 'Please don't let me stop you from finishing your meal.'

'What are you planning, gentlemen?' Erhama asked presently. 'The *Eden* has been moored here for several days.' He was not foolish enough to risk confronting her with all her cannon on board; that was why he had dropped anchor at night away from the harbour. 'So what are you plotting, eh?'

Loch allowed Bruce to speak as he knew that his relationship with the pirate went back many years.

'It's true, we do need to talk to you about something quite important,' stammered Bruce.

Loch saw one of the pirate's henchmen slap Abbas on the cheek and tell him to bring some tea and tobacco for his master.

'Hurry back from the kitchen if you don't wish to be hit again,' warned Dirar.

Loch immediately thought of using that as a way to send a message to Sadek. 'That's right,' he said to Abbas. 'Go now to the coffee house and ask Sadek for some good tobacco for our important guest.'

Abbas understood the coded message and tried to go out of the door but the guard standing there would not budge.

Loch turned to Erhama and said, 'Bruce has the most awful tobacco – let this man bring us something decent to smoke.'

'There's no need for that,' replied Erhama. 'I've come in secret and will go the same way. I don't want anybody to know I'm here. And now let's discuss the reason why you wanted to meet me.'

Bruce looked nervously at Loch. What were they supposed to say now? Erhama had them cornered.

Chapter 34

Manfuhah, Central Arabia

WHEN SADLEIR AND HIS companions arrived in Manfuhah, they saw horrendous scenes. After Ibrahim Pasha had razed Diriyah to the ground, all its inhabitants had fled to Manfuhah where they settled in its farms and wastelands and ate anything they could lay their hands on to keep body and soul together. People slept where they had collapsed from fatigue and hunger, the story of their wretchedness and tribulations written on their faces. The streets and alleys were filled with desperate women and children, some of whom followed the newcomers, pointing to their mouths.

The terrible sights spoke of a heinous crime that had been committed against these people. Sadleir did not wish to stay in Manfuhah and headed instead to Diriyah without even taking the time to rest; indeed, even the loneliness and perils of the desert were more welcome than these scenes of abject misery.

When they came within sight of Diriyah, they saw many parallel lines drawn in the sand.

'These must be the traces of the artillery wagons of Ibrahim Pasha's army,' said Sadleir.

Met'ab examined the marks on the sand carefully. 'Is it possible they used camels to transport their guns?' he asked. 'It's clear that these wheels were pulled by camels.'

Sadleir made a note of that. The British army had never thought of using camels to pull artillery wagons. Yet it made perfect sense in sandy terrain and deserts.

Diriyah was a ghost town.

It was completely devastated: its outlying farms were burnt-out shells, its wells were filled with dust, and the buildings in the centre had been razed to the ground. Doors were missing or hanging off their hinges, and they could see from the empty interiors that all the houses had been looted. There was no sign of life left in the town: Ibrahim Pasha's army had taken away all the livestock, and the men of the town had been killed or captured while the women and children had fled to Manfuhah.

The little group walked in eerie silence to the centre of Diriyah, examining everything they saw and trying to imagine the last moments for the residents of the town. In fact, the only sign of life was stray dogs feeding on decomposing flesh.

Bashir, who could not bear to see such atrocities, wept bitterly. The others, too, felt sick to their stomachs. Sadleir took the small water bottle from his camel, drank a little, wet his hands and wiped his face. He reached over and spat angrily on the ground.

No one complained of exhaustion or about how long they had already walked that day. All they wanted was to leave this place of horror behind as soon as possible and so they kept moving, heading northwest in the direction of Unaizah.

Unaizah was considered a strategic point on the caravan trade routes leading to Al-Zubair, the Levant, Al-Ahsa and Qatif. It was in fact regarded as the very heart of the Arabian Peninsula and an important centre for trade and politics.

Unaizah had so far managed to survive despite the ravages

wrought by Ibrahim Pasha's army. While a number of its buildings had been destroyed and some of its inhabitants had been killed, its farms and wells remained largely intact. Before Ibrahim Pasha's hasty departure, he had asked his deputy to get rid of those town leaders he did not trust. The deputy had stayed behind along with some of the army, with instructions to follow the vanguard a few days later.

During his time in Unaizah, the deputy had invited four of the town's leaders for dinner. While they sat as his guests, he had ordered his soldiers to cut off their heads and display them in the town square. He had then left Unaizah along with the remaining part of the army to catch up with Ibrahim Pasha.

On entering the town, Sadleir and his companions saw the decomposing heads in the square; nobody had yet dared take them down.

They managed to get new provisions from Unaizah and to rest a little from the exhaustion of travelling, while trying hard to wipe out the memory of the scenes of devastation of the past few days.

Sadleir began to think seriously about abandoning his mission. He felt that Ibrahim Pasha had been so brutal that it would be almost impossible for the Sultan of Oman and other Arab allies to join in a pact with the pasha.

But he soon reminded himself of all that he had been through to deliver the Indian sword. He remembered all the reports he had written and those he had received from the Governor of Bombay and, ultimately, he called to mind the strong sense of duty to king and country that he had as an officer in the British army. Even if the probability of success was nil, he had no choice but to see his mission through to the end.

Sadleir learned that Ibrahim Pasha's army had camped in a small village near Al-Rass. So he decided to go there and deliver the gift and come to an agreement with him. He wanted to set off at dawn the next day before he changed his mind.

On arriving at the pasha's camp, Sadleir and his companions were stopped by the soldiers manning the gate. The guards were fair-skinned Albanians who spoke Arabic with a heavy accent. They were so stocky they seemed capable of lifting anyone and snapping them in two. In fact, the Albanian contingent represented the core of Ibrahim Pasha's army because they came from the same region of the Ottoman Empire as the Khedive of Egypt, Mohammed Ali Pasha – Ibrahim's father.

Bashir looked at the Albanian soldier talking to Sadleir and was amused to see his thick moustache which became thinner at the ends and then coiled upwards like horns. It was an unfamiliar look to the people of Arabia.

Having learned that Sadleir was an acting British ambassador to Ibrahim Pasha, the soldier went to summon his officer.

The officer who came to meet Sadleir was also a burly man with a round face and a moustache similar to the guard's. But his fez was smaller than that of the lower ranks and he had a pistol and a curved sword in his leather belt. He wore very large breeches and Bashir had difficulty recognising this bizarre outfit as a military uniform.

After listening to Sadleir, the officer went into a tent not far from the entrance. This tent was different in size and colour from the others in the camp and, given the guards outside it, Sadleir assumed it belonged to a high-ranking official.

Presently, the officer emerged in the company of a man dressed in civilian clothes who approached Sadleir and introduced himself. 'I'm Rashwan Agha, Ibrahim Pasha's deputy,' he said. 'I welcome you to our camp.'

Rashwan Agha spoke quickly with an Egyptian accent that was distinct from the slow Nejdi accent Sadleir had become familiar with, and he struggled to follow what the man was saying. 'I'm here to meet Ibrahim Pasha on an urgent matter, sir,' said the major. 'May I see him now?'

Rashwan Agha shook his head. 'We're about to advance for a battle at Al-Rass, so you won't be able to meet him today. But you and your companions will be our guests until the pasha is free to see you.'

He turned and signalled to Sadleir to follow him into the tent.

Chapter 35

Bushehr

ERHAMA WAS WAITING FOR an answer to his question; Loch and Bruce wanted to dispatch a messenger to Sadek to tell him the pirate was in town. No one said anything or moved a muscle, as if time had come to a standstill.

Erhama eventually broke the silence. 'Captain, have we not already agreed that you would leave me to deal with my enemies in return for the Indian sword? Now you've asked to see me and you won't tell me why. Do you think I came all this way just to look at your pretty English faces?' He spat on the floor. 'Now tell me what exactly you want of me.'

'Two British subjects,' said Loch, thinking quickly.

'What?'

'An Englishwoman and her young daughter were abducted on their way to Basra,' he explained. 'We have reason to believe you were the kidnapper.'

'What?' repeated Erhama incredulously.

'That would be in clear violation of our agreement.'

Erhama roared, 'I thought you had some sense in that big, empty head of yours. I am not the kind of man who breaks agreements. Besides, I don't kidnap women or children. I may attack and burn your allies' ships, but I would never harm a woman.' Merely the idea that people might think that of him made him furious.

218

'But how can we trust what you say?' interjected Bruce. 'You're a pirate who makes a living out of robbing ships. Or one of your captains might have done it without your knowledge.'

Erhama was livid. '*We* do not break agreements and *we* do not attack women – unlike you rotten, drunken foreigners!'

Loch was infuriated by Erhama's rudeness. 'Hold your impudent tongue,' he shouted back. 'Let me remind you that you are addressing a representative of His Majesty's Government and a commanding officer of the Royal Navy.'

The words were barely out of his mouth when Dirar struck a small table with his sword, breaking it in two; he was itching to use his blade on them.

This caused Erhama to smile appreciatively at Dirar. 'Perhaps you should cut off their heads. We're tired of their presence in the Gulf – that way they could all go to hell.'

Loch considered it wiser to keep quiet.

'So tell me, Captain, did you call me all this way to ask me this silly question? My time is too precious to spend it with you. But before I go, you need to know that Erhama keeps his word at any price. The information you have about abducted British subjects is totally wrong.'

Then, turning smartly on his heel, he said to Dirar, 'Let's go. I'm tired of talking to these people.'

Dirar followed his master and, as he reached the door, he warned, 'One of our men will stand outside the door and will kill anyone who tries to leave. You're all guests in this house until the morning.'

Bruce immediately took a handkerchief from his pocket to wipe his brow. 'That was a close shave, eh?' he said. 'I always had my doubts about that story of the kidnapping.'

'It looks like Erhama must be innocent, then,' offered Matthews.

'I'll never trust that wily snake, Gulap, again,' Loch said soberly. 'But I'm afraid, gentlemen, that the problem has now become more intricate. We have an angry pirate and we don't know what he's planning to do now that he suspects we might violate our agreement with him.' He scratched his chin pensively. 'And then we have Sadek.'

'Yes,' agreed Bruce. 'What shall we do? Sadek is bent on killing Erhama and Erhama has already left. And if he can't kill the pirate, we won't be able to help him overthrow his uncle. Sadek is likely to become quite an irritation for us. What rotten bad luck.'

'Bad luck indeed,' exclaimed Loch. 'I wonder what kind of ill fortune brought me to this port. I'll enjoy killing Gulap when I return to Muscat.'

'So what shall we do, Captain?' repeated Bruce.

'I believe Sadek represents a greater threat than Erhama.' After all, the pirate was an old man who had never attacked a ship flying the Union Jack; he had attacked Sadleir's ship precisely because it had not been flying the flag. 'Sadek could threaten our presence in Bushehr and our control over trade with the interior of Persia, and even with a port as important as Basra.'

'Are you suggesting that we get rid of Sadek?'

'Of course.'

They emerged from the room the next day and, while he prepared for another trip, Loch sent Matthews to the *Eden* to collect five strong marines. Abbas was also ordered to travel with the group. Bruce would remain in Bushehr. At midday, the group gathered outside Government House and made ready to ride to Shiraz to meet the Prince.

The following evening, they arrived outside Shiraz just as the city gates were about to close for the night. They stopped in front of a gate that was guarded by a large number of soldiers. Loch asked to be admitted for an audience with the Prince of Shiraz on an important matter; and his request was relayed to the palace while they waited outside the city walls.

They were told they would have to wait a long time and, while Loch was not pleased at having to hang around outside the city, he took the opportunity for a wash and a change of clothes, and ordered his men to rest until they received further instructions.

The next morning, the gate opened to let two men out – a Westerner and a Persian – both dressed formally in smart suits. They approached Loch's small camp and introduced themselves. The first was Agh Bahman, the Prince's master of ceremonies, a short, stocky man with several rings on the fingers of both hands, a sign of his status in Persian society. The other was a British merchant called Frank Hopkins, who had become close to the Prince and was responsible for the education of his children. The two men shook hands warmly with Loch and asked him to accompany them to the palace where the Prince was waiting for him.

Loch asked if his companions might enter the city and stay at one of its lodging houses as the journey on horseback had been long and exhausting. Agh Bahman immediately ordered the guards at the gate to admit them, and while Matthews and Abbas accompanied Loch, the rest of the group was led to a lodging house.

The Prince of Shiraz was weak. Like his nephew, Sadek, he belonged to the ruling Qajar family. During the war against the

Russians from 1804 until 1813, he had been the commander of a Persian regiment and had demonstrated his inefficiency both as a figure of authority and as a military man. The Shah had tried to send him to a remote area of the Persian Empire, but the womenfolk in his palace had interceded on his behalf and had saved him from such an ignominious posting. He had subsequently been appointed as the Shah's deputy in Shiraz and the surrounding area.

It was a time of cautious anticipation. The Persian Empire was too weak to stand up to Russia's military superiority and had been courting Western powers. There had been a rapid influx of European merchants and officers, many of whom were appointed at the Shah's court or the provincial courts of his governors as advisers and tutors to teach their children Western languages and horsemanship, among other skills. This was aimed indirectly at strengthening Western–Persian ties against the Russian southern advance.

Loch entered the main royal hall followed by Agh Bahman, Hopkins, Matthews and Abbas, who tried to hide behind the person in front of him. Abbas was intimidated; even though he worked for Sadek, he now felt he was in the presence of true royalty. One of the guards grew suspicious of his furtive behaviour and caught him by his shirt, pushing him to the rear to keep him out of sight of the Prince. Abbas stood anxiously behind a wall, still not quite believing that he had ended up in the palace.

The Prince welcomed Loch with exaggerated cordiality since he knew that any conversation between them would eventually reach the Shah. He felt certain that his hand at the royal court would be strengthened if he managed to forge a robust relationship with an eminent officer of the British navy. So he rose from his throne, extended his arms towards the captain and embraced him with a warmth that Loch did not particularly care for.

They all took their seats around the Prince, who clapped his hands for desserts to be brought to his 'dear guests'. They exchanged pleasantries and the Prince used the opportunity to play up his involvement in the Russo-Persian war in which, according to his heroic account, he had defeated the Russian hordes and obliterated their cavalry. Then they talked about Shirazi wine and about the pirates in the Gulf and how Persia needed to build a strong fleet to protect her trade in the region.

After these preliminary discussions, Loch requested a private audience with the Prince.

'Please feel that you can talk freely,' encouraged the Prince. 'Everyone here has my absolute trust – I surround myself only with men I have faith in. Should any of them dare betray my trust, I would break their necks.'

'Very well, Your Highness,' Loch said. 'This relates to your nephew, Sadek. How is your relationship with him, sir? Do you trust him?'

The Prince was surprised by the question and his smile froze on his face as though he were still waiting to be asked something.

'My nephew?' he said at length. 'Yes. Sadek is a very ambitious man. Why do you ask?'

Loch was about to respond when the Prince continued, 'His father passed away when he was very young and he was raised by several palace women. He was spoiled by his mother, who would not let him out of her sight. So he was brought up in an environment of female conspiracies and spite. As you must know, I've appointed him my deputy in Bushehr.' He added with concern, 'I trust he hasn't done anything shameful.'

Loch cleared his throat. 'I saw him two days ago and I can inform Your Highness that he's planning –' he paused, 'to kill you, sir.'

He stopped to gauge the impact of his statement.

The Prince remained perfectly still, again as though he were waiting for Loch to complete his sentence. Then he stood up and walked among the guests in silence, his hands behind his back, until he reached the end of the hall. He stood in front of a window looking out onto a garden.

'Are you sure of this?' he asked finally. He had long had his suspicions about his nephew.

'I'm afraid so.' Loch had a card up his sleeve: a spy who worked for Sadek and whom he had encouraged Bruce to retain on his staff. 'If you would allow me, Your Highness, I would like to call one of his men.'

The Prince's silence was a sign of acceptance, so Loch raised his voice to call Abbas. When there was no answer, Matthews got up and hurried towards the door where he found Abbas on the floor, his head buried in his turban. Matthews took hold of him and brought him to the Prince.

Abbas trembled as he drew nearer and then went down on his knees with his eyes turned towards the captain. He could not bear to look at true royalty.

Loch asked him, 'What did you hear, Abbas, during our meeting with Sadek at his mountain camp? Tell His Highness everything you heard and omit nothing.'

'Why are you doing this?' Abbas sobbed miserably. He raised his hands to the sky as though asking heaven to save

224

him from this misfortune. 'I'm a poor man and all I want is to continue to provide for my family.' Answering the question would mean certain torture and death. 'Please, sir,' he wept, 'I cannot.'

Chapter 36

Diriyah, Central Arabia

IBRAHIM PASHA'S DEPUTY, RASHWAN Agha, and Sadleir emerged from the tent when they heard a bugle call, swiftly followed by the sound of excited commotion. They stood and watched the army as it moved out of the camp. The military force was made up of Moroccan, Turkish and Albanian horsemen; infantry; artillery driven by camels; mules loaded with guns, ammunition and food; and camels carrying Arab fighters.

The movement caused a huge dust cloud, forcing the onlookers to cover their mouths and noses.

'May I ask the size of this army?' Sadleir had to shout above the din.

'We have around three thousand Albanian, Turkish and Berber horsemen,' Rashwan Agha shouted back, 'and an equal number of infantry. We also have around five thousand Arab fighters on camels.' He then signalled to an officer to provide the guests with horses so that they might accompany the army to Al-Rass.

They all mounted the horses provided by Rashwan Agha and followed the army, trying to avoid the dust storm it created as it snaked its way across the desert.

The colossal army reached the village of Al-Rass where around five hundred Wahhabi fighters had made a stand.

Ibrahim Pasha ordered his army not to pitch camp or even dismount from their horses and camels until the village was occupied and everybody within it had been killed.

Artillery guns were brought forward and directed at Al-Rass. The artillery commander ordered his regiment to fire the guns and a volley of shells struck the defensive walls. They could see thick palls of smoke rising and hear distant screams, but still the walls stood; the besieged repaired them constantly between volleys and poured water on them to make them more shock-absorbent. The bombardment continued for several hours.

Believing that resistance had ebbed after so much shelling, Ibrahim Pasha ordered his infantry to advance. For a while, the infantry division marched in neat lines, but as they drew closer to the village they began to run, roaring with battle fury.

The besieged fired a volley of shots and a huge number of Ottoman soldiers fell as the bullets found their targets. It was clear to Sadleir that the Wahhabi fighters were sharpshooters.

The second and third lines of foot soldiers were given orders to march. But they did not fare any better and many fell near the wall. The battlefield became littered with dead and injured soldiers. At sunset, the call to prayer that could be heard from the village seemed to echo the same call coming from Ibrahim Pasha's camp.

Sadleir stood by his horse close to Rashwan Agha. Near him was Bashir, who was appalled by the sheer number of dead. He had never seen so many corpses. As he heard the call to prayer from both sides he uttered with disbelief, 'They pray to the same God and towards the same Kaaba, and yet they butcher each other.'

Bashir meditated on this, wondering about the meaning of piety and worship. He thought of the killings and blood shed.

If human beings truly believed they would stand before God one day and be asked about their deeds in life, why all the fighting and killing? Was life not fairly short, a trial period before the final reward? If people were here only for a short time, why destroy each other?

The two camps retired for the night and the sounds died down except for the wounded, who moaned all night long.

At break of dawn, the call to prayer again sounded from both sides and attacker and besieged alike implored the same God to give them victory over their enemies.

The two sides prepared themselves for combat. Ibrahim Pasha ordered the horsemen to get ready. The first riders attacked the wall but were shot down. Successive waves of cavalry charges made inroads and managed to cross the barrier only to disappear a few feet into the compound: the besieged had dug a deep trench just beyond the wall, and camouflaged it with palm leaves and tree branches.

The heavy death toll as well as the trench stratagem undermined the morale of Ibrahim Pasha's army. They were particularly demoralised by the thought that the enemy facing them numbered no more than five hundred men with old muskets.

Ibrahim Pasha could not bear to be defeated, so he announced a handsome reward for every pair of ears brought by any soldier, and an even larger reward for anyone who managed to break through the wall.

This inducement proved successful. In a renewed, all-out assault, the entire army attacked all the tiny breaches that had been made by the cannon fire and soon the Ottomans were able to enter the village and hunt down the Wahhabis in fierce hand-to-hand combat.

Eventually, all the besieged in Al-Rass were killed and its

main square was filled with corpses. After the firing had ended, Rashwan Agha invited his guests to accompany him into the town.

The group advanced on horseback through the ruins of the main gate. As they entered, they had to pick their way through the bodies strewn everywhere in the area beyond the wall, moving in single file to avoid stepping on the dead with their horses' hooves. They saw the corpses of resistance fighters torn to pieces by spears and swords and with their ears chopped off.

Bashir covered his face with his turban to hide his tears and sorrow, Sadleir spat on the ground with sheer disgust and Met'ab – the once merry Bedouin – could think of nothing except the horrible wholesale destruction of that village.

When some of the soldiers saw Rashwan Agha approaching, they dragged the corpse of a fighter by the feet and placed it in front of his horse. As the horse came to a halt so did the whole group.

One of the soldiers went up to Rashwan Agha and greeted him. 'Here's their leader, sir,' he said proudly.

Rashwan Agha looked at the corpse, which had several bullet-holes in the stomach and the head. He guessed that the man had been shot in the head after being wounded. 'What was his name?'

The soldier looked at the corpse and shrugged. 'We don't know, sir. But we may delay killing some of the prisoners until we have cross-examined them.' He indicated two soldiers standing behind him. 'They wish to cut off his ears in order to receive the reward. They also want to offer his head to Ibrahim Pasha as a gift.'

'Do as you please,' Rashwan Agha said, moving away.

As the rest of the group moved past slowly, Bashir looked

across in time to see the soldiers preparing to hack at the dead leader's throat.

He screamed out, 'Stop, damn you! Let me look at him.'

He jumped off his horse and ran towards the corpse. He wiped the blood off the forehead and recognised the lifeless features of Bin Ofaisan.

'It's Bin Ofaisan, Sadleir,' he moaned. 'They killed this brave man.' He glared at the soldiers around him. 'May God curse them.'

Sadleir and Met'ab had dismounted and stood sadly beside their friend. Although Met'ab had never met Bin Ofaisan, he was touched by the sight of Bashir, who could not stop crying.

'How I hate war now that I've seen it!' Bashir wept bitterly. 'It's torment before death.' Seeing Bin Ofaisan had been the last straw: he released all the pent-up grief he felt, which had grown with every step on the battlefield and every scene of death and destruction.

An Albanian soldier stood nearby with his sharp sword already drawn, waiting to cut off the head. But Rashwan Agha ordered him to leave and he stepped away reluctantly.

Bashir asked Met'ab to help him place the corpse on the back of his horse so that they could take it somewhere for burial far from the eyes of soldiers who would not hesitate to dig it up again to cut off its ears.

Having put the body on the horse, Bashir and the others began looking for a place where they could lay it to rest after performing funeral prayers.

As they continued to pass through the village of Al-Rass, they saw the corpses of women, children and elderly men whose ears had all been severed.

The men were overcome with disgust and Bashir could not

mask his revulsion as he said to Rashwan Agha, 'Your soldiers will do anything for money. Look at these corpses of women and children. Isn't it a crime for an army to behave like that?'

'Shut up and have some self-control, man,' Rashwan Agha retorted crossly. 'If you weren't my guest, I would do worse than that to you. This is war – don't you know what that means? It means you suppress all human feelings because otherwise you will be defeated.'

Sadleir looked at Bashir and patted him on the shoulder to console him.

Al-Rass was no longer a habitable place. Dogs came out to eat the corpses and birds of prey descended to partake of the banquet. Once Ibrahim Pasha had left the village, not a single human being remained alive.

At sunset, Bashir prayed for Bin Ofaisan's soul. He laid him in a hole in the ground, well outside the village, and placed a stone on either side of the makeshift grave. He wrote neither a name nor a date. Ibrahim bin Ofaisan's grave stood alone in the desert.

Chapter 37

Shiraz, Persia

THE PRINCE OF SHIRAZ could not bear to hear the man on the ground, bawling like a child. He signalled to one of his guards, who approached Abbas and kicked him. When that only increased the man's plaintive wails, the guard unsheathed his dagger and placed its tip on Abbas's neck. He pushed it, drawing a drop of blood that trickled onto the blade.

Abbas immediately stopped his howling.

Sensing that things were moving in the wrong direction, Loch asked if the guard could step aside and then, taking hold of Abbas's arm, he helped him up and said to him, 'Don't worry. Nobody will hurt you. You'll stay with me and you'll be out of Sadek's reach. Just tell His Highness everything you heard.'

'Do you promise you'll protect me, sir? Do I have your word?'

'Yes, I give you my word. Now speak up.'

This was all Abbas needed to hear. From that moment, he could not stop talking: he mentioned everything that he knew about Sadek and his plan to usurp the Prince, including events and information that Loch was unaware of. Over the years, Abbas had informed Sadek about the activities and affairs of Government House. But, similarly, he had overheard many nuggets from Sadek – conspiracies and intrigues that he had never dared repeat until that moment.

The Prince shook his head as Abbas related every snippet of information and eavesdropped conversation. Many things became clearer to him, from the disappearance of important people to missing taxation money and inexplicable changes of loyalty. The Prince started to believe that his nephew was a demon in human form.

Abbas ended with Sadek's intention to kill his uncle and seize his property. He fell abruptly silent and was suddenly exhausted as though an impossibly heavy burden that he had been carrying for many years had been lifted.

The Prince looked pensively out of the window at the garden. Then he turned resolutely to Agh Bahman and asked him to look after the guests and put them up for a few days in one of his own houses. He also instructed that they should be offered gifts before they left for Bushehr.

He waited for his guests to be led out before summoning his head guard. The Prince whispered in his ear and the guard bowed and left in a hurry.

Agh Bahman led the guests to a sumptuous house and excused himself, leaving Hopkins behind with Loch and Matthews.

The three sat together in a comfortable drawing room. Hopkins took a snuffbox from his pocket and, placing a pinch of tobacco on the back of his hand, inhaled it through one nostril. He offered some snuff to the other two, who declined. 'Not the only thing I've become addicted to here,' Hopkins said cheerfully. 'Quite a show you put on for the Prince. I thought that our politicians were the cunning ones, but I see that the military can be equally devious.'

Loch grinned broadly at that. 'And how is it for you in Persia?' he asked politely.

'In the years I've spent in this country, I've seen little beyond conspiracies,' he told them. 'People here live and breathe plots.'

He described Persia's recent defeat by Russia and the threat of a new war between the two empires – a conflict for which the Shah was desperately trying to gain the backing of Western powers. Palace politics did little to help their situation. 'After today's events,' he said, 'I should be surprised if the Prince allows you to leave before he has got rid of his nephew. He will want you to be sure that he has removed him before the news goes out.'

'Why is that?' asked Loch with a frown.

'Because the report you'll write to the Admiralty will carry more weight than the one he'll send to the Shah.' When the captain looked at him blankly, he explained, 'The Shah knows that such things happen between members of the ruling family on a daily basis. But the report the Prince will want you to write about the foiled coup by Sadek will strengthen his position because he will claim it proves he has British support. That will please the Shah. Mark my words.'

Loch and his entourage enjoyed the Prince's hospitality for two days. On the third, Loch heard a great commotion coming from the city square and learned that the Prince had ordered Sadek to come to him as quickly as possible. No sooner had he arrived than he was tied in chains and brought to the square where he was fastened to a pole. A judge sentenced him to death on charges of treason.

That same day, Sadek was beheaded and his body remained tied to the same pole while his head was impaled on a long spear and left to rot overlooking the marketplace. The captain knew his mission had succeeded. This was quite evident to his companion, Agh Bahman, who smiled with him at this turn of events.

Loch and his companions returned to Bushehr, where Bruce was waiting impatiently for them. The governor barely gave Loch time to dismount before asking him about his visit to the Prince of Shiraz.

Loch led the way to Bruce's office and helped himself to some wine for a toast. 'To a successful mission, dear chap,' he said, raising his glass.

'Successful, Captain?' Bruce asked. 'Please explain.'

'Our friend Sadek has lost his head.'

At first, Bruce did not take the literal meaning.

Loch described the events that had led to Sadek's execution. 'You will not have any more trouble from that quarter.'

'Thank God for that,' said Bruce, delighted. 'If he had lived on, we would have been at the mercy of that spiteful tongue of his. Now we only have Abbas, who knows far too much, don't you agree?'

'Don't worry. I'll take Abbas on my ship and he will disappear completely from your view. And we will then deal with Erhama.'

'Yes,' said Bruce, refilling their glasses. 'Let's celebrate today.' The Prince of Shiraz had become their close ally since they had protected him from one of his relatives. This would doubtless mean an expansion of Britain's trade interests.

'The Prince offered us most generous gifts as a reward for having unveiled the plot against him. I haven't forgotten you in this, for I told him that you were the one who suggested disclosing the scheme and asked me to go to inform him of it. He sent you some wonderful gifts which I've asked Matthews to take straight to your house.'

The governor was overjoyed. 'My dear Captain, I am indebted to you. Thank you.'

Sailors who passed by Bruce's house that night heard what they assumed to be a fairly drunken celebration going on. But by midnight the Shirazi wine had taken full effect and the noise had died down. The next morning, Bruce and Matthews stood at the wharf and waved farewell to Loch as he stepped into a boat to take him to the *Eden*. Behind him, in his best outfit and carrying all his belongings in a bundle, was Abbas, thrilled to be leaving the wretched port where he had spent his entire life.

As soon as the captain climbed on board HMS *Eden*, Mansen shouted, 'Captain on deck!'

The sails were spread and the ship moved slowly in a south-westerly direction, leaving behind Bruce and Matthews who both wished they too were on board.

The ship had barely gone a nautical mile when something suddenly fell from the deck, splashing into the ocean. The following day, sailors found Abbas's body and entrails floating on the surface. Nobody could explain the accident.

Chapter 38

Al-Rass, Central Arabia

Having buried bin ofaisan in the desert, Sadleir and his companions returned to the camp outside Al-Rass. Sadleir repeated his request to meet Ibrahim Pasha, and Rashwan Agha promised that an answer would be forthcoming.

In the evening, as Sadleir sat with Bashir in their tent, Rashwan Agha came to give them the good news that the pasha had agreed to have breakfast with Sadleir the following morning.

Bashir waited for Rashwan Agha to leave and then said, 'So you'll meet the monster tomorrow, will you? If it was me, I would hide a dagger in my clothes and stab him in the heart after all he has done to this country.'

'Don't worry,' said Sadleir gently, 'his day of reckoning will come. Whether he is stabbed or shot or dies in any other manner, he will disappear from this land – hopefully sooner rather than later.

'I'll hand him the sword, give him the message I have for him and wait for his response. Then I'm done with him. But to tell you the truth, Bashir, I don't expect much from this meeting.'

'Nor do I. He's a murdering bastard.' Bashir's eyes were still red as he thought of Bin Ofaisan's grave and remembered the man's kindness. He had been Bashir's uncle and father at the same time; the young man had been able to tell him everything without any reservations, even his secret love for Salwa. 'May he rest in peace,' he said mostly to himself. 'If my father learned what had happened to Bin Ofaisan, he would surely follow him immediately to the grave.'

The next morning, Sadleir woke up early and put on his uniform. He dusted and polished the wooden box, then brought out the sword and wiped it with a clean cloth as he waited to be summoned to the meeting.

Rashwan Agha arrived to take him to the pasha's tent at the centre of the camp. It was surrounded by a select group of Albanian guards. On seeing Sadleir, Ibrahim Pasha greeted him and invited him to sit down and have breakfast.

As he took his seat opposite the pasha, two black servants served them fresh hot bread.

Sadleir examined the man's face to see if he could glean anything of his personality. He was a young man in his early thirties, dressed in a Turkish military uniform whose design had been slightly modified by his father, the Khedive of Egypt, so as to appear somewhat different from regular Ottoman issue.

He had a thin beard and a fastidiously well-groomed moustache. His facial expression suggested a kind of soft cruelty; Sadleir guessed he was the type of person who could smile pleasantly and not bat an eyelid while committing murder.

Judging from the way he spoke to his servants, Sadleir assumed he was probably bad-tempered and impatient, able to mistreat those around him without giving it another thought. He acted as though the whole world revolved around his father and him.

'Tell me, Major Sadleir,' said Ibrahim Pasha, 'how did you manage to reach my camp from Al-Ahsa?'

'I have come from further than Al-Ahsa, Your Excellency,' said Sadleir. 'My unit is in India.'

'India?' said the pasha, impressed. 'India? You've come all the way from India? Well, tell me about India. I've often heard about it but have never been.'

'What would you like to know about India, sir? It's a vast country with many races, religions and languages.'

'Do Indians, for example, know anything about my father, Mohammed Ali Pasha?'

Sadleir shook his head. 'Indians know little about what goes on outside their country. But the Governor of Bombay sends you his greetings and he was the one who told me a great deal about you and your father.'

'Good. Good. But tell me about the most important wares exported by India. We may find a way to trade with that country and make some profit. I hear that India is a rich land – is that so?'

'India exports almost everything, most importantly spices, wood and perfumes. There is a flourishing trade.'

'What about wheat? Do they grow it there?'

Sadleir was not impressed by the pasha's questions. 'I'm a soldier, Your Excellency, not a merchant. But if you wish to receive information on trade I would be happy to refer you to some of our traders.'

'Yes, a soldier like me. So tell me, what brings you here? Did you take part in our battle?'

'No, sir. I just observed and I saw enough.'

'You haven't seen anything yet. I'll come back soon to the area of Abar Ali which is controlled by a large tribe. I intend to confiscate all their property. Although I expect them to fight desperately to defend it, I will crush and exterminate them all. If you wish to see some real fighting, come along with us there.'

Sadleir felt he was being invited to a hunting party. 'I have a gift for you, sir,' he said suddenly. 'It's from the Governor of Bombay, Sir Evan Nepean, and with your permission I would like to hand it over to you. In addition, I wish to have a private conversation with you if you would allow me such an honour.'

The pasha snapped his fingers and said something that immediately caused the servants to lay everything down and leave.

Sadleir reached down for the box and placed it in front of the man. Ibrahim Pasha quickly opened it and took out the sword. Drawing the blade from the scabbard, he ran his fingers along the edge without uttering a single word. His eyes bulged and his mouth was open – he seemed to Sadleir like a spoilt child who had been given an appealing toy that he would never let go of.

Sadleir waited for the pasha to finish examining the sword. He fiddled with it and read the engraved words on the scabbard and box. Sadleir would have had longer to wait if one of the guards had not entered to tell the pasha that they were waiting for his orders to move out.

The pasha gave the order with a flick of his hand and then placed the sword on his lap, with both hands over it.

Sadleir brought out the letter from Sir Evan and handed it to the pasha. 'This is a message to you personally from the Governor of Bombay.'

The pasha opened the letter and read it carefully. Sadleir followed his facial expressions as he tried to anticipate what his decision would be regarding the pact. Having finished reading, the pasha put the letter down on the table beside him and said nothing.

Sadleir already knew the content of the letter: a call to unite against a common enemy. The Wahhabis had got as far as the eastern coast of the Arabian Peninsula and they now had ships that threatened trade. It was the same plan for the three armies, including the Sultan of Oman, to join forces and mount a massive campaign to eradicate the Wahhabis.

'Your Excellency,' prompted Sadleir. 'Do you approve of this plan? I will need to inform my superiors of your decision.'

Ibrahim Pasha looked away reluctantly from the sword to fix his gaze on the Englishman. 'I can't do anything without consulting my father, the Khedive,' he admitted. 'This British plan will require a lot of money and soldiers. As you see, my army has become worn out by these battles. So I will need my father's support for this.' The Khedive's orders had been to destroy Diriyah and quash any resistance inside or outside it, which Ibrahim Pasha had done. He was still awaiting further instructions.

'When should we expect your reply, Your Excellency?'

'Come with me to Medina where my family lives,' he said. 'From there we'll go to Yanbu where we can receive my father's answer in a matter of days. Our ships sail on a daily basis from Yanbu to Suez carrying messages.'

Sadleir thought of the long journey. They were now in Al-Rass, in the middle of the Arabian Peninsula, and the pasha wanted him to accompany him to Medina, the city revered by all Muslims. And from there he proposed to travel even further, to Yanbu on the Red Sea coast.

'Thank you, sir, but I wish to return to Muscat as soon as possible. From there I should head back to Bombay where the governor will be impatient for my report on this visit.'

'But the route to Muscat from here is dangerous – how will you get there?'

Sadleir was not too sure. Certainly travelling across the desert would be perilous. 'I'm thinking of leaving Al-Rass for Damascus and going from there to Baghdad, Basra and then Muscat. Or I might go to Basra directly if I can find someone I trust from the tribes to protect me. I still don't know exactly, sir,' he confessed, 'and I may need to study the situation before I decide. But I must have your answer to take with me whichever way I go.'

'Why the hurry, Captain? Stay with us and enjoy the war a little. Accompany me at least to Yanbu and from there you can decide your route. I hope we will be in contact.'

The pasha stood up, thereby announcing the end of the meeting. He shook the breadcrumbs from his clothes and put on his fez. 'I too have a gift for the British governor in India that I'd like to give you.'

Sadleir rose to his feet. 'That is most generous of you, Your Excellency. I'll be honoured to carry whatever you wish to offer the governor.'

The pasha raised his voice and, calling the head servant, who came running right away, he ordered, 'Prepare a valuable gift for the British governor in India as a token of appreciation for his generosity.'

Sadleir would have another gift to protect for the return journey to India. He felt light-headed as he thought of everything he had been through since his meeting with Sir Evan in Bombay.

He went back to his tent where Bashir was waiting for him.

'The plan will not work, Bashir,' Sadleir told him. 'The pasha needs to consult his father about collaborating with us.' Sadleir could tell that Ibrahim Pasha wanted to leave the Arabian

Peninsula as soon as possible, perhaps because his army had been worn down by the battles of the past few months and the length of the supply lines. Moreover, Sadleir suspected that the Khedive in Cairo was too far removed from this battle with the Wahhabis to really care. 'Personally, I would say he's not very enthusiastic.'

Bashir's face lit up. 'That's good news, Sadleir,' he said. He had been haunted by the thought that the plan had been endorsed and by visions of the whole region turning into a titanic battlefield, with famine spreading everywhere. Bashir could never forget the women and children begging for food in Manfuhah, or the horrendous sight of all that blood and death. 'I've had my fill of scenes of suffering and don't want to see any more, Sadleir.'

Over the past months, Bashir had become a close friend and Sadleir shared his views and felt the same pain. But the Englishman was torn by conflicting emotions. While he was relieved that Ibrahim Pasha had not accepted the pact outright, he was also aware that his superiors would not be pleased: everyone, from Sir Evan to Loch, had hoped that the pasha would give his consent the moment he set eyes on the priceless Indian sword.

'But it could still happen,' Sadleir told his Arab companion. 'Ibrahim Pasha's father may agree to it in the end. It's just that there are currently some obstacles.'

'I hope God never removes those obstacles, Sadleir. Damn all wars.' Bashir paused and resumed in a gentler tone, 'I know you're a soldier carrying out the orders of your commanders. But I also know that you wouldn't wish to see more massacres like the one we've just witnessed. Your military commanders push you one way and your heart pushes you in the opposite direction.'

Sadleir sat down, suddenly overcome with exhaustion. He put his head in his hands. 'That's true, Bashir. When you're in the army, you learn to follow orders. I'm loyal to my commanders and I won't hesitate to do anything to make the plan work – even if it makes me sick to the core.'

'I understand,' Bashir said. 'You would think differently if this land was your land and if these people were your people. You need to know that I will never want this plan to work and I'll celebrate the day it fails.'

That afternoon, the pasha's head servant came to Sadleir's tent and, greeting him formally, asked Sadleir to receive the pasha's gift to the Governor of Bombay. When Sadleir walked out of the tent followed by Bashir, they saw a thoroughbred Arabian horse. A guard was leading the saddled animal by its reins.

Sadleir began to examine the horse, stroking its head and neck with admiration. Then his attention was drawn to the edges of the saddle, which were frayed.

'The saddle has been used before,' he said to the servant, pointing at the worn edges. 'This is not a gift worthy of the Governor of Bombay.'

At first, the servant thought the Englishman was joking.

'Please tell the pasha that I refuse to accept this gift.'

The servant's face changed colour; he simply could not believe Sadleir's rudeness or bear to think of the pasha's anger when he heard of this.

'It's a used saddle,' Sadleir complained to Bashir while the servant was still within earshot and walking away with the guard and the horse. 'I don't know who has used it before. How can I take it to the Governor of Bombay? What would I say to him? It's an affront!'

In the evening, Rashwan Agha came to the tent clearly upset. He tried to convince Sadleir to accept the gift. But the major continued to refuse.

Rashwan Agha had no choice but to tell the pasha. He decided, however, to take his time doing so in case Sadleir changed his mind on the way to Yanbu.

The next morning the pasha and three hundred of his best soldiers set out on the long road to the Hejaz. At the rear of the caravan were Sadleir, Bashir, Met'ab and Mirza. They did not look at all happy to be heading west.

Chapter 39

Ras al-Khaimah, Eastern Arabia

E RHAMA SAT ON A beach with Sheikh Hassan al-Qasmi, surrounded by a group of armed men. Behind them was the wall of Ras al-Khaimah, which encompassed a town of some ten thousand inhabitants. Built from a mixture of coral stones and mud, the wall was fifteen feet wide at the base and grew increasingly narrow at the top. It stretched out like two arms embracing the town and reaching towards the sea, each arm ending with a large tower at the water's edge. Inside those towers were cannon that had been taken from ships.

Erhama sat in the middle of the gathering and drank a cup of coffee that had been offered to him by a servant. He took a couple of sips and handed the cup back, only to receive a refilled cup. The man pouring the coffee could not leave the meeting until everyone had handed him their cup after shaking it from side to side as a clear indication that they did not want any more coffee.

The meeting on the beach was far from formal. Erhama and Sheikh Hassan spoke quietly together while the rest of the gathering talked amongst themselves – everyone was armed with a variety of pistols, daggers and swords.

'My dear Sheikh Hassan,' said Erhama softly, 'the British don't keep their word and don't honour agreements. Would you believe that they can sign a pact one day and break it the next? They tried to tempt me several times to be their ally so that I would go back on my agreements with you.' He was clicking his sword in its scabbard. 'But I've always refused. The latest was an arrangement whereby they would leave me to deal with my enemies and I would leave them to trade in peace.' He thought it unnecessary to mention the Indian sword. 'They also reneged on that. Have you ever met people who don't keep their word like this?'

'I've often warned you, Erhama, against cooperating with them,' said Sheikh Hassan. 'They think everything is allowed. In their view we are nothing. If we don't resist them, they will treat us like the Portuguese did and cut off people's ears and noses.' Then he quoted from the Qur'an: '"How can there be such a league, seeing that if they get an advantage over you, they respect not in you the ties either of kinship or of covenant."'

'I just can't believe how quickly they break their promises and agreements,' insisted Erhama. 'Sometimes I feel that they enjoy doing that.'

'But tell me, where is your friend Ibrahim bin Ofaisan? I was hoping he might be able to mend your ways and make you a more pious person,' Sheikh Hassan said, changing the subject.

Erhama turned to stare at the sea as though waiting for something to come into view. 'Ibrahim left me some time ago,' he said. 'He told me he had to go back to Nejd because he couldn't stay away while Ibrahim Pasha was wreaking havoc in his country. I hope he's enjoying peace on his farm.'

'He did well to leave. I didn't want him to stay too long with you.'

'Why?'

'Because you have only one aim, Erhama, and that is to fight the Al-Khalifas, even though they are your cousins. I don't understand your willingness to die to achieve a meaningless aim. Why don't you fight the infidels with us? They are God's enemies who occupy our land. At least that way you'll go straight to heaven after your martyrdom.'

'You sound like Bin Ofaisan,' Erhama said glumly. 'But my destiny has been chosen for me by God and it has to be fulfilled. As for death, I don't fear it. I'm nearly seventy or perhaps older – I don't really know when I was born. I only know my age by comparing myself to the people I know and my ailments to theirs.'

'You will outlive us all,' said Sheikh Hassan. 'But tell me, Erhama, what news of that British captain, Loch? Have you heard of him since his defeat?'

'He's like a wounded lion now, waiting to take revenge for your victory over him. I believe he will move against you soon, so you must be cautious.' Erhama gazed out at the horizon again. 'He likes to declare to people he meets that his mission is to rid the sea of pirates. Those pirates are you and me, Sheikh Hassan. Can you believe it?'

'We are not pirates, Erhama. We are fighters defending our homes and our people against invaders. They are the pirates and killers.'

'Yes,' Erhama said absent-mindedly, his eyes fixed on a point on the horizon.

A long way from Ras al-Khaimah, beyond the horizon, a fleet of naval ships was advancing towards the coast, spearheaded by the *Eden* and flanked by two other men-of-war, HMS *Liverpool* and HMS *Curlew*. The fleet included nine smaller vessels belonging to the East India Company, a group of transport ships, as well as the fleet and soldiers of the Sultan of Oman.

The ships carried a total of three thousand fighters. Half of these were British soldiers who had been transferred from the 47th and 65th Regiments, in addition to an artillery regiment. It was the largest campaign in the history of the Gulf.

On the *Eden*, Loch stood in front of a group of officers, dressed in full uniform. He felt that he was on the point of completing the task he had been entrusted with and which would greatly enhance his military reputation. He had called a meeting in the wardroom to explain – with maps and charts on the wall and a pointer in his hand – the details of the military operation.

He tapped the map behind him with the stick, the tip striking the settlement on the coast. 'Ras al-Khaimah is the best fortified of all the towns in the Gulf,' he said. 'Our mission in the region will be accomplished once we destroy it.' As he described the topography, the pointer moved to a strip of land stretching into the water, which ran parallel to the coast in a northeasterly direction. It was about five miles long and a mile wide and was bounded on one side by the sea and on the other by a small creek that was deep enough only for the lighter Arabian vessels.

The pointer came to rest on a sketch, next to the map, of two towers guarding the entrance to the creek. 'Cannon have been installed in these towers. But as far as we know, they are antiquated guns that were captured many years ago and have not been properly maintained since. We expect them to be rusty and virtually out of service and to have a poor stock of ammunition.

'Now here's the plan, gentlemen,' he said, the pointer returning to the map. 'The *Eden* will sail as close as possible to Ras al-Khaimah and then shell the wall and the towers. We expect the response to be fairly weak. If we manage to demolish the wall and destroy the guns, the town will be at our mercy. The *Liverpool* will stop at the entrance to the creek facing the town gate to shut it off, barring ships from all entry and exit. As for the *Curlew*, she will be positioned off the coast to prevent any pirate ships at sea from providing relief to the besieged.'

The pointer moved to a particular stretch of the coast. 'Meanwhile, our soldiers will come ashore here and will block access by land to the town. In this way, we will have cut them off on all sides.' He tapped the map in rapid succession as a reminder: 'The *Liverpool* in the north, the *Curlew* in the west, the infantry in the south – and, of course, the creek in the east will become a trap for any of their ships trying to escape. Is this clear, gentlemen? Any questions?' He waited a moment and when none were raised, he said, 'Good. Let's get to it then.'

Loch loved to devise strategies even if, on the ground, their implementation turned out to be radically different from the theoretical plans. He lived for these moments, despite knowing that, once the shelling began and the number of casualties increased, some unforeseen variable could turn the whole plan on its head and ruin it completely.

In the harbour of Ras al-Khaimah, Dirar stood talking to one of the sailors bringing fresh supplies from town when another man pointed at the horizon.

The sun was about to set and the weather was fresh and cool. It was the end of autumn and the short rainy season would begin soon, bringing with it the much needed water to revive the land and improve living conditions. When Dirar turned to look at the horizon, he expected to see clouds laden with heaven's bounty. But the sky was cloudless; Dirar was about to question the man when his mouth dropped open in utter surprise.

He blinked at the huge number of dots in the distance advancing towards them. Without a moment's hesitation, he yelled at the sailors to weigh anchor and spread the sails. Dirar was in such an agitated state that no one dared ask him why they were leaving Erhama in town and sailing without his permission. Dirar screamed at them to leave the creek as soon as possible.

From their meeting place on the beach, Erhama saw the *Ghatrousha* slipping out of the creek towards the open sea in a southwesterly direction. He asked Sheikh Hassan to hand him a long telescope and, when one of his men rushed to provide him with one, Erhama focused on the deck of his ship. He saw Dirar waving his arms frantically at him and pointing to the sea. Swinging the telescope round, Erhama saw the fleet advancing towards Ras al-Khaimah.

Erhama gave the telescope to Sheikh Hassan. The ships were now becoming visible to the naked eye. Sheikh Hassan saw all the ships and knew that it was the battle Erhama had mentioned a little earlier. '*Allahu akbar*,' he muttered slowly.

All the men stood up to watch the black specks on the sea that grew more menacing every minute.

'What are you waiting for?' Sheikh Hassan screamed. 'Go to your positions and get ready to fight. Tell everyone what you have seen so that every able-bodied person will carry their weapons.'

The men ran to their positions and began to chant old battle songs to boost morale and prepare for the fight ahead. Soon, only Erhama and Sheikh Hassan remained on the beach.

'What will you do, Sheikh Hassan? They're coming for you with all their soldiers and guns,' Erhama said. 'I would advise you to negotiate with them – you can't fight them all.'

'That's the difference between us, Erhama,' Sheikh Hassan said sternly. 'I look for a fight while you run away from it. Why should I negotiate? They came to our land and we will fight them with all our strength until we destroy them or they destroy us.'

'Many will die if you do so,' said Erhama slowly. 'There will be a great deal of destruction. Let's talk to them – I know Captain Loch and we might find a solution.'

Sheikh Hassan shook his head doubtfully. 'Whoever comes with such a massive force certainly doesn't want to negotiate.'

By the afternoon, the fleet had reached the coast of Ras al-Khaimah. Sheikh Hassan's men secured their positions on the walls and in the towers, and in the palm groves near the town. Some Arab vessels tried to leave the creek but were too late as the ships of the fleet had already come within sight. The *Liverpool* approached and fired – two vessels were destroyed while the rest returned to the safety of the creek.

Meanwhile, the *Eden* had taken up position facing the town and began to bombard the wall. Volleys of cannonfire destroyed the towers and killed many of the defenders. By nightfall, Ras al-Khaimah was fully under siege, and gunfire from both sides continued until sunrise.

Dirar had managed to steer the *Ghatrousha* away before the noose had tightened. He had aimed for a small hiding place, southeast of the town, behind the line of landing troops. By nightfall, these troops had created a barrier between him and the town, and he watched the battle from a distance – powerless to do anything other than monitor the situation.

Throughout the night Sheikh Hassan and Erhama remained in hiding in a house overlooking the sea. They were with some guards who were watching the coast warily, anticipating the deployment of troops. They were unaware that a landing party had already captured the southern approach to town, thereby closing the circle and cutting the town off from the rest of the world.

In the early morning, a craft was lowered from the *Liverpool*, with an officer and three armed soldiers raising a white flag to parley. Sheikh Hassan asked Erhama for his advice.

Erhama thought about all the ships they had seen from the beach and the fact that now only two of them were visible: the warship blocking the entrance to the creek and the other man-of-war. 'We don't really know what happened during the night,' he said pensively. 'But we do know that their numbers are huge. I advise you to negotiate.

'But don't tell them I'm here or Captain Loch will feel he's trapped his two arch-enemies in one go.'

Chapter 40

Between Al-Rass and Medina

I BRAHIM PASHA'S CARAVAN PASSED over bare, rocky mountains, arid valleys and barren deserts. Although from time to time they spotted people watching them from hilltops, they had no clashes with the local Bedouins. The pasha's personal guards were alert to any unexpected movement and surrounded their master at all times.

Once they reached the outskirts of Medina, they entered a camp that had already been prepared to receive the pasha. When Sadleir noticed the presence of a large number of thoroughbreds, he asked Rashwan Agha about them.

'They belong to the pasha and he will take them with him to Egypt,' the man replied. 'The pasha is mad about horses, Major. He sends them by sea to Suez and from there to Cairo. I've seen how some of them die on the way or on board ship, for transporting them is extremely difficult. But such is the wish of the pasha.'

In fact, there were so many horses that they caused miniature sandstorms just by trotting and cantering in the camp. Rashwan Agha tried to avoid a sudden cloud of dust and Bashir took that opportunity to explain the truth of the situation to Sadleir.

'These are all stolen horses that have been confiscated from their owners,' he told him. 'The army has instructions to steal all thoroughbreds for the benefit of the pasha.'

Met'ab wanted to be part of the conversation. 'They say Ibrahim Pasha hasn't left a single thoroughbred horse in the Hejaz and Nejd,' he said. 'That's why the prices have become so high. All the horses he finds are sent to Egypt. If this continues much longer, people here will forget what horses even look like.'

After they had settled in the camp, Sadleir was left alone while his companions went to visit the Mosque and Tomb of the Prophet. Rashwan Agha came to see him again to ask him to reconsider his rejection of the pasha's gift to the Governor of Bombay.

'I'm reluctant to tell the pasha of your refusal because I know he will become extremely angry with you, Major Sadleir.'

Sadleir felt it should have been easy enough to find a new saddle. 'I insist, sir. His anger will be much easier to take than the governor's.'

'I can't delay telling the pasha any longer. I hope with all my heart that he will understand your point of view.'

In truth, though, the gift was not the real issue. Sadleir had come to the pasha to convince him to enter into a pact against the Wahhabis and, consequently, to move east. Instead Ibrahim Pasha had gone west, unable to take a decision without his father's blessing. Sadleir knew that his mission had failed and not even the finest gift in the world would change that fact; all that remained for him to do was to return to his regiment in India.

In the evening, Bashir and Met'ab came back from their visit to the holy sites and described them in such detail that Sadleir's curiosity was aroused. But when he expressed his wish to see them and walk along the alleys that were congested with beggars, Bashir told him he was barred from stepping into the city as a non-Muslim.

255

Met'ab, in contrast, did not object, pointing out that there were many people from different countries visiting the sites, and Sadleir would be regarded as one of them.

The next day, Sadleir took Met'ab by the shoulder and led him outside the tent. He repeated his wish to visit Medina.

'I suggest you wear the Turkish clothes usually worn on these occasions as well as a turban on your head. I'll teach you a few words that you may need in case someone asks about our nationality,' Met'ab said.

Met'ab taught Sadleir the phrase 'There is no god but God and Mohammed is his messenger.' Then he taught him how to perform ablutions and prayers. After Met'ab was satisfied that Sadleir was convincing, they prepared to leave for Medina. But Sadleir changed his mind at the last moment when he realised what an ordeal it would be if he were discovered. So he decided to gather information about Medina and write down all he could. In the evening he wrote the following:

I can give only a partial description of Medina because non-Muslims are barred from entering. I have managed, however, to gather some information about it.

Medina lies in the middle of a chain of bare mountains and is built of mud, plaster and stone. Its houses are covered in plaster, which makes them look magnificent when seen from the open space around them.

The city has three gates. The first is Al-Sham, where a green flag is flown each Friday near the cannons on top of the gate. The second gate is the Misr gate, while the third is the Al-Jumman. Three small cannons are placed on each gate.

During ordinary festivities a red flag is raised on two of the gates. Many parts of the city boast farms of pomegranate, figs and vegetables as well as palm groves. It has a supply of water from the Blue Springs in addition to other wells.

Medina also houses the Prophet's grave and that of his daughter, Fatima, in addition to the graves of his disciples Abu Bakr and Omar. It has two large mosques, a judge and two muftis *(religious counsellors)*. One of the muftis *belongs to the Hanafi sect and the other to the Shafei sect.*

There are thirty schools for children in the city. Six hundred money purses are dedicated to the maintenance and improvement of holy buildings. It seems to me that constant renovations have led to the disappearance of the original buildings, with the exception of the Prophet's grave, which has remained untouched. The residents of Medina depend for their livelihood on the sums of money offered by people wishing to perform pilgrimage.

Pilgrims are naturally an important financial source for the inhabitants of Medina in addition to charities sent by the Islamic world to the poor.

It is strange how people buy water in the city in spite of its abundance. Equally strange is the fact that they pay to visit the graves. The money collected is then distributed proportionately after the arrival of pilgrims. The residents of the city pay no taxes at all.

The number of houses in the city recently totaled six thousand, half of which are dilapidated and deserted. The population is around eight thousand. There are palm groves to the north of the city where large numbers of inhabitants live. In the area west of Abar Ali there are destroyed villages and farms in the valley stretching to the mountain cliffs in the southwestern areas.

Sadleir finished writing his remarks about Medina and thanked God he didn't carry out his plan. The pasha would likely be furious enough over the rejection of the gift and he didn't wish to become involved in another scandal.

Mirza, their Persian companion since Qatif, decided to remain in Medina. He had become acquainted with a group of Persian pilgrims and wanted to stay with them. Sadleir did not hesitate to give his consent, since Mirza made an insignificant contribution to their party and his departure would cut down the amount of food and water they would need for the journey.

The following day, Rashwan Agha came back looking distressed. The pasha had not taken the rejection of his gift well. Indeed, he was so furious that he ordered Sadleir to leave the camp at once and said the rude Englishman should not expect any response from him concerning his proposal.

Rashwan Agha went on to advise them that their safety could no longer be guaranteed, especially once the troops learned of the pasha's displeasure.

Sadleir's party of three was ready to leave the camp before word got around. They headed west, with Sadleir and Bashir walking side by side, followed by Met'ab.

Chapter 41

Ras al-Khaimah

S HEIKH HASSAN WENT OUT to meet the officer from the ship, accompanied by three guards. The eyes of the fighters on both sides followed what was happening from a distance. As they saw the two parties engage in talks, they could only imagine what was being said between them.

It was one of the shortest parleys in history.

On the beach, the British officer drew some lines in the sand. Sheikh Hassan looked at them for a second, shook his head and promptly returned to the besieged town.

Sheikh Hassan was livid. His men gathered around him to hear the outcome of the meeting. Erhama, too, was keen to know.

'They have laid siege to us from all sides,' he told everyone, 'and we must decide whether we wish to fight or surrender. They have cut us off from the south with troops on the ground and their ships have obstructed navigation in the creek, so we can't ask for help from outside.' He looked around at his men. 'We are on our own with only God's help. And today, I will not take a decision alone – this affects us all and all of us must therefore decide. They have given us until tomorrow morning.'

A young man at the meeting stood up and asked for permission to speak. 'God has commanded us to struggle to defend ourselves, our families and our property. I don't see how we can avoid that.' He added passionately, 'We haven't gone to them but they have come to us. If we don't fight them today, they will occupy our land tomorrow, shed our blood and take our property. If the choice is between death and humiliation, I choose death.'

Sheikh Hassan turned to Erhama. 'What do you think, my friend? Your opinion would be highly appreciated because you have become one of us.'

'My dear Sheikh Hassan, I haven't changed my mind,' he replied. 'Let's negotiate with them and we may get something out of it. But if we fight and lose, which I think likely, we will become captives and they will do to us as they wish.'

Sheikh Hassan spoke. 'Now please go, all of you – I need to think. May God help me decide what's best.'

Dirar was watching events unfold from the deck of the *Ghatrousha*, his long telescope tracking the ships and the besieged town. He could not bear to remain separated from his master and so, that afternoon, he gathered some of the men to ask them if anyone was willing to join him in a bid to return to Ras al-Khaimah. He warned them that the enemy had landed on the coast and formed a barrier between them and the town and that they would have to try to break through enemy lines under cover of darkness.

Five of them agreed to take part despite the perilous nature of the operation and the very real possibility that they would not survive.

That night, the group of six men bid farewell to the rest of the crew, removed their clothes and swam to shore with their weapons in bundles strapped to their backs. Once they reached land, they moved swiftly north parallel to the coast until they saw the lights of the enemy camp and heard their voices.

With a gesture of his hand, Dirar ordered the group to lie on the ground and crawl forward. They crept as far as they could without drawing attention to themselves. Dirar took out his dagger and, placing the blade on his own neck and the palm of his other hand on his mouth, he made the others understand how they were to kill the guards: by slitting their throats so that they would be unable to raise the alarm.

He held up his hand for all to see and signalled the charge. No sooner had he lowered his hand than the group rushed forward like phantoms. A few moments later, the soldiers were lying on the ground either dead or dying, stabbed in the neck and left to bleed to death.

Dirar's men took the weapons of the dead guards and crawled towards another group of soldiers in a desperate attempt to get inside the besieged town. But when they were close to this second group, one of the guards spotted them and fired a shot in the air to alert the others. Dirar's men responded with gunfire.

Thus began an unequal battle between an army and a small band of men.

When the ships anchored near the coast heard the shots, they opened fire without waiting for orders. The besieged town was shelled from all sides. Houses collapsed and the wall was destroyed. Caught unawares, many people died in the furious barrage.

Sheikh Hassan looked at Erhama, his eyes blazing with fury. 'What's happening, Erhama? Didn't we have until tomorrow? God damn them. They are never to be trusted.'

Erhama tried to protect his head with his hand as a hail of rocks suddenly came down on them. The sound of cannonfire was now constant and drowned out the screams and shouts from the town. Dust filled the air and women and children wailed, which only made the men howl with fury.

During a brief lull in the artillery fire, Erhama could hear the pleas for God's mercy and the groans of the wounded. He lifted his head a little to see Sheikh Hassan and make sure that he was still in one piece: his face was ashen due as much to the pervasive dust as his raging anger.

Sheikh Hassan's top priority was to protect the lives of his people; he would never have intentionally and recklessly exposed them to such bombing. Erhama was aware of this every time the sheikh publicly asked him his views so that the war enthusiasts would hear about the destructive and deadly effect of wars. But the British had once more violated a truce and had shelled the town even though they knew it was full of women, children and elderly people.

'What did I tell you, Erhama?' roared Sheikh Hassan. 'These are not God-fearing people. They are forcing us to see them as our eternal enemies. May God take revenge on them!'

His curses were drowned out by a shell that landed next to their position and turned a whole section of the wall to rubble. His musket already loaded, Sheikh Hassan led the way to a sandy mound near the beach and was followed by others, including Erhama. They crawled on their bellies to reach the top and prepared to fight off a landing party.

The shelling ended as abruptly as it had begun; only distant gunfire could now be heard from the south.

'How many men do you have protecting the southern part of town?' asked Erhama.

'Not more than ten,' replied Sheikh Hassan. They had been

stationed there purely as a precaution, believing that most of the fighting would come from the sea.

South of Ras al-Khaimah, Dirar and his band responded to the heavy gunfire that fell on them from every direction like rain. They were all veteran fighters who aimed precisely and used their ammunition sparingly. They managed to kill a large number of soldiers until one of the fighters was shot in the head. Soon after, a second of Erhama's men was shot in the chest near the heart and moaned for hours before he died.

For two days, the fighting continued intermittently in the town, after which Sheikh Hassan decided to evacuate women, children and elderly through the creek at low tide. He sent one of his men to pass on his decision so that, with the exception of the fighters, everyone else would be ready to leave the town.

The creek was an inlet of shallow water and muddy land just over a mile across. As soon as one of Sheikh Hassan's men gave the signal, a long line of wretched people moved towards the shore: wounded women, maimed children and elderly men on mules, donkeys and horses.

The crescent moon was large and clear, and shed its light on this procession of misery – crying infants, wailing mothers – that headed towards the water as though declaring war on life itself and preferring to perish at sea. The long line of people walked in single file, each forgetting the pain of others in order to concentrate on their own wretchedness and despair.

From a distance, Loch watched the death march through his telescope and asked his officers to watch it too. It was not something one saw every day. Then he called Mansen and asked him about the latest developments in the field.

'Apparently the group of fighters in the south are still trying to break through the siege and get into town, sir,' replied Mansen. 'The other fronts around the town are fairly quiet now. We haven't observed any movement except for that.' He indicated the line of civilians. 'The *Liverpool* is awaiting your orders to open fire on them, sir.'

'Leave them for now,' said Loch. Most of them would probably drown anyway as the tide was coming in. 'We need to save our ammunition for the fighters. Leave them to their fate.'

The procession looked like a necklace of black pearls decorating the small bay.

By dawn, the tide had flowed in and screams could be heard every now and then. Those who were injured or could not swim drowned; by mid-morning, dead bodies, mostly of women and children, were seen floating in the water.

Erhama's band of men had fought valiantly. Two had died and the rest had wounds all over their bodies; blood trickled from cuts and scrapes from the fighting and from the thorns and rocks they had crawled over. Dirar knew that time was not on his side and that he had to withdraw from the battle. He ordered his men to retreat and leave the bodies of their friends behind.

They succeeded in swimming back to the *Ghatrousha*. It was obvious that things were not going well for Sheikh Hassan and his men. The two parties had to reach a final agreement. The sheikh would not be able to resist much longer and the British could not continue to besiege the town for long without fresh supplies. Dirar decided to stay put for a few days before deciding what to do.

When he saw the dead bodies of his people littering the shore, Sheikh Hassan wept so bitterly that Erhama hugged him and kissed his head in an attempt to console him.

Sheikh Hassan called one of his men and asked him to raise the white flag.

Chapter 42

Yanbu, Western Arabia

SADLEIR'S PARTY STOOD ON a hill overlooking the port of Yanbu, a cloud of dust hovering over the small city. The port was the link between Ibrahim Pasha's army and Cairo: supplies from Egypt reached the army, while, going in the opposite direction, stolen goods and horses were dispatched to Cairo. Ill and wounded soldiers also waited at Yanbu for transport to take them back home.

Sadleir's face was coated in a film of dust and sweat which had the effect of a mask and made him almost unrecognisable. Despite the grime, however, Sadleir's frown was clear. He looked pained whenever he saw something unpleasant, and Bashir had come to recognise that look. It was the same look he had seen after the pasha had taken the sword and expelled them from the Ottoman camp outside Medina.

In the distance they could see a lot of activity – stables, army camps, ships, small houses and many people moving around. It was as if the entire population of the Hejaz had suddenly decided to depart from Yanbu.

The group headed down to the city, and the closer they got to it the more suffocating the atmosphere became. The heat and humidity were made worse by the dust. Bashir covered his face with the end of his turban, as he always did when the air grew clogged, and the other two followed suit.

When they entered the city, they were immediately followed by a throng of people: the poor who had lost their way in the war and had no means to return home, as well as disabled soldiers in dire need of money. Human misery was gathered in this tiny, unbearable place on a vast scale. Children clung to their legs, whining for money, and women cried as loudly as they could to draw attention to their plight. These desperate people followed the group for a while but gradually started to lose interest until they left them altogether.

'Thank God you didn't put your hand in your pocket for some money,' Sadleir said to Bashir. 'If you had, we would never have got away from them.'

'It makes me really sad. The more desperate the situation, the more difficult it is to provide help. It breaks my heart that I can't do anything for these people.'

Yanbu contained a strange mixture of people that Sadleir had never imagined finding in this part of the world. There were Moroccan horsemen with their distinctive turbans and gilded swords, stocky Albanian foot soldiers with their twisted moustaches, Bedouins in their flowing white robes, in addition to Egyptians and Africans who wore an array of mismatching clothes and clashing colours and carried an assortment of weapons. All these disparate groups of people had become a tool of death in the hands of Ibrahim Pasha, who moved them wherever and whenever he wished.

Sadleir asked Met'ab to look for accommodation for them where they might rest until they found a way out of Yanbu. Before Met'ab went off, he arranged to meet them at one of the small cafés found all over the harbour.

In the café, the waiter came and stood in front of them without saying a word. His clothes were soiled with remains of food.

267

Bashir asked him to bring some drinking water and grilled fish. The waiter didn't answer or comment and his face was expressionless. A little later, he returned with some food and water, which he carelessly laid on the table.

Bashir took the fish in his hand and began to peel it. But feeling repelled by its smell, he left it and ordered something else. Sadleir in contrast ate heartily. They stayed long at the café waiting for Met'ab's return. When he finally arrived, he was exhausted after having spent a long time looking for accommodation.

'I found a nice place. It may not be exactly what you hoped for, but it's more comfortable than a tent in the desert,' Met'ab said smiling.

'Anything will be better than a tent, Met'ab,' said Bashir, 'I can't wait for a comfortable bed after such a long and tiring journey.'

The group went to the hotel in the middle of the city near the harbour. It was built of clay and its walls were covered in white plaster. It was reasonably clean compared with the surrounding buildings. Bashir and Sadleir chose a room while Met'ab preferred to sleep alone. They put their belongings in the room and sat together on the roof of the hotel where wooden chairs had been placed to catch the sea breeze and escape from the heat.

Bashir pointed to the horizon, the deep blue where the sky joined the sea. 'The sea is in front of us now, and we must decide what we should do.'

'We'll go to Oman, Bashir. You can easily get home from there. As for me, I'll go back to India. Met'ab will have to decide where he wishes to go.'

'But what route will we take?'

'The most direct,' Sadleir answered. 'We'll go down to the

harbour and ask about the best and safest way. The war has turned the whole region into chaos where you can't tell friend from foe.'

Met'ab didn't say much, for what he had seen of the war upset him greatly. He wanted sleep to carry him away from his memories. 'Let's get some sleep now. The past days have been rough and God only knows what the coming days will be like.'

At midnight Sadleir woke up with terrible stomach pain and a high fever. He ran towards a pail at the end of the room and threw up. The sound of vomiting was so loud that it woke Bashir. He got up and went to Sadleir, and held his head in his hands to relieve Sadleir's nausea. When he touched Sadleir's head, he felt how hot it was and knew that his friend was in very bad shape. Sadleir, gripped by a strange hysteria, felt his soul was leaving his body. He began to tremble uncontrollably, which forced Bashir to sit on his chest and hold his hands to stop the violent shakes.

Bashir was afraid Sadleir was about to die. He hurried to Met'ab's room and asked him to come with him. Met'ab went running into the room with Bashir. When he saw Sadleir's state, he began to recite verses that he knew by heart to protect Sadleir from the devils and demons possessing him. After a few minutes of tension and fear, Sadleir grew quiet and passed out.

Bashir asked Met'ab to help him put Sadleir in bed. Having done that, Met'ab placed his ear near Sadleir's nose to make sure he was still alive and breathing. He then lifted his head saying, 'He's alive, Bashir. The devils couldn't kill him. But why should they possess him instead of one of us? Is it because he's Christian and we're Muslim?'

'He has fever, Met'ab. Get a wet piece of cloth and put it on his forehead. Stay with him while I go to fetch a doctor, if I can find one in this city.'

Met'ab sat cooling Sadleir's head with the cloth. Sadleir opened his eyes as though he were opening them for the first time, and the light coming through the window seemed too strong for him. 'Met'ab, what's happening to me? Please help me. I feel like I'm dying,' he said.

'Don't worry, Sir. You've been possessed by the devils of this town. You must have done something to anger them. But don't worry, I'll stay with you and recite some spells to banish the evil spirits.'

'Get me a drink of water, please, my mouth is horribly dry.'

With an explosive sound from the lower part of his body, Sadleir had an attack of uncontrollable diarrhea. Met'ab looked at him in astonishment:

'The devils have decided to leave your body, but they went out the wrong way! They should have gone out of your mouth, but they're obviously obnoxious devils.'

'I'm sorry, Met'ab, I can't do anything to clean myself,' Sadleir said.

Covering his nose with a piece of cloth, Met'ab began to clean Sadleir. Then he moved him to Bashir's clean bed and removed the soiled sheets. He refilled the water in the jar and opened the windows. He covered Sadleir and put the wet piece of cloth on his forehead while repeating more spells to exorcise evil spirits.

A few hours later, Bashir returned with a young Egyptian who was working as a male nurse in Ibrahim Pasha's army. The young man asked Sadleir to stick out his tongue and then felt his pulse. He asked him a few questions and then turned to

Bashir and told him that Sadleir had food poisoning. He had to rest and drink liquids that had been boiled beforehand.

Met'ab listened to the conversation, believing that the Egyptian was an expert in exorcising evil spirits and that he had tried to communicate with those spirits by touching Sadleir's tongue and looking into his eyes. When the young man was about to leave, Bashir placed a few coins in his palm and thanked him.

Met'ab said to Bashir, 'What are you doing, man? Why did you let him go? We don't know how to talk to spirits. You've seen what they did to us when we tried to comfort Sadleir. Let him stay. We may need him.'

'We won't. He said Sadleir has food poisoning and we have to look after him until he gets well.'

'Poisoning? Of course he'll be poisoned if the devils decide to escape from his stomach. Do you think stomach devils are nice, clean spirits? They may leave their shoes inside the man's stomach. Had you been here earlier, you would know that they are dirty devils capable of anything.'

Bashir said a little irritably, 'Haven't you heard me, Met'ab? It's not the work of evil spirits. It's food poisoning from the fish Sadleir ate. Now go your way. You've really got on my nerves with your talk.'

Sadleir spent a whole day in bed with fever, and Bashir and Met'ab took turns looking after him. The following day, Sadleir opened his eyes. His temperature had dropped a little and he asked for some water. On the third day, he was substantially better and began to eat some fruits and vegetables.

Several days later, Sadleir and his companions went to the docks and asked around for a ship that would take them to Oman.

They were informed of a vessel that was due to sail to Muscat via Aden and soon found the captain to discuss the possibility of joining him and to negotiate a price. They reached an agreement, settling on a fee that Bashir found preposterously steep. But although the ship looked old and dilapidated, and was almost unfit for travel, Sadleir insisted on leaving at any cost.

Chapter 43

Ras al-Khaimah

ONE OF SHEIKH HASSAN'S men came out and stepped onto the shore, a white flag in his hand. Out at sea, on the British ships, all eyes watched him as he drew closer, wading into the water until it reached up to his knees. He stopped and began to wave the flag in long, sweeping motions. The tears in his eyes trickled down to his beard. But this was lost on the officers in the ships, despite their long telescopes focused squarely on him and his white flag.

Nothing seemed to happen. The ships exchanged signals and an eerie silence descended.

Finally, a small boat was lowered from the *Eden*, with an officer, four armed guards and four oarsmen on board. When the craft reached the shore, the men disembarked and the officer ordered one of the guards to hand him the Union Jack, which he proceeded to plant forcefully in the sand in a deliberate act of provocation. His hands on his waist, he stood haughtily as he looked towards the ruined wall where the besieged men were hiding.

If anything, his expression became even more arrogant as Sheikh Hassan, accompanied by Erhama and a group of fighters, gradually emerged from behind the wall. Their appearance spoke volumes: faces covered in dust, congealed blood on their garments. They had not eaten or slept in two days and, as the dishevelled party shuffled towards him, the British officer narrowed his eyes on the leader. Could this be the same Sheikh Hassan whose very name filled British sailors with dread? The officer took in the features of the short man, from the turban and unkempt beard to the shabby clothes and broken sandals.

This was far from his usual attire. Sheikh Hassan had even dispensed with the weapons that he always carried, the gold dagger, the pistol inlaid with silver and the sword slung over his shoulder. That day, he was simply a man representing his people in this humiliating surrender. The ruler stood there, nonetheless, with his head held high, buoyed by the sense of duty towards his people.

'Are you Sheikh Hassan?' demanded the British officer.

'Yes, I am Sheikh Hassan. What exactly do you want?'

Putting his hand into a pocket of his jacket, the officer brought out a folded sheet of paper. 'We expect you to sign these terms of surrender without delay,' he said bluntly.

Sheikh Hassan read the paper then handed it to Erhama, who did little more than scan it before passing it in turn to one of the sheikh's aides. Erhama was busy watching Sheikh Hassan; he saw his friend's face progressively turning a deep red, his cheeks swelling as though they were about to explode.

He decided to step in. 'We will need some time to consider this,' he told the Englishman. 'And then I will need to speak to Captain Loch.'

'Just who do you think you are to demand to see the captain?' the officer asked, his tone barely concealing the contempt he felt.

'Tell him that Erhama bin Jaber wishes to speak to him,' the pirate replied evenly. 'He knows me.' He pointed toward the

274

ships at sea with an accusatory finger. 'And now return to your vessel and take your flag with you. We will be here tomorrow morning at the same time.'

Erhama nodded to Sheikh Hassan, who led the party back to the devastated town.

The British officer ordered his men back onto the boat, leaving the Union Jack behind. A young Arab ran forward, pulled out the flagpole and threw it in the direction of the officer, who had no option but to pick it up and pass it to one of his soldiers.

In the evening, Sheikh Hassan sat on the beach surrounded by his advisers and men to discuss the terms of surrender that had been delivered to them.

According to these terms, they had to hand over their weapons and warships to the British, pledge not to fight them again, and open their ports and markets fully to British trade. Moreover, they had to vow not to harbour the enemies of Britain, not to enter into any agreements with other military powers without their consent, and to accept the presence of British troops on their soil. In return, Britain would pledge to protect them from attacks by other forces.

Sheikh Hassan looked up. 'They also talk about the riches they will extract from our land and promise to give us a percentage.' He paused as he took in the expressions of his advisers. 'Now tell me what you think of these terms.'

Closest to the sheikh sat an old man with a white beard. 'What if we don't accept them?' he asked.

'They will resume their fire,' the sheikh replied simply. 'They will kill twice as many again and they will occupy our land.' He added sombrely, 'God only knows what they will do with any survivors after that.'

The white-bearded man nodded slowly. 'I've known you since you were young,' he said. 'Even back then, you struck me as wise, with the interests of your people at heart. Today, we must choose either to die and lose our land and people, or surrender and lose some of our dignity.' His eyes fixed on Sheikh Hassan. 'Life is more important than the loss of some dignity. And besides, even with this agreement, who could possibly stop us from trading? Those foreigners will be here for a short while, but sooner or later they will have to leave. But we will remain. We will prevail.'

Erhama smiled thinly as he listened to the words of the old man. There were some people who supported his view, but others – especially the more headstrong young men – had previously spoken belligerently. He now expected some of them to put in a word for continuing the fight. Erhama glanced around the gathering, his eyes finally settling on the sheikh's son-in-law, who had been among the most vocal in calling for a holy war against the invaders.

But the young man was quiet and he did not even seem to be following the discussion. His eyes, filled with tears, were fixed on a point in the distance, on the creek that had so recently engulfed dozens of people in the fury of war. Erhama noticed the white flag twisting in the young man's hands as though he were throttling a beast. This was the same flag that had signalled their surrender to the British ships.

'And what do you think, Erhama?'

Erhama blinked, focused on the subject at hand and turned to Sheikh Hassan who had just asked him to reply.

He paused and then answered with a gentle nod towards the tearful young man. 'Look at us,' he said dejectedly. 'This man has lost his parents, his wife and two of his children, who were

276

not yet five years old.' He shrugged helplessly, desperately trying to control his own emotions. 'You know my opinion, Sheikh Hassan.' He indicated the white-bearded man. 'I agree with our brother here. We've already lost a great many of our loved ones and we don't need to lose more.' He placed his hand squarely on the old man's shoulder. 'Yes, we are seafarers and the whole world is our oyster. We can still trade. And what of these riches buried in our soil? What are they? I say we let them dig for them and if there is anything of value, they will have to give us our share.'

Sheikh Hassan looked at the men sitting around him and said finally, 'I'll sign their terms tomorrow. If anyone has any objections let him speak now and in front of everyone, for I won't change my mind afterwards.'

There was a long silence, interrupted only by the sound of waves breaking on the shore.

'Very well then,' said Sheikh Hassan. 'I pray to God that this is for the good of our people.'

The following day at the appointed time, Sheikh Hassan and his companions returned to the same spot on the beach, while a boat carrying a group of British officers and guards came to shore. As soon as the boat landed, Captain Loch jumped out and held out his hand to Sheikh Hassan. He then shook hands more warmly with Erhama.

'I was happy to learn that you were here,' he said to him. 'At least we can resolve two problems at the same time. I wanted to tell you about the kidnapped Englishwoman and her daughter.' He turned to address Sheikh Hassan. 'But first, have you signed the terms?'

'Yes, we have,' replied Sheikh Hassan tersely. 'I hope that you will keep to your side of the bargain.'

'We don't fight for the sake of it,' countered Loch. 'We fight to protect our interests. So as long as you don't pose a threat to those interests, we will not have to fire our guns at you.' He continued in a more conciliatory tone, 'We would like to be your friends, Sheikh Hassan.' He ordered one of his officers to pitch a tent on the beach and added with a grin, 'We'll have supper together – we'll call it a supper of peace.'

Sheikh Hassan declined with a sharp shake of his head. 'How can I have supper with you when my people haven't tasted food in many days? We're in a state of mourning, Captain. I hope you will respect that.'

Loch ordered one of his officers to bring food from the supply ship to distribute to the people. Everyone heard Loch say to the officer, 'Bring as much food as you can. We need these people as much as they need food.'

In the evening, the area that had been a battleground only a day earlier had been transformed into something completely unwarlike. There was a tent with lights inside that was so grand that Sheikh Hassan's men could not help but look impressed. British soldiers sat around the tent enjoying meat cooked on spits while, a few paces from them, their Arab counterparts did the same, all to a loud chatter of different languages. To a casual observer, the scene looked almost festive. But there was, none-theless, an unmistakable undercurrent of antagonism, judging from the hostile glances between the groups, and a sense that the wounds were too deep and too recent to be healed merely by a handshake and a shared meal.

'What did you mean when you said, "We need these people as much as they need food"?' Erhama asked Loch.

'Oh, you heard that, did you?' he replied. 'I really must be more careful.' He shrugged. 'Orders straight from the top.'

278

When Erhama pressed him, Loch explained, 'His Majesty's Government has changed its opinion about the western coast of the Gulf and all who live here. Basically, we are to become allies – providing food is simply what friends do.'

Chapter 44

Aden, Southern Arabia

A FEW DAYS LATER, THE boat carrying Sadleir, Met'ab and Bashir sailed into Aden. Sadleir could see a great number of ships docked there and felt like going ashore to stretch his legs. But the captain shook his head adamantly, opened the trapdoor leading below decks and asked them to hide.

'You mustn't be seen by the harbour officials,' he said anxiously. 'They would ask for your papers and imprison you.' They would also cause the captain trouble.

Sadleir peered down: he could see dead rats in the hold. 'It's absolutely filthy,' he complained. 'We can't go down there.'

The captain pleaded with them. 'Please be patient until the harbour officials have finished their inspection,' he said. 'They'll be here soon. Don't make a sound now. If they don't find you, they'll just ask for their usual bribe and then leave.'

They went below and were overpowered by the dank, musty air, which was only exacerbated by the heat. Some sea water had seeped into the hold to form puddles everywhere that swilled around whenever a wave hit the ship, causing the dead rodents to float to other dark corners.

Met'ab threw up and his vomit mixed with the stagnant water under their feet.

When Bashir started to feel sick, he forced himself to think of Salwa and how he had kissed her delicate hand at their last meeting. He wanted to get back to her as quickly as possible, and that thought alone took his mind off the repulsive surroundings.

The minutes passed excruciatingly slowly.

Eventually, the trapdoor was opened, letting in some fresh air. They raced to climb up on deck.

'Have they been?'

'Yes. As expected they asked for a bribe. It seems to be the only way to make a living for those working in the harbours these days.'

After getting fresh supplies, the ship sailed east, following the southern coast of the Arabian Peninsula as it headed back to the Gulf.

The days were long, uneventful and hot as usual until they felt the ship change direction to the north. Eventually, from a great distance, they saw the black peaks of rocky mountains and the weather became particularly humid. They knew that they were nearing Muscat.

When the ship entered Muscat harbour, Sadleir stood at the bow trying to see the British vessels that were docked there. He noticed that three ships he did not recognise were anchored together. Then he spotted the *Eden* on its own, which meant that Loch was in town and would be able to facilitate his return to Bombay.

It felt odd to be back. He had been cut off from his command and his fellow countrymen for so long that he was uncharacteristically nervous. How, for instance, would he take to hearing English again after all this time?

The ship docked in the harbour and Sadleir jumped onto the wharf and headed first to Gulap's office since it was the closest. He was stopped at the entrance by a guard who wanted to know the purpose of his visit. The guard had mistaken him for a native because of his attire. When he heard Sadleir speak English fluently, he raised his eyebrows and allowed him to enter. It was the first time he had ever seen an Englishman who looked and smelled like that.

Sadleir went into Gulap's office and was surprised to find someone else sitting at the desk.

'Where's Gulap?' Sadleir asked.

'And who, sir, might you be?'

'I'm Major Sadleir. I've just returned from a long mission and this is the office of the East India Company, is it not?'

'It is,' the man confirmed.

'So where's Gulap?' repeated Sadleir.

The man invited Sadleir to take a seat. 'He is no more,' he said simply and asked a servant to bring some water and sherbet for the officer.

'You mean he has been transferred out of Muscat?'

'I thought the whole town knew Gulap's story.'

'What story, sir?'

'Gulap claimed that Erhama the pirate had kidnapped two British subjects on their way to Basra. But the whole story was invented, which caused us a lot of trouble. Captain Loch –' He paused to ask, 'Have you heard of him?'

Sadleir nodded.

The official resumed his story and described how Loch had entered that very office and, seizing hold of Gulap, had threatened him. When Gulap had not confessed straight away, he had been tied to the seat Sadleir was sitting in while the captain's men searched his office. They had found two purses filled with pearls in one of the locked drawers and Gulap, when asked how he had come by them, had told Loch they were a gift from a merchant. He had changed his story soon enough, though, when the captain's men had begun to beat him. Then Loch had taken out a dagger and bent over Gulap.

At that moment, the man got up from his chair and, bending over Sadleir, he showed him a sharp groove in one of the armrests. Placing his finger in the groove, he said, 'This was made by the knife that went through Gulap's hand.'

It was then that Gulap had gone to pieces and confessed that the whole story had been made up. A Bahraini merchant had wanted Loch to pursue Erhama in revenge for the ruler's son who had been killed at sea by the pirate.

'So what happened to Gulap?'

'Captain Loch sent him to Bombay after confiscating all his property in Muscat. He also wrote a message to the Governor of Bombay asking him to seize all of Gulap's property in India in reparation for the cost incurred by the Royal Navy in looking for the British subjects who had supposedly been abducted.'

'What a sad end for the man.'

'The story doesn't finish there, I'm afraid,' the official said and described how the Indian had been taken on board a merchantman and locked up in the hold with some pirates who had been captured. Halfway to Bombay, he had forced a piece of cable down his throat – the same thick rope used for tying up ships – and choked to death. His body had been unceremoniously thrown into the ocean.

'May I ask once again who you are, sir?'

'My name is David Matthews and I worked at the governor's office in Bushehr until I was appointed to replace Gulap in Muscat.' He was thankful to be gone from that fly-infested hellhole where everything and everyone had got on his nerves; by contrast, nothing seemed to bother him here, except the heat.

Sadleir left Matthews's office and met Bashir and Met'ab outside; they looked as dejected as he felt.

'It's obvious things are changing much faster than I ever anticipated, my friend,' he said to Bashir.

'Did he have any news of my father, Sadleir? I'll have no peace of mind until I know what's happened to him. He's the sort who can't live quietly,' he added reflectively. 'If he doesn't have enemies, he creates them.'

'Let's get some rest now, Bashir, and tomorrow we'll enquire about all that.'

Sadleir led them to a lodging house he had stayed at before, near the harbour. He longed to take a bath and change his clothes; and he realised with a start that he had not had a proper wash since setting foot in Qatif. He needed to have a bath and a fresh start in life.

Sadleir knew where to find Loch; whenever the captain was in town, he always seemed to set up his base in the office of His Majesty's representative in Muscat, Sir Rupert. He had met Sir Rupert on his first day in Oman, when he was still nursing his wounded pride after Erhama had taken the Indian sword during his trip from Bombay.

Sadleir and Bashir managed to make their way to Sir Rupert's office with great difficulty since they needed to explain the purpose of their visit to everyone they met, from the guard outside the building to Sir Rupert's clerk.

Loch was pleasantly surprised to see Sadleir enter the room followed by Bashir. He interrupted his conversation with Sir

Rupert and stood up to greet the officer. Sadleir, by contrast, was far from pleased to see the captain again after all this time; no officer or gentleman would torture a man the way Loch had tormented Gulap.

Sensing Sadleir's cool response, Loch became less effusive in his welcome and, smiling wanly, the two shook hands. He looked over at Bashir and asked him to wait outside, explaining to Sir Rupert that the young Arab was the pirate's son and should not be privy to their conversation.

Sadleir addressed Sir Rupert instead. 'With your permission, sir, this man has proved indispensable to our mission. With all due respect to the captain, he seems to have forgotten that we would never have got the Indian sword back in the first place without him.' He placed his hand squarely on his friend's shoulder. 'We crossed the desert together to reach Ibrahim Pasha. He deserves to be here.'

Loch was about to argue the point when Sir Rupert thought it best to intercede and he offered them two seats in front of his desk. 'Tell us about your mission, Major.'

Sadleir sat down. 'I think we all knew from the start that my quest was doomed to failure. Ibrahim Pasha's crimes in the towns and villages of Nejd would make the devil himself blush. Could we really have entered into a pact with such a monster?'

They discussed the unsuccessful mission at some length and Loch explained how plans had to change over time to take account of evolving situations or different circumstances.

Sadleir looked the captain straight in the eye as he asked him, 'Was your treatment of Gulap part of that new plan, sir?'

'I say, how dare you speak to me like that!' said Loch; the man had barely concealed the insolence in his tone. 'I need to remind *you*, sir, that I am your commanding officer until such time as you leave the Gulf. Besides, that snake got his comeuppance for lying about the kidnapped woman and her daughter.' He gave Bashir an evil look as he added, 'And that pirate father of yours will soon get his just desserts as well.'

Sadleir spoke slowly, 'I have seen a lot during my trek through the desert – and you will get my full report – and what I have witnessed is piracy on a far wider and more organised scale by people who call themselves civilised.' He paused and then added deliberately, 'I, for one, will not call Erhama a pirate.'

Feeling that the discussion was getting out of control, Sir Rupert asked Sadleir to tone down his speech and ordered sherbet to be brought for everyone.

Loch ignored Sir Rupert. 'Call him what you will,' he replied sharply. 'He killed four of my men a few days ago and I'm on my way to look for him. He's finished, as far as I'm concerned. I'll kill him with my own hands if I have to.'

He rose to his feet and reached for his cocked hat.

Bashir stood up and said, 'May I accompany you, Captain? I would like to see him and talk to him at least one more time before he dies.'

Sadleir looked at him in astonishment and shook his head as though he thought his friend had gone completely mad.

Chapter 45

Ras al-Khaimah

IN RAS AL-KHAIMAH, SHEIKH Hassan sombrely took his leave from Loch and retired, followed by his aides, as the victory celebration continued around them. Erhama was about to join them when Loch invited him to his tent for a private conversation.

'Don't you find it strange, Erhama, that only yesterday we were fighting while today we're sitting like friends sharing a meal? Isn't it rather bizarre?'

'I'm used to this kind of thing from you,' said Erhama. 'I never wished to see all this bloodshed and, besides, I knew that the time would come when we had to sign a peace agreement with you – we couldn't stand in the face of your mighty ships and guns forever.'

'I wish everyone had your wisdom, Erhama. I know that people will hate us for many years to come,' Loch said pensively, 'but I'm hopeful that commercial interests will overcome the hatred one day. We'll start the process of reconciliation from here, from this camp and from this tent.'

It was a one-sided process, thought Erhama, where the victor dictated the terms. 'It's clear that you have taken the whole coast,' he said. 'So have you signed similar agreements with other tribal leaders?'

'No, not yet. The news from Ras al-Khaimah will take a few days to get out. We will offer reconciliation to all those who oppose our presence in the region. After hearing what happened, they are likely to agree.'

'Then your battle is over.'

'Not quite.' There was still the small matter of a pirate at large. Loch produced his pipe from his pocket, filled it with tobacco and lit it. Then, puffing steadily in order to fill the tent with smoke, he told Erhama the fabricated tale of the abducted woman and her daughter and how the representative of the East India Company in Muscat had led him on a wild goose chase to Bahrain and Bushehr. 'I returned to Muscat and squeezed that lying rat until he confessed that he'd made it all up. It seems a Bahraini trader bribed him in order to accuse you of the crime.'

Erhama's eyes narrowed; he was not at all surprised that the Al-Khalifas had been behind such a plot. 'I'll devote my time from now on to my own battle. Now that you have got rid of your enemies, Captain, let me remind you of our agreement – I also need to get rid of mine.'

Loch inhaled the pipe smoke deeply and then exhaled so that a screen formed between them. He explained that the plan had changed. It seemed less likely now that Ibrahim Pasha would join a pact against the Wahhabis and victory had been redefined. All that mattered now was trade – the Empire had changed its mind about Arabs. Britain would deal with the devil himself so long as he bought their merchandise. 'Orders straight from the top.'

Erhama frowned. 'What do you mean?'

He meant that victory had now been defined by the Admiralty as removing every single obstacle to that trade, but he said, 'I don't quite understand why I honour my deal with you, Erhama. I've done many things in my life, but I haven't gone back on our agreement.'

'That's because you know you'd lose many men,' said Erhama frankly. 'At any rate, I don't care about all that as long as I have my revenge on my enemies.'

Loch shook his head. He had made that deal to retrieve the Indian sword; now that the tripartite pact was not in the offing, the sword and, consequently, the deal had become irrelevant. 'I'm afraid your presence is causing us a lot of problems.'

At that point Loch called the guards standing outside his tent. After his experiences in Bushehr, he had learned not to leave his ship without armed protection.

Two guards stood behind Erhama and held him down while they waited for the captain's instructions.

'Tie him up and take him to the *Eden*,' he ordered. 'Place him in the brig and make sure he doesn't talk to anyone.'

Erhama's stunned look turned to fury. 'Curse you and your damn agreements,' he shouted. 'You don't have an ounce of honour in you. You'll pay dearly for this.'

Loch said nothing but signalled to the guards to take the prisoner away. Then he uncorked a bottle of vintage wine and poured himself a glass. He felt he deserved a celebratory drink.

He toasted himself as he imagined the Gulf region after all the parties had signed the peace agreement. He pictured the accolades he would receive from His Majesty's Government – perhaps even a knighthood – in recognition of his successful mission. This victory would erase the memory of his earlier defeat and he could now look forward to a promotion in the Royal Navy.

The guards tied Erhama's hands behind his back and pushed him towards the beach where a boat was waiting to take them to the *Eden*. They placed him between them at the front and the two oarsmen who sat in the middle began to row. The boat moved slowly towards the ship.

Halfway between the shore and the *Eden*, something struck the bottom of the boat and caused it to capsize, throwing all its passengers into the water. As he struggled to breathe, Erhama felt a hand take hold of him and lift him up to the surface. Looking into the man's face, he realised it was Dirar and all around them he heard muffled screams as his men drove their knives into the bodies of the British soldiers. Erhama's bonds were cut and they swam towards the shore where the *Ghatrousha* lay waiting for them.

The next morning, Loch was awakened by flies buzzing around his head. He waved his hand in irritation and opened his eyes. He yawned, tried to ignore the taste of stale wine in his mouth and got up to walk outside. He almost tripped over a guard lying fast asleep on the ground, so he kicked him in the foot, causing him to stir. Looking around, he saw his men sprawled everywhere like beached porpoises, filling the entire area between his tent and the shore. They, too, had slept through the night and early morning under the influence of drink after celebrating their victory.

The guard who had been kicked woke the others with a loud yell and, a few minutes later, the whole camp was a hive of activity. Tents were folded and fires extinguished, and the soldiers moved to the water's edge, waiting to be ferried back onto the ships.

Suddenly someone shouted, 'There are bodies floating in the sea!'

Some officers and soldiers hurried to drag the bodies out of the water and onto the beach. There were four of them, all with slashed necks and discoloured faces.

'They're ours, sir,' an officer said to Loch as he came to investigate.

He stared down and immediately recognised the two guards who had been charged with escorting Erhama to the *Eden*.

'Damn!' he exclaimed. 'Damn, damn and damn!' He pointed up and down the beach frantically. 'Look for Erhama the pirate, and quickly!' he bellowed to his men. 'He can't be far.' But he suspected he was already a safe distance away; the corsair had slipped through their fingers once again. He wished he did not have to head straight back to Muscat to report on the subjugation of Ras al-Khaimah, since all he really wanted now was to track down the scoundrel and blast his boats to oblivion.

A long way south of the British camp, Erhama was reunited with his ship and his men. He asked them to sit around him as he described the ferocious battle between Sheikh Hassan's fighters and the British.

'In the end they forced him to sign a peace agreement. It will deprive us of one of our havens where we used to hide and get supplies. We still have our fort in Dammam.

'But I believe we will soon lose that as well because the whole coast will remain under the British yoke for a long time to come. I have a plan, my brothers. Our only hope is Bahrain. We will take the island. If we succeed, we will all become rich for I will give you more land than you can imagine.'

There were loud cheers. Most of Erhama's men had been with him at sea for decades and many were keen to settle down and start families.

Erhama held up his palm and silenced them. 'But our battle for Bahrain will not be easy. We will face two enemies: the Al-Khalifas and the British, who are now demanding my head. From now on we will not be able to appear in public and our life will be much harder. But we have each other, my brothers, and I can promise you this: either we make our life and don't allow others to make it for us, or we die with honour.'

There was rapturous applause. The northern tip of Qatar was Erhama's favourite hiding place whenever things got difficult. The *Ghatrousha* dropped anchor at her usual place between the Qatari coast and a low-lying islet that appeared and disappeared according to the tide. Once the ship was anchored, the sailors began to relax, cook, make tea and talk, enjoying a respite from the hardships of travelling or fighting.

Erhama summoned Dirar and asked him to go in secret to Zubara to bring Abu Matar to the ship; he had missed his friend and wished to know the news of the area from him.

Dirar went ashore at night, hired two horses the following morning and was in Zubara by the evening, making his way surreptitiously through the town's alleyways to Abu Matar's house.

Abu Matar opened the door when he heard the knocking, greeted Dirar and, on reading a handwritten message from Erhama, immediately got dressed and rode back with Dirar to the northern tip of the Qatar peninsula. Along the way, Abu Matar kept wondering what Erhama's reaction would be when he heard that Bashir was still alive; would he accept the fact that he had survived or would he still wish to kill his son?

They were on board the *Ghatrousha* the next day and Erhama hugged Abu Matar warmly and kissed his head; he was one of the few people Erhama trusted completely. Abu Matar accepted his seat beside Erhama while they were served tea and dates. 'I have some news, Erhama,' he said cautiously, 'which I feel will make you happy.'

'Tell me, my dear friend, for I haven't heard a single piece of good news for a long time. Tell me what it is.'

'As far as I know, your son Bashir is alive. He managed to swim to safety.' Abu Matar thought it wise not to mention that he knew it was Erhama himself who had thrown his son overboard.

For a second, Erhama remained unmoved as though he were still waiting for the news. Then, deliberately, he turned his face away and covered it with his scarf. Abu Matar noticed how Erhama's upper body heaved and he was relieved because it sounded as if he was crying for joy.

'Tell me more, Abu Matar.'

He related Bashir's account of how he had swum to shore and arrived in Zubara with blisters on his feet.

'And Ali?'

'He didn't make it,' Abu Matar said sadly. 'He drowned. May he rest in peace.'

Erhama lowered his head and fixed his gaze on a spot on the deck as he tried to bring to mind the events of that day. At length he lifted his head and said, 'Where is Bashir?'

Abu Matar shrugged. 'I advised him to stay close to you and I know he travelled to Qatif. But I don't know whether he's still there.'

Erhama was torn by conflicting emotions and his hand trembled as he reached for his tea. The veins bulged on the back of his hand and his entire arm was covered in scars and burn marks where Abu Misfer had administered his scalding therapy. His hand was shaking so much that he had to support it with his other, partly lifeless hand.

Nodding towards the burn marks on his arm, Abu Matar teased gently, 'If you roasted your whole arm, Erhama, it would not stop trembling. You've aged and you need to admit it. Stop torturing yourself.'

'I know that, dear friend.' He knew he had little time left to do what he needed to do.

'Will you make peace with your son, Erhama?' Abu Matar asked him directly.

'You remind me of Bin Ofaisan. He always talks about reconciliation and forgetting the past. But I can't forget the past, my friend. I wish I could. But I'm the sort of person who takes his decisions very seriously and does everything in his power to stick to them.' He nodded sadly. 'I envy people who can forget the past or change their decisions according to circumstances. Unfortunately I can't. I will die soon and all I can hope is that my life will have had some value.'

Abu Matar tried to change the subject. 'I've also heard that the British are moving in huge numbers along the coast, giving away quantities of rice from India. Do you like rice, Erhama?'

Erhama was not listening.

Abu Matar continued, 'Apparently people like this rice – they say it's lighter and easier to cook than the wheat from Al-Ahsa and Nejd.'

'All I hope for now is to see my son before I die.'

'Why are you going on about death like this?' Abu Matar scolded him. 'You used to talk about life and now you talk about death. What's happened?'

'A lot,' replied Erhama simply. 'Since the death of Sheikh Salman's son I've known that my days are numbered. I had one enemy in the past – my cousins, the Al-Khalifas. I knew that I would lose my position in the Gulf if I fought the British. That's why I never attacked their ships and concentrated on fighting only my enemy.

'But now that the British have forced Sheikh Hassan to sign a peace agreement and are about to make similar agreements with other Gulf sheikhs, I'll be the outsider in this new order – an outcast. If I fight anyone, I'll be branded a rebel.'

He knew what he needed to do; the news of Bashir's survival, as well as the new political situation, had made it clear. He called Dirar and asked him to prepare some things and then, turning to Abu Matar, said urgently, 'I can't wait any longer. We're preparing to raid the Al-Khalifas before they attack us. I'll say goodbye to you, Abu Matar. This is the goodbye of someone saying farewell to life.'

Dirar returned with the things in a bundle. 'My will is in here,' Erhama said. 'Please keep it and give it to Bashir when you see him. This bundle also contains some money for him. Don't give it to him until you are certain that I'm dead. Do you understand, my friend?'

Abu Matar nodded. 'If I can't understand you, who can?'

'Thank you.' Erhama turned to Dirar and said, 'We set sail for our fort in Dammam at dawn.'

Chapter 46

Muharraq

S HEIKH SALMAN AL-KHALIFA SHOOK his cup of coffee to indicate that he did not want any more. He turned to the merchant sitting on his left in the *majlis* of his Muharraq palace and said, 'Tell me what happened, Abu Saleh. Has your plan failed?'

Abu Saleh drank another cup before replying, 'I believe it has, Sheikh Salman. The representative of the East India Company in Muscat confessed everything to the British, and the Indian who used to work for me and who introduced Gulap to me has vanished without a trace.'

'Did he take your money when he fled?'

'No, sir, he didn't. But I depended on him for my business as he was well connected to the Indians working in the Gulf area.'

'And why didn't the British hold you responsible for the plot?'

'Gulap told them the truth,' said the merchant. 'He said that I had paid him with pearls to get rid of Erhama. But he also admitted that the whole story about British citizens being abducted was his own invention. That's why the British closed the case after his confession.'

Sheikh Salman turned to his other guests in the *majlis*. 'Listen, gentlemen,' he said loudly. 'As you all know, Erhama brutally killed my son at sea. I buried him in the same clothes he was wearing and I didn't accept condolences for his death. Since then, I have waited for the right time to take my revenge. I hoped Abu Saleh's plan would put an end to this criminal, but unfortunately his plan has failed. I tell you now that I will move within five days to fight Erhama.' His eyes picked out each guest individually as he added, 'Whoever wishes to come with me should meet me at the harbour. I will not force anyone to join me, but I wish everyone to know that the sea will not be safe for us as long as this man remains free to come and go as he pleases. Get ready for we may have a decisive battle ahead.'

One of the guests spoke out. 'I heard that Erhama killed his own son by throwing him overboard. This man is a monster in every sense of the word – a person who is heartless enough to kill his own son is capable of doing anything. He is a man who has lost all human feelings. My advice is that you should leave him alone – this type of person makes many enemies and does not survive long.'

Sheikh Salman shook his head emphatically. 'But I can't let him live after he murdered my son.'

One of the religious leaders spoke next. 'Islam urges us to forgive and God rewards those who forgive and show mercy. Why do we forget that? With this decision you will take all your brothers, friends and fighters to the sea to do battle with some-one who may die today or tomorrow.'

'Revenge runs in our veins. The thought of it prevents me from sleeping and eating. So let me carry out what I have set my mind to do.'

He raised his palm in a gesture to signify that he would brook no further discussion on the matter.

During the next few days, the harbour of Muharraq became a hive of activity. Groups of men carried supplies to ships while others fixed hulls and sails and made sure they were seaworthy, and still others gathered weapons and ammunition and distributed them to the vessels.

On the day of their departure, Sheikh Salman and his men performed the dawn prayer on the decks of all the ships and then the flotilla set sail for Dammam.

Buoyed by thoughts of revenge, Sheikh Salman turned a deaf ear to the wives and children crying on the wharves as his men waved goodbye to them. The wind picked up and carried the ships to the northwest until the men on board could no longer hear their families.

In the deep blue space ahead of him, Sheikh Salman saw a rapid succession of images of his dead son: the little boy who tried to wear his headdress like his father, and the cheeky little imp who had pushed his swimming instructor into the water in all his clothes as a prank.

For a second, Sheikh Salman even smiled at that distant memory until his eyes focused on the real horizon and on the unrelenting agony of never being able to hold his son again.

The *Eden* sailed from Muscat to Dammam with another man-of-war and a supply ship in tow. On board were Loch, Sadleir and Bashir.

Loch was intent on getting rid of Erhama as soon as possible. In the past, the western coast had been a safe haven for those who opposed the British presence in the Gulf and for the pirates who attacked every ship that sailed there. But now that all the ruling tribes had signed truces with His Majesty's Government, Pax Britannica could finally prevail and Loch proposed that the whole Gulf should be called the 'trucial coast'.

Although Loch had initially been reluctant to accept Bashir's request to accompany him, he had finally acquiesced because he believed that the pirate's son would help them find Erhama's hideout and tell them about his movements.

As for Bashir, all he wanted was the chance to see his father again, even if it was only for a moment before he lost him for ever.

On the deck of the *Eden*, Bashir was contemplating the sun as it set on the horizon when Sadleir placed his hand on his shoulder. He had asked him his reason for coming on the trip several times already and had been given little more than monosyllabic answers. So he tried again. 'I know you hated your father and didn't want to see him again, so what made you change your mind?'

'You'll be going back to Bombay soon to join your regiment,' replied Bashir without taking his eyes off the setting sun. 'But I will remain here. People in this area don't know me; they only know my father. When I tell them that my name is Bashir, it means nothing to them. But when I say that I'm Bashir bin Erhama, their eyes widen and they react with anything from admiration to hatred.

'I'm Bashir bin Erhama whether I like it or not. But as I'm his flesh and blood, I owe him the duty of a son. I don't want him to die cursing me. I wish to have his blessing – I want his approval for my marriage to Salwa.'

'But you can do that without joining Loch,' stated Sadleir.

Bashir shook his head. 'I wouldn't be able to find my father before he does. All I can do is beg people to take me on their small boats. I have no money, Sadleir. How could I travel and search for him?'

'But I promised to give you some money as soon as I accomplished my mission,' countered Sadleir.

'When?' said Bashir dejectedly. 'First you have to go back to Bombay, write your report and wait for official approval. And then, if you get that approval, you would have to send the money to me all the way from India. By then I'd probably be dead anyway.' He stepped away from the bulwarks and said abruptly, 'I'm going to get some sleep now. Have you ever heard of someone begging his father's executioner to take him to the execution?' He shuffled away to the quarterdeck.

Sadleir looked at the dying rays of the sun and thought of everything he had gone through with Bashir, since the moment – more than a year ago – when he had woken with the tip of the Indian sword pressed into his chest. Little could he have suspected back then that Bashir, the son of the corsair, who seemed so ready to kill him, would become his friend. They had crossed the desert together, travelled several seas and their mutual trust had grown with every passing day, blossoming into genuine affection.

Sadleir had learned a great deal from his relationship with Bashir, Met'ab and those he had met in this land. They were not savages, as many of his countrymen maintained. In the midst of all their struggles to gain money, power and influence, humans carried out abominable acts against each other. They forgot how small they really were and what an elevated role they could instead be playing through love and mutual respect.

Sadleir looked at the stars that were beginning to appear in the night sky and brought to mind several passages from the Qur'an which Bashir had read to him.

Chapter 47

Dammam

E RHAMA DID NOT REMAIN long at his fort in Dammam. On arrival, he had ordered everybody to gather all the gunpowder, food and weapons they could find and transport them to the ships. They were abandoning the fort that he had ruled over for so long, and only two men were to stay behind to guard it. The loading took a whole day. With a final glance, Erhama shouted for everyone to board the ships.

Erhama's three vessels left for Bahrain. They were led by the *Ghatrousha* and were full of men, arms, fighting gear and gunpowder. As soon as they were in the open sea, they came face to face with the Bahraini flotilla advancing to meet them.

'They're Al-Khalifa's ships!' Dirar yelled. 'They're heading straight for us! What are your orders, sir?'

'Stay on course!' bellowed Erhama to his men. 'Prepare to fight the mother of all battles!'

Dirar gave the orders to his men, who sent signals to the other two vessels.

The ships on both sides suddenly came to life. Cannon appeared from portholes and swords glinted in the sun as they were drawn out of their scabbards and waved at the foe. The riotous sounds of battle cries and chants rose from all the ships so that they could be heard even from a great distance.

Loch looked through his telescope and realised that the coming battle would be decisive. He could see the Bahraini ships confronting, on his left, Erhama's three vessels. The pirate did not intend to flee.

He ordered the anchor to be dropped in order to watch and wait for the outcome of the battle. If Erhama died at the hands of the Al-Khalifas, there would be little reason for him to interfere.

The two sides shot their first salvos of cannonfire and the gates of hell opened wide. Dense, acrid smoke filled the air as parts of the hulls and decks exploded in a blaze of pyrotechnics and mayhem, and human bodies were torn limb from limb. There was so much smoke that the spectators on the British ships had trouble following the progress of the battle.

After various volleys, the ships drew closer and hooks appeared suddenly, arcing through the air to lodge in the enemy's bulwarks. Fighters jumped onto the decks of their foes and engaged them in hand-to-hand combat. Soon, the water around the battle was thick with floating bodies and debris.

Bashir could not just stand and watch. He suddenly dived off the *Eden* and swam vigorously towards his father's ship, hoping he could reach the *Ghatrousha* before it was too late.

Mansen saw him jump and informed the captain.

'Fancy a wager, John?' said Loch. 'I'll bet you a bottle of fine malt that he won't see his father – one or both will die before they can meet.'

Mansen watched the young man's powerful strokes in the sea. 'I'll take that bet, sir,' he said at length. 'I think he'll reach his father in time.'

'Makes this show all the more interesting,' said Loch with a broad grin as they shook hands to seal the wager.

Bashir's pace slackened. He was growing tired and there was still a great distance between him and his father's ship. By slowing down a little he hoped to conserve his energy.

On the *Ghatrousha*, Erhama and his men fought desperately with all their strength. Their clothes were torn and drenched with blood as fires blazed all around them.

On the leading Bahraini ship, Sheikh Salman exhorted his men to fight and, as the smoke began to lift, he spotted his enemy. He shouted for his sailors to bring the ships closer to the *Ghatrousha*. Soon, three ships surrounded Erhama's vessel and threw their hooks onto her deck so that she was snared on all sides. Erhama's men fell one after the other until Dirar said to his master, 'We're cornered, sir. We have no more men to defend the *Ghatrousha*.'

'Light a torch for me before they come any closer.'

Dirar took a torch from the mast and lit it from one of the many fires on the ship. 'What would you like me to do, sir?'

Erhama took the torch wordlessly and, accompanied by Dirar, retreated to the stern, ducking the bullets and spears aimed at them. Erhama kicked open the door to the quarter-deck where they had stored the gunpowder.

'Are you ready to die, Dirar?' he asked.

Dirar deflected a blow from one attacker and drove his sword into another. He caught Erhama's eye and gave him the briefest nod before turning to face a sea of angry faces.

Sheikh Salman led the struggle on the deck of the *Ghatrousha* with a group of his men. But as fighters fell from both sides, the distance narrowed between him and his enemy. He screamed at his men, 'Leave Erhama to me! He's mine!'

Bashir had drawn very close to his father's ship and

continued to swim as he spotted him in the stern. Sheikh Salman was standing in front of Erhama with his sword ready to strike and Bashir saw that his father carried a torch. He could guess what his father was going to do and he stopped swimming.

Sheikh Salman was surrounded by a group of his men and his sword dripped with blood. Dirar had been wounded in several places and yet was still able to fight on valiantly. Erhama looked straight into Sheikh Salman's eyes and said, 'The end will be in my hands and nobody else's.'

Erhama never heard his son's screams, a last-ditch attempt to stop his father from carrying out his plan.

'Noooooooo!'

He screamed when he saw his father almost casually tossing the torch.

With a deafening roar as though she had always been destined to end her days in a mighty blaze, the *Ghatrousha* exploded into a flaming ball, which consumed everything and everyone in its path.

Bashir dived underwater as a mass of debris and human remains were catapulted through the air. When he resurfaced moments later, nothing was left but a charred section of the hull and corpses floating in the water.

'I believe I won our wager, old friend,' said Loch to Mansen with a grin.

'You certainly did, sir.'

Sadleir looked at the two officers in stunned disbelief. He could never share their despicable lack of respect for the dead, their horrible grins as they took in the carnage. They congratulated one another on a mission accomplished – even though they had done nothing but foment trouble and had left others to do all the underhand dirty work for them.

'We're now rid of that bloody pirate,' Loch said. 'Weigh anchor and spread sails. Let's go back to Muscat.'

'What about Bashir?' Sadleir demanded.

Loch looked at him with irritation. 'He can go to hell, Major Sadleir, for all I care.'

Sadleir had to think quickly; his friend's life was at stake. He cleared his throat and said in his most deferential tone, 'Piracy has almost come to an end and you, sir, will be known throughout the Empire as the officer who made navigation safe in the Gulf.'

Loch raised his eyebrows at that, with clear approval.

Sadleir indicated the figure bobbing in the sea. 'But there's one pirate left, sir.'

'He's not a pirate,' countered Loch.

'I've been with him long enough to know that he's his father's son. If we just leave him there, sir, he will lead the next generation of corsairs against us.' He looked straight into Loch's eyes. 'Allow me, Captain, to pick him up and take him to Bombay clapped in irons and he'll never bother us again.'

Loch thought for a while. 'Very well, Major,' he said finally, and ordered two oarsmen to accompany Sadleir in a boat.

Sadleir was still not sure what it was he hoped to achieve; all he knew was that he could not leave his friend out at sea to die.

They reached him just in time since the men on the Bahraini ships, incensed by the death of Sheikh Salman, had taken it upon themselves to kill any of the surviving pirates found in the water.

Sadleir shouted at them to leave Bashir alone as he was a prisoner of the British forces and that if they killed him now, the British ships behind them would bomb them and their town in Bahrain. The men lowered their weapons reluctantly.

Sadleir held out his hand for his friend.

Bashir had been convinced that he would soon be joining his father, so when he heard the familiar voice he looked up in surprise. 'A prisoner?'

In English and for the benefit of the oarsmen, Sadleir said, 'You are under arrest. Come with us now.' And then in Arabic he added, 'Did you really think I'd let you die out here?'

'I lost my father, Sadleir.'

'Yes,' he said, 'but you've gained a brother.'

Bashir reached for Sadleir's hand and squeezed it, hoisting himself into the boat. They rowed back to the *Eden* with one final look over their shoulders at what was left of the pirate's ship.

Bashir then turned and stared stonily ahead, wondering what the future would be like without Erhama bin Jaber, the corsair.

A NOTE FROM THE AUTHOR

Although *The Corsair* is fiction, it is based on true events. British foreign policy in the Arabian Peninsula in the early nineteenth century was focused on combating piracy on the seas and stemming the advance of Wahhabism on land, and His Majesty's Government sought to bring a number of different allies into its campaigns. The naval and land battles described are based on historic incidents. The leaders mentioned in the book – in Egypt and Bahrain and elsewhere – were rulers at the time. Several of the main characters on the British side are based on actual people. And of course Erhama bin Jaber, the Arabian corsair himself, lived a long and eventful life, often in the company of his slave, Dirar. Erhama had a son, Bashir, though little is known about him. Most of the other, secondary characters who populate this novel are the creations of my imagination.

A NOTE ON THE TYPE

The text of this book is set in Adobe Garamond. It is
one of several versions of Garamond based on the
designs of Claude Garamond. It is thought that
Garamond based his font on Bembo, cut in 1495 by
Francesco Griffo in collaboration with the Italian
printer Aldus Manutius. Garamond types were first
used in books printed in Paris around 1532. Many of
the present-day versions of this type are based on the
Typi Academiae of Jean Jannon cut in Sedan in 1615.

Claude Garamond was born in Paris in 1480. He
learned how to cut type from his father and by the age
of fifteen he was able to fashion steel punches the size
of a pica with great precision. At the age of sixty he
was commissioned by King Francis I to design a Greek
alphabet, for this he was given the honourable title of
royal type founder. He died in 1561.